GABRIEL'S GAMBIT

PATRICIA D. EDDY

If you love steamy romantic suspense, I'd love to send you an exclusive short story set in Dublin, Ireland. Castles & Kings is ONLY available for my newsletter subscribers. Visit my website and let me know where to send your free short story.
http://patriciadeddy.com

ONE

Willow

In the past three weeks, I've gone from a boring adjunct college professor dreaming of tenure to seeing my own ghostly doppelgänger around every corner.

All because I got close enough to an ancient book to activate magic I never knew was inside of me.

Now, a secret government organization is trying to force me to wield my power for the vilest of tasks.

Just as they're about to bring the pain, I'm saved by an honest-to-God—yes, *that* God—angel.

He smells nice. His voice is like spun gold. And when his hair billows in the wind? I'm ashamed to admit...I swoon. But I can't trust anyone.

Not even a celestial.

I'm so screwed.

Three Weeks Ago

Willow

I SHIVER, despite the heat of the early October afternoon. When my department chair heard I hadn't yet visited St. Mary's Cathedral, he insisted I take the small group of graduate students on today's tour.

"You specialize in the occult and you haven't seen the vault at St. Mary's?"

I didn't tell Anton that I'd tried to visit the cathedral a dozen times since I'd moved to San Francisco five years ago. But something always kept me away.

Warned me away.

I don't know where the thought comes from.

"Dr. Saunders," Ruby says, "we're going to be late."

She tosses her dark curls over her shoulder and links her arm with Candice, her research partner. The two women are only a few months away from masters' degrees in architecture, and Ruby's writing her dissertation on the great 1906 San Francisco earthquake and how it affected the look and feel of the city.

I stare up at the tower, the Gothic spires piercing the clear blue sky. Time clings to the ancient red brick walls, their cracks and crevices swelling with a power I feel in my bones.

"I wonder if we'll see any of the ghosts who haunt this place?" Ruby whispers as we step through the heavy wooden doors.

"This is still a working church," I chide. "No talking about ghosts until after we leave."

Or...ever.

I might be the only person alive with a doctorate in the occult who gets the heebie-jeebies when she thinks about ghosts.

The doors creak loudly, almost groaning through the weight of their heavy, rusty hinges. Rows and rows of well-worn wooden pews stretch out across the vast, dimly lit nave. Incense—along with something older and way more sinister—fills the air, so thick it's almost choking.

Along one wall, a rack of votives casts flickering shadows,

creating the illusion of movement where there should be none at all.

"Are you Dr. Saunders?" An older nun with a few strands of gray hair peeking out from her habit hurries over, her sensible shoes making almost no sound on the threadbare red carpet. "I'm Sister Cecilia. Father Shin sent me to greet you. He's still busy with the previous tour group. Welcome to St. Mary's."

"Thank you, Sister. Is it okay if my students take a few photos while we wait?"

"Of course!" She beams as she turns toward the sanctuary. "The cathedral is well-loved—and well-used—but she is still a stunning building. When I was first assigned here, I would spend hours sitting in the pews this time of day. The light is breathtaking."

I don't have the heart to tell her that's not the word I'd use. That the three frescos painted behind the altar are cast in an eerie glow. The cherubs and angels seem to almost fly off the wall.

The sun beating against the stained glass windows to my left should be warm. But instead, it leaches the heat from my limbs. My stomach does backflips, and I swallow hard. I need to sit down.

Sister Cecilia takes Ruby and Candice up to the altar and starts telling them all about the paintings, but back in the pews, an oppressive silence settles over me. Disoriented, I drop my head into my hands. I shouldn't have skipped lunch. Or...breakfast, for that matter. But I've felt *off* all day. Allergies, maybe. Or a POTS episode threatening. The vascular disease causes dangerous drops in blood pressure when I stand up too quickly.

If I'm not careful, I can even pass out.

I dig a hard candy out of my crossbody bag and pop it into my mouth. The strawberry sweetness usually helps.

It's a full ten minutes before Father Shin emerges from a door behind the altar. He's pale. Dark bags swell under his eyes. Deep lines etch his forehead. Sister Cecilia startles when she sees him, crosses the cathedral, and rests a hand on his elbow. He looks like he feels as awful as I do. Maybe he needs a candy too.

The priest stares up at the golden crucifix behind the altar and makes the sign of the cross. After a moment, he runs a hand through his thinning salt and pepper hair, shuffles over to me, and forces a smile.

"Dr. Saunders, please accept my apology for being late." The middle-aged priest has an easy way about him, despite how rattled he'd looked only seconds ago. "The previous tour had many more questions than usual."

"It's no problem, Father. You're doing us a favor. The woman I talked to at the rectory said you'd stopped giving tours a few months ago."

He offers me a weary smile as Ruby and Candice finish taking photos of the frescos and head over to us. "I had. The cathedral needs renovations, and the work was to begin this week. But there was a delay, and when your call came in, I'd just scheduled with the previous group. The scaffolding will go up soon. I'm afraid this is the last tour I'll be able to give for the foreseeable future."

The two young women are eager to get started, but my stomach is still in knots. So I hang back and pull another hard candy from my bag.

Father Shin leads Ruby and Candice through the sanctuary, his voice almost reverent as the cathedral's history spills from his lips. I gaze up at the vaulted ceiling, intricate designs almost coming to life in the shadows.

The stained glass windows, though beautiful, depict macabre scenes. Saints and sinners, their faces twisted in expressions of torment and ecstasy, are bathed in hues of crimson and gold by the setting sun.

I can't shake the feeling of *wrongness* here. I grew up in churches like these back in Boston. My parents baptized me and sent me to a Catholic grammar school. They believe in a higher power. Though I suspect more in the general sense than one true God.

The strange sensations skittering down my spine grow stronger with each step. Awareness prickles along the back of my neck. I glance around, my shoulders hiked up to my ears, but the few parishioners seem oblivious to anything out of place, and Father Shin prattles on about the fire that gutted the church more than a century ago.

"After the earthquake, the flames burned so hot, they destroyed everything but the bell tower and the walls. The marble altar *melted*," he says, his voice reverent.

"Stone can melt?" Ruby presses her hand to her throat with a gasp.

"I was as surprised as you, my dear. But yes. It can. There are only a few grainy photos from that time, but it must have been a sight to behold." Father Shin pulls a heavy, purple velvet drape behind the altar aside to reveal a narrow alcove. "Now, watch your step. The stairs down to the antechamber are steep, but this is one of the most interesting parts of the entire cathedral. And one of the most mysterious."

A cold blast of air washes over me, carrying the scent of the bay. Salty. Dank. *Old.*

I should stay in the sanctuary.

Where it's safe.

"Dr. Saunders? You *have* to see this!" Candice calls. The girls were so excited to come here. Even happier when I agreed to go with them.

There's no reason to be scared. It's a basement. Nothing more.

I find a scrap of courage and make my way down the winding steps. As I reach the last one, I falter, grab onto the metal hand rail, and suck in a deep breath through my nose. Father Shin's voice fades as a strange, almost imperceptible hum fills the air. My body *vibrates* with it. Something deep within me strains to break free.

My hesitation burns away in a heartbeat. Suddenly, I'm desperate to keep going. To get past Shin, Ruby, and Candice and find out what's just beyond the reach of the dim bulbs running along the ceiling.

The world tilts on its axis. I stumble toward the far corner of the space. My vision blurs and the room starts to spin. A haunting melody seems to come from everywhere and nowhere all at once.

I reach out. I'm so close. My fingers ache. There's so much power here. Power I need. Power I want. Power that's *mine*.

Everything goes soft and dark, and an ethereal whisper from somewhere beyond is the only thing I can hear.

"Welcome, Whisper Keeper. We have been waiting..."

"DR. SAUNDERS? WILLOW?" A woman's voice cuts through the fog swirling around me. Someone touches my neck. I jerk away—or try to—but my limbs feel like they're encased in cement. "Take it easy. Try opening your eyes first, dear."

Oh. Right.

The old light bulbs swim in and out of focus over my head. The scent of the bay—of salt water—is so strong, it burns my nose. Under it, the subtle spice of incense and something else. Something familiar. From long ago.

Sister Cecilia kneels next to me, her face ghostly pale. Ruby and Candice hold onto each other over her shoulder. Candice's cheeks are stained with tears. Ruby—always the calm, composed one—is shaking.

Father Shin sits on the steps a few feet away, a rosary clutched in his hands.

"What...happened?" I croak. My throat is dry. Scratchy. Like I've been screaming for hours.

"You just...collapsed," Ruby says. "You went all pale, then the whole room got cold, and you...went down. We tried to catch you, but... It all happened so fast..."

I struggle to sit up, and Sister Cecilia slides her arm around my back to help me. My head spins for a brief moment, but after a hard blink, the dizziness subsides. As does the knot in my stomach.

"Welcome, Whisper Keeper."

The strange voice is only a memory now. What the hell is a Whisper Keeper?

"I thought I heard someone...calling to me."

"God protect us," Father Shin whispers.

"From what?" I turn carefully, hoping I won't pass out again.

He shakes his head as he pushes to his feet. "The tour is over. I'm sorry. You all need to leave. Immediately."

Sister Cecilia frowns. "Father, Dr. Saunders is in no condition—"

"Now, Sister Cecilia." Gone is the kindly older man who was so excited to tell us about this place. He lowers his voice to murmur, "Observe the time and fly from evil," before fleeing back up the winding staircase and leaving the four of us staring after him.

RUBY CALLED a Lyft to bring me home—even offered to ride with me—but all I want is a chocolate chip cookie and my bed.

My nervous system hasn't worked right I was a teenager. A rare form of cancer stole any chance of having children and gifted me with one more lingering side effect—POTS. For years, I've tried to keep the symptoms in check. Stay hydrated, don't get up too quickly, don't skip meals... But postural orthostatic tachycardia syndrome doesn't always play by the rules.

I drop my keys on the kitchen counter, pour myself a glass of water, and pull two cookies from the tin. There's a flicker at the edge of my vision—a shadow that shouldn't be there.

A trick of the light?

But then it happens again. The cookies slide from my hand as a gauzy form hovers between the kitchen and my tiny living room.

It's *me*. Or...a ghost of me. Her eyes are filled with sorrow, despite being mostly translucent. The water glass hits the floor, shattering into a thousand pieces, and when I look up again, the ghost is gone.

Gabriel

Crumbling bricks pop and crack as they hit the ground. Sparks from the twisted electrical conduits rain down at the edges of the destroyed power station.

My wings are in tatters. The scent of burned feathers makes my stomach roil. Flying through a magical portal and into the fires of Hell was reckless beyond measure. But only an angel could have saved Zoe and Sinclair from Lucifer's endless torment and lived to tell about it.

I am overwhelmed by the suffering all around me. And very angry. Only an hour ago, Thorn, one of the worst demons to ever walk the earth, and his fae concubine, Regina, were auctioning off the *use* of six women. He'd held, starved, and tortured them for days, then branded them with spelled ink so their minds belonged to him and him alone.

A pure-bred incubus, the asshole had fed off their fear. Until Zoe—a daughter of Seraphim—had fused her consciousness to his and dragged him to Hell. Sinclair, her mate, had risked his life—and his soul—to save her.

Across the destroyed space, Sin cradles Zoe in his arms. She passed out moments after I yanked their souls from the Underworld and has yet to stir.

Along another wall, a panther shifter named Dion sobs in a mage's arms. "I can't! The mark...you have to remove the mark!"

I stride over to the young mage. The woman looks entirely overwhelmed trying to comfort the hysterical shifter. "Can you not see the rune, magic bearer?"

Dropping to one knee, I tear a strip of cloth from the sleeve of my robes and gently swipe it over Dion's forehead. The mark fades slightly, but whatever the incubus bastard used to create it is strong, even now that he is dead.

"Water. Or alcohol," I demand. "Now!"

Dion shudders and a fresh wave of tears tumble down her cheeks. "Who...are...you?" she whispers.

My shoulders straighten, sending waves of pain rolling down

my back. "I am the archangel Gabriel. The bringer of justice, the revealer of truth, and the interpreter of the Almighty's plan."

Her bloodshot, amber eyes water. "The Almighty's plan...for me...fucking sucks."

"I swear to you, shifter, this was *not* part of any plan." Her emotions are almost too much for me to bear. My angelic senses are wide open—have been since I, along with Michael, Azrael, Rapheal, Ariel, and Cassiel, lent our powers to one of the most powerful warlocks in all eternity—and I cannot seem to close them off to the suffering in this room.

Lieutenant Grayson Eve, head of the Bureau of the Occult and the Other, strides over to us with a bottle of vodka in her hand. "You wanted alcohol?"

"Yes." I take the bottle and pour a generous splash over the cloth. "Whatever that bastard used to put that rune on her forehead is resisting me."

"She's bleeding all over the place. We need a healer!" Eve shouts.

"I...can heal myself. If...I can shift." Dion's voice is fading too quickly. She's barely holding on. "Please..."

The alcohol helps, and the moment I cut through one of the rune's lines, black fur ripples over the shifter's skin. Within seconds, she sighs and passes out.

"How did you know?" Grayson's nails lengthen into talons as she sweeps her gaze around the remains of the power station.

With a groan, I push to my feet. My body aches, and the act of drawing breath to speak is not one I look forward to. "It was quite obvious. You could not see the mark?"

"See it? Of course, I could. My sight is better than your average shifter, *angel*. How did you know what it was doing to her?" Her voice takes on a screeching edge, and her blond hair sticks up in all directions with the start of her shift. But after a moment, she regains control of her emotions.

"Millennia of knowledge." Bored with this conversation, I turn, seeking out Sinclair and Zoe. The half angel, half incubus demon sits against one of the crumbling walls, his gaze pinned to his mate's tear-stained face. Their souls have returned, but Zoe will need days—if not weeks—to heal.

She may be a daughter of Seraphim, but she was given a very human body, and Thorn visited horrors upon her that should be beyond imagination.

Sinclair's brother, Maddox, and his warlock mate, Killian, lean against the wall next to them. It was Killian's magic that created a tether to the mortal realm and allowed Sinclair's soul to descend into the Underworld to rescue Zoe's.

Azrael touches my arm gently. His wings flutter against his back, and I am unprepared for the odd pang squeezing my heart. Is that...jealousy?

"Are you coming, Gabriel? The rest of us are returning to the celestial realm. We can bring you with us."

The other angels stand together, shoulder to shoulder. Without the use of my wings, I cannot return to the celestial realm on my own. The only way back is with another angel. I should accept Azrael's aid. I do not belong here. Amid death and destruction and *humans*. So why do I not immediately agree?

"Gabriel?"

I shake my head. "I...will stay. Sinclair and Zoe might...need me."

Azrael arches a brow. "For what?"

Shoving at the Angel of Death, I drop my voice to a growl. "We did this to them, Azrael. It may have been Seraphiel's plan, but *we* stood by and let it happen. I will stay until I am certain Sinclair and Zoe are safe. The rest of you can fuck off back to the celestial realm. But tell Seraphiel that if I ever see him again, I will tear the feathers from his wings one by one."

With a chuckle, Azrael smooths his hands down his robes. "Good luck with that plan. Seraphiel has the Almighty's ear. You would be banished before the first feather fell." He eyes my damaged wings, and concern softens his tone. "It could be weeks before you heal enough to return. If you grow tired of waiting, call to me. I will hear you."

I clasp his arm briefly and nod. Of all the archangels, he is the only one I would consider...a friend. Though I do not think he feels the same about me.

"Time to go," he says to the others. "Our work here is done."

"Do *not* disappear inside this building!" Grayson shouts. "That much power will kill us all."

The angels grumble but make their way outside, and the eagle shifter stands beside me, her hands shoved into the pockets of her tailored black pants. "You know, Gabriel, the Bureau could use someone with your particular talents."

I stare down at her, my brows lifting. "An archangel? *Working? For you?*"

"Not full time. A...consultant, perhaps?" Amusement dances in her piercing blue eyes. "I'm not sure any of us could take your particular brand of hubris every day. The Bureau of the Occult and the Other handles many different types of *Other* crime. This case was our worst—ever—but I've seen things I can never unsee. This world has more evil than it should—particularly now. We would be grateful for the help."

Across the room, Maddox and Killian kneel, forming a protective circle around Sinclair and Zoe. Magic crackles in the air, the salty tang stronger than it has any right to be after the amount of power the warlock expended to save them.

The four disappear a second later. I am unprepared for the sharp stab of worry through my heart. Or how very alone I feel, despite the dozen Bureau agents still in the room and their leader at my side.

Turning to the Lieutenant, I shake my head. "I must decline your offer. I have a job, and the Almighty would not take kindly to...moonlighting."

She shrugs and offers me a small smile. "I had to try."

Letting my angelic powers wash over the whole of the world, I search for Sinclair and Zoe. Until I know they are safe, I will protect them. Whether they want me to or not.

TWO

Gabriel

The lights of San Francisco twinkle like some sort of celestial disco beyond the floor-to-ceiling windows of Sinclair's penthouse. I should have left eighteen hours ago—as soon as I knew Sin and Zoe were safe. But my wings burned and blistered so terribly, I will not be able to fly for weeks, and much of my angelic strength is gone.

After hours of rest, I am finally well enough to travel. Yet I have also found myself with two "minders" who huddle together across the spacious living room, talking in muted whispers.

"He's going to get himself killed," Maddox says.

"Or worse." The half-breed angel's mate, Killian, shakes his head. "He'll come back covered in tattoos, pierced, and with a raging case of syphilis."

"Fuck me. The Almighty will smite us for not taking better care of him." Maddox's cheeks drain of all color. "We can't let him leave."

"Do *you* want to try to stop him?" Killian asks. "He's a bloody archangel!"

"You do know I can hear you, yes?" I straighten to my full

height, wincing as searing pain lashes across my back. Perhaps I am not as recovered as I thought I was. A strange feeling—almost a shudder—rolls through me.

My existence could have—*should* have—ended in Hell. But the collective power of five other angels gave me the strength to help Sinclair and Zoe escape with their lives.

Maddox draws in a quick breath and clutches Killian's arm. "I knew you should have cast a spell first."

I arch a brow. "As if that would have stopped me. I can eavesdrop from halfway across the world. And you, of all the beings in the earthen realm, should know that."

Maddox bristles. His mate presses a kiss to his cheek. "He's baiting you, luv."

"He's an ass."

I chuckle. "That I may be. But I am also the bringer of justice, the revealer of truth, and—"

"The interpreter of the Almighty's plan. Yes, *we know*." Maddox runs a hand through his hair, tugging on the strands until his eyes crinkle with pain. "But while you're here in the earthen realm, you're subject to earthen rules. You can be injured. Killed."

I brandish the tip of one wing. A single burned feather falls to the floor. "Obviously. I am not an idiot, half-breed."

Killian steps in front of Maddox. "You have seen what I can do, Gabriel. Insult my mate again and you and I will have...*issues*." Power glows from within the warlock, crackling over his fingers. "I may not be able to stop you, but I can make your existence quite painful before you end me."

In all truth, the warlock probably could stop me. Creating a magical tether to anchor Sinclair to the earthen realm so he could pull his mate from Lucifer's endless torment should have been impossible, even with the help of *six* archangels. Yet Killian managed to do so without dying. Though it cost him. The dark circles under his eyes have not faded, and he looks almost... hollow.

"Apologies." I force the foreign word from my lips. In the

celestial realm, I am revered. By most. Seraphiel would like to see my end, I am certain. But the others...I have cultivated my reputation carefully over millennia. The lesser angels know not to challenge me. It does not end well.

"Are we done here?" I smooth my hands down my white robes, dispelling the last of the soot into thin air. "I do not wish to dawdle. Immersing myself in this realm will occupy me while my wings heal. And perhaps allow me to better understand those I am tasked with watching over."

"No. Not even close." Maddox thrusts a wad of green paper at me.

"What is this?" I wrinkle my nose at the scent. It reeks of...old. Of greed and desire and sweat from hundreds—if not thousands—of humans. I can sense them all. Different races, ages, religions. Their stories race through my mind. None of them linger for more than a blink. Unimportant, yet...not, at the same time.

"Money," Killian says. "You will need it for everything. Lodging, food, travel—"

"I am an angel. I do not need lodging. Or food. Or to rely on human means of transportation. Nor do you, for that matter."

Killian links his fingers with his mate's, a small smile curving his lips. "I have rather mastered teleportation. But you cannot simply appear and disappear in front of humans, Gabriel. They will talk. A lot. And your power alone could kill or injure them."

"Then I will ensure I am away from them first." I try to hand the money back to Maddox, but he rolls his eyes.

"For the love of all that is good and holy in both realms, listen to us," Maddox says. "This is the longest you've ever spent here, Gabriel. Your powers...change once you leave the celestial realm. Trust me. Please."

The muscles in my back ache with a bone-deep pain, and my stomach has felt hollow all day. Maddox is not wrong. It has been a millennium since I passed more than a few hours in the earthen realm. And this time, I am not on a mission from the Almighty.

In truth, she may not even know I'm here.

Last night, after Maddox directed me to one of the guest suites in Sinclair's penthouse, I thought I *chose* to sleep. To experience this very human activity as part of my education about this realm. And to speed my healing. But did I? Or did my body simply...give out?

"Fuck."

"Did no one explain what would happen?" Killian asks.

I arch a brow at him. "Who, exactly, do you think would bother? Seraphiel? He hates me with his very soul. The Almighty is too busy to care—though I suppose she might have made the time if I'd told her what I was planning."

Maddox gapes until Killian elbows him in the side. "He may be a proper arse, luv, but you told me the story of the first time *you* visited this realm."

The half-breed's cheeks flush bright red. His embarrassment should not bother me, but I avert my gaze. Why? I care nothing for the warlock and his mate. A strange sensation rolls through me, and I ask, "What happened?"

Shoving his hands into his pockets, Maddox pins his gaze to the floor. "Sinclair took me to a bar. I had never tasted whiskey before. I had no idea it could lead to...poor decisions. And vomiting. So much vomiting."

"I will remember this. Whiskey can cause vomiting."

Killian shakes his head. "Only in large quantities over short periods of time. The point, Gabriel, is that there is much you do not know about this realm, and you cannot simply take off and hope for the best. If you do, you will quickly find yourself injured, dead, or worse."

"Worse? What fate is worse than death?" I ask.

The two men reply in tandem, "Marriage."

I stare from one to the other, confused. They are mated—the supernatural equivalent of marriage. And yet they are opposed to the institution? This must be some sort of human joke I do not understand.

"I do not enjoy being fucked with, warlock. I have had enough of these delays. Helping Sinclair and Zoe convinced me that I know too little of this realm. As I cannot return to the celestial realm until my wings are fully healed, I have decided to spend some time on earth among those I am tasked with watching over to better understand them. After a week—perhaps two—I will return to the celestial realm for the rest of eternity."

In truth, understanding humanity is not my only motivation. The past several days have been some of the most interesting of my existence. I am not ready to go back yet. I want...more.

I shove the crumpled bills into the pockets of my robes and step back so I do not injure the two men when I disappear. My power has been known to burst ear drums and render even the strongest of humans unconscious for hours.

"Wait!" Killian snaps and grabs my wrist. "You need more than money."

"What else?" I ask, bored of this conversation. "Get on with it quickly so I may be off."

Maddox shakes his head. "And I thought *I* was naive when I came to this realm."

Killian chuckles and presses a kiss to Maddox's temple. "You were, luv. But at least you knew what *pants* were." The warlock looks me up and down. "What do you think? Thirty-four long?"

"At least. Maybe thirty-six. He's taller than either of us." Maddox drops to one knee and jerks the hem of my robe up to expose my feet. "Holy fuck. Size twelve shoes. No. Thirteen."

"Is there something wrong with my sandals?" I wrench the robe from Maddox's hand. "They are comfortable."

"It's October." Killian shakes his head. "San Francisco may be mild this time of year, but the rest of the country is not. And if you visit Canada or Russia or Iceland..." He shudders. "You'll find rain, sleet, snow..."

"I am an archangel. Rain will not touch me. Snow will melt at the very sight of me. Enough of this fussing. I am certain Sinclair and Zoe need some sort of assistance. Perhaps you should...check on them?"

Maddox rolls his eyes. "When I knocked on Sin's door this morning, he said, and I quote, 'Fuck off.'" Killian gapes at him, and he adds, "He did text me five minutes later and apologize. But Zoe hasn't woken up yet, and he doesn't want to be disturbed until she does."

"He's lucky I wasn't the one who checked on him," Killian says, "or he would have found himself turned into a raccoon for a few hours. I know he's worried about Zoe, but after what we did for him..."

The warlock's shoulders slump. He expended so much magical energy creating the tether from this realm to the Underworld, I was almost...worried about him.

"He's been alone for a long time." Maddox scribbles on a small pad of paper, tears off a sheet, and hands it to his mate. "I think this should do it. Do you want to go? Or shall I?"

"I'll take care of it," Killian says. He embraces Maddox, slides his fingers into the half-breed's hair, and kisses him for so long, I wonder if Maddox is breathing. Angels do not *need* to breathe, but with a human mother, Maddox's angelic powers are surely muted.

I let my senses blanket the room. Desire. Arousal. Love. An undercurrent of annoyance—with me—and much worry. Sinclair is half angel, half incubus demon. He left his body in the earthen realm when he traveled to the Underworld, so he was not physically injured. But Zoe had been beaten, starved, and branded by the demon Thorn. Though she is the daughter of Seraphim, her body is outwardly human. She will heal, but it will take some time. The strength of Sin's fear—along with the love he has for his mate—causes a physical ache inside me.

The two lovers part, and Killian tosses a glance at me over his shoulder. "If you leave looking like that, angel, you will regret it. Stay here until I return."

Seconds later, he closes his eyes and disappears. Impressive. He can teleport without an incantation. Not many witches and warlocks are that powerful.

Maddox strides into the kitchen of Sinclair's apartment, finds the coffee pot, and pours himself a cup. "You want one, Gabriel?" he asks. "I need the caffeine hit, and Sinclair has terrible taste in tea."

"I do not require food or drink," I say, returning my focus to the glittering lights of the city outside the windows. "Or caffeine."

"For fuck's sake. Coffee is delicious. Try some." He sets two cups on the glass table in the center of the living room, then sinks onto one of the black leather sofas. "And sit down. You look knackered."

I fold my damaged wings, banishing them from view with a wince. Pain is a new experience for me—one I do not enjoy. Perhaps sitting would be wise. The cushions are soft, and the rich scent of the leather comforting.

I do not care for how the warmth from the mug makes my burned fingers ache. I almost spill some of the dark liquid when I switch from holding it in two hands to gripping the handle.

I choke on the first sip. Disgusting. "Humans drink this *willingly?*"

"Millions of gallons of the stuff," Mad says with a smile. "Trust me. It gets better."

I am skeptical, but to my chagrin, the second taste is much different. "Interesting. You are certain I need...new clothes?"

"Yes, mate. Absolutely. You want to blend in. Robes won't cut it."

Straightening, I set the coffee down and narrow my eyes at Maddox. "I do not plan on *cutting* anything. I am an angel—an archangel, to be precise—and I can hide myself anywhere I choose."

"Really? You're an archangel? You *never* mention it." Mad runs a hand through his light brown hair and sighs. "Hiding won't let you experience the world, Gabriel. You need to talk to people. Listen to them. Have real conversations."

"As opposed to...?" I pick up the mug again, and this time, the taste is pleasant. With a subtle jolt I find...odd. Azrael would enjoy this, I think. He was the one to rally the others to join us. I should call him down here for a cup before I return to the celestial realm.

Maddox drains the last of his beverage and leans back against the cushions. "All you're doing is making excuses for why you know better. But you've only spent two days here. You've never been hot or cold. Hungry or full. You've never *wanted* for anything. I have. All humans have. Is it so unfathomable that Killian and I *might* have some wisdom to impart?"

I push to my feet, stifling my wince. My eyes are gritty. The scent of burned feathers grates on me. Perhaps I should avail myself of Sinclair's bathing facilities.

A subtle power stirs the air before I can snap back at Maddox, and Killian appears with several large bags clutched in each hand.

He sways on his feet for a moment, and Maddox jumps up from the couch. "Fuck me. I should have been the one to go. Why didn't you tell me you were so weak?"

The two hold onto one another for several seconds before Killian straightens. "I'll be fine, luv. Nothing a solid night of sleep and a proper meal won't cure."

The warlock does not look fine. He looks as if he is about to fall over. "Give me those." I take the bags from his hands and peer inside. Trousers, shirts, a jacket, two pairs of shoes, and a dozen other items I do not recognize.

Maddox points to the hallway. "Take a shower before you put on any of those clothes, Gabriel. You reek of Hell. I'll order us some food. If you hope to survive the next week, you're going to need it."

"CAN you think of anything else we need to teach him?" Maddox asks. He pours his mate more wine, then offers me the bottle, but I wave him off. The rich, red liquid tastes of berries and tobacco and spice, but my head started to feel odd after the first glass. Much like my stomach. Not in an unpleasant way, though.

The meal—pasta in a heavy cream sauce—was interesting. Rich and smooth. Almost sweet, but not. I must remember to ask Azrael if he has ever partaken of a meal. If he has not, I will suggest he remedy the oversight. Quickly.

I stare at the unfamiliar items around me. A small leather

pouch contains a toothbrush, toothpaste, and deodorant. Several changes of clothes are folded neatly in a duffel bag on the floor. And a dozen bills of various denominations are spread out on the glass table. "I suppose I can always use these to pass the time should I find myself...bored."

Across from me, the two men stare at one another, horror in their eyes. "No strip clubs," Maddox snaps.

Lifting a brow, I pick up one of the five-dollar notes. "I was referring to origami. The Japanese art of paper folding?" Creasing the bill in half, then in half again, I spend the next few seconds creating something that almost resembles a crane.

"He knows origami, but not money." Killian shakes his head. "He's a lost cause."

"I know many things, warlock." I set the crane on the table. The new clothes feel...strange against my skin. Not unpleasant. Different. I am not accustomed to wearing pants. Or socks. Or underwear. The shoes, at least, are comfortable. Maddox called them loafers.

With a yawn, Killian rests his head on Mad's shoulder. "He knows how to use his mobile pay. Text messaging. We explained hotels, taxis, brushing and flossing, and the odd obsession the United States has with tipping. Anything else, he's on his own."

THREE

Willow

Every day for the past two weeks, I've seen her. My *whisper*. She appears at the most unexpected and inconvenient times, blending into the shadows of my life, but always just out of reach.

I'm not sure why I call her that. Except, the weird voice at the church called me the Whisper Keeper. Why, if this new thing—*being*—is anything other than a whisper?

Behind me in the bathroom mirror some mornings, she mimics my movements, but with a detached sadness that sends chills down my spine.

On the bus, she sits across from me. The other commuters don't notice her. Or...if they do, they don't react.

The worst part is when I see through her eyes. It's disorienting—like being ripped from my own body and thrust into hers. One moment I'm in my office at UCSF, grading papers or answering emails, and the next, I'm on a roof. Or in a park. People pass by without reacting, their faces blurred and distant. Leaves rustle. The sounds of the city are muted when I'm in her head, but not that far away.

She can move on her own. Wherever she wants to go—I think.

If I'm seeing through her eyes, I'm helpless to resist—a supernatural passenger in my own doppelgänger.

Last night, she woke me twice. Once, she was standing in the middle of the street outside my apartment, and a car drove right *through* her.

A few hours later, the foghorns blasted, and I jerked awake. My whisper was two blocks away—that seems to be as far from me as she can go—and the fog was so thick, it was all I could see through her eyes.

I try to ignore her. To tell myself it's stress or lack of sleep, but it's getting harder to believe my own bullshit.

God, I wish I had someone to talk to about this. I even tried calling Father Shin, but he transferred out of the parish. Sister Cecilia too.

I'd go back on my own, but I've been too scared. So I've spent my workdays locked in my office, praying my whisper will leave me alone, and searching for anything I can find about the *Whisper Keepers*.

So far, I haven't learned anything helpful.

Am I losing my mind? I don't tell anyone what's happening. How can I? No one would believe me. But fear is chipping away at my sanity every single day.

The rain cascades down my office window in sheets. My whisper stands on the other side of the desk, staring out at the sidewalk. Her reflection in the glass is almost solid—more real than any other time I've seen her.

I take a tentative step closer. My heart races. Shit. If I'm not careful. I'll have an episode and pass out.

"Who are you?" I ask.

She turns, her expression mirroring the confusion and fear that have been my constant companions for weeks now. For a moment, our emotions are so tightly linked, we might as well be one being.

And then I'm pulled into her world again. Cold drops of rain pelt my skin. Thunder rumbles in the distance. Lowering my gaze, my own hands—as solid as they were in my office—reach for something unknown.

"Please." I don't have a voice when I'm seeing through her eyes. But maybe she can still hear me? *"Please tell me what's happening?"*

But she doesn't answer. Only walks away, leaving me stranded in this strange, whispered version of my life. Until I blink.

The warmth of my office surrounds me. I'm soaked to the bone. Rainwater pools on the floor, though the window hasn't opened in years.

I sink down to my knees, tears mixing with the rain on my cheeks. How much more of this can I take? Reality and illusion blur together, and I'm terrified that one day, the two will mix so thoroughly, I'll never find my way back.

Gabriel

The small duffel bag swings from my hand as I wander the streets of San Francisco. Despite my desire to be off the previous night, I found myself unwilling to leave the city yet. Instead, I took the credit card Maddox had given me—the one linked to Sinclair's bank account—and rented a hotel room a few blocks away.

It was only natural to begin my education about this realm in the one place I have some familiarity with. That was what I told myself as I tossed and turned in the king-sized bed.

A warm, comforting scent calls to me. My stomach rumbles. I have not eaten since last night. I should have asked Maddox how often humans partake of a meal.

The delicious smells get stronger until I find myself in front of a shop with a glowing sign in the window.

Pizza by the Slice

A man and a woman stand at the counter, and I eavesdrop as they each order a slice of pepperoni. I do the same, and after waving my phone over the payment terminal, take the thin paper plate with the slice of pizza over to a booth and sink down onto the red vinyl seat.

It is hot, almost burning my tongue. Gooey. The crust crackles as I bite down into a pillowy softness. I flick my tongue to swipe at the corner of my lips. Such an odd motion, but instinctual, somehow.

The flavors meld together. Some of the cheese tears off, leaving the dough naked save for a light sheen of sauce. It glistens and, fuck me. Why is that so appealing?

The meat is salty and rich, with a burn totally unlike that of the molten cheese. I must have more.

After two more slices, my stomach starts to feel...uncomfortably full. I push to my feet, and the man behind the counter stares at me in disbelief. "You can't still be hungry, dude. I serve the biggest slices in the city."

"Dude?" I straighten to my full height, prepared to smite the man for his familiarity. "I am an an—" *Fuck.*

"It's just an expression. Geez." He turns and pulls another pizza out of the oven. "I need a vacation. This job is getting to me."

I hurry out of the shop. I almost told the man I was an angel. The very thing Killian and Maddox warned me not to do. Does hunger—or its opposite—affect one's intelligence or judgement?

I could call the warlock and his mate and ask. But given how much fun they had at my expense last night, perhaps that is not wise.

The sun is starting to set. I cannot stay in San Francisco any longer. I should go to New York City next. The desk clerk at the hotel said that was the most exciting place he had ever been. I will start there.

But first, I need to find an alley where no one will notice me to disappear.

A cathedral looms at the end of the block. It calls to me, the Gothic spires standing proudly against the sky. A few more minutes in San Francisco will not cause any harm.

Willow

My whisper darts up the aisle, runs *through* the altar, and stops at the heavy purple drape before staring back at me.

"What do you think you're doing?" I hiss. "Stop!"

"The Almighty does whatever she pleases," a deep voice says from behind me. "I have found that asking her to stop has always been rather futile."

I yelp and glance up into a pair of golden, amber eyes filled with amusement. His hair tumbles over his shoulders in waves. God, he's almost too beautiful to look at. If only I were in the mood for company.

"You know God personally?" I ask. "Because if not, mind your own business."

He holds up his hands and backs away. "My apologies. I do not have much experience talking to people. I meant no disrespect."

I snort. "I doubt that."

The man's brows knit together. "I do not lie."

"You look like a model. I'm sure you have women falling all over you."

I scoot to the end of the pew, but when I stand, my blood pressure bottoms out and my heart races. Dark spots swim in front of my eyes. Swaying, I flail my arms, desperate to grasp on to something—anything—to keep me upright.

A spicy, rich scent wraps around me like a warm blanket. I want to live in it. To stay here forever. But then my vision clears, and I'm staring up at those mesmerizing golden orbs. Only now, the amusement is gone, chased away by concern.

"Are you all right?" He sinks down onto the pew with me still held against his chest, and I end up with my legs draped over his.

Am I?

A strange man has me nestled in his lap, and I'm not trying to get away. I'm seeing ghosts—well, *one* ghost who looks just like me —and I came back to the place that scares me most in this world.

"You need a doctor." He shifts, and his hard length presses against my ass. I suck in a breath, trying to wriggle free.

Shit. That's not helping. He's only getting harder. He knows it, too. His cheeks take on a red tinge, and he stills.

"No. I...I don't. Need a doctor, I mean."

Not that kind of doctor, anyway. A shrink? A stay in a nice, padded cell for an undetermined amount of time? That's debatable.

"You almost passed out." The man brushes a lock of hair away from my forehead. I lean into the touch before I can stop myself. "My name is Gabriel. And you are?"

"Willow. Willow Saunders. *Dr.* Willow Saunders. I have a Ph.D. in Mythology and the Occult." Shit. I'm babbling now. Why can't I stop myself?

Because he's hot as fuck.

I need to get out of here. Between his addicting voice and those mesmerizing eyes, he must have a girlfriend. And I'm not looking for anything. Not now. Not when I'm terrified I'm losing my mind.

"Anyway, what happened—almost passing out—is kind of par for the course with me," I say and scramble off his lap. Thank God I don't have another episode this time.

He frowns. "Par...for the course? I do not know this phrase."

Is this guy for real?

"It means...this happens a lot. I have a medical condition. It's not life-threatening," I add when he tenses. "But if I get up too fast, my blood pressure drops and I can get dizzy. Thank you. For catching me. But...I need to go."

I run for the back door, but stop and look over my shoulder before I escape into the early evening air. Gabriel stands in the center of the aisle, staring back at me. His full lips curve into a gentle smile. In his arms, I could breathe again. If only I could have stayed there a little longer. Maybe I wouldn't feel like my entire life were spinning out of control.

Gabriel

The desire to chase after Dr. Willow Saunders surprises me. As does the ache in my cock. I have not had sex in centuries, and I'd forgotten what it was like to *need*.

In the celestial realm, such things are simply…not done. I have walked among among humans five times in my existence, and last *fucked* in the early 1800s. I enjoyed the acts, but once I left this realm, I no longer felt the same urges.

When Willow Saunders tumbled into my arms, all of those desires—and more—came flooding back. Her curves fit against me perfectly. I can still feel her soft blond locks slipping through my fingers.

"Enough," I say quietly. It is time for me to leave San Francisco. I had thought to call Azrael to meet me here so I could talk to him about coffee and pizza. But now, I think it would be best if I moved on.

I slip through the heavy wood doors and glance up and down the street. Dr. Willow Saunders is gone, and while I will treasure the memory of having her in my arms, I have many more memories to make before I return to the celestial realm.

New York is waiting.

FOUR

Willow

My whisper glides between the stacks, her fingers trailing over the spines of the theoretical physics books. She smiles at me, then darts *through* the bookshelf. For a brief moment, ink blurs before my eyes.

She's running now. Chemistry. Calculus. Italian. Renaissance Art. The French Revolution.

Standing, I fight against the dizziness. Is this another POTS episode? Seeing through my whisper's eyes? Or both? I brace my hands on my thighs and drop my head toward my knees. My heart pounds hard enough to feel it in my temples, and a roaring sound fills my ears.

I hit the ground, the pain in my ass jarring me out of my whisper's head. As if she's mad at me, she flickers back through the shelves with such force, one of the physics books tumbles to the ground.

Holy shit. She's...not just a ghost anymore.

One finger jabs me in the chest. It's not exactly solid. More like...the *idea* of a jab than an actual poke. But in the weeks she's been with me, she's never managed to affect the physical world. Until now.

"Go away!" I shout.

Five students halfway across the library stare at me. Anton rushes over to me, disapproval pinching his dark brows together. My whisper is gone.

"Willow, what the hell?" he hisses.

"Sorry." I accept the hand he offers to help me to my feet. "There was...uh...a wasp. I'm allergic."

"You look tired." He leads me back through the study area to the front of the library. "You haven't been yourself for weeks. You're looking over your shoulder all the time, you've missed the last three review sessions with Ruby, and now you're shouting in the library?"

My shoulders slump. "I haven't been sleeping well."

"Then go home. Better yet, take the week off. I'll handle today's review session. Friday's too." The judgement in his tone is too much. Tears prick at my eyes, but I refuse to let them fall.

"Anton, I need to work. I'm sorry I yelled. The...wasp...scared me. I can handle Ruby's session. She's so close to finishing her dissertation. I want to see this through."

I hate the desperation in my voice. But I can't go home. My whisper will be there. She's *always* there. I don't sleep because she wakes me at least half a dozen times a night.

"No. As your department head, I can't let you continue to shirk your duties. Either take the week off, or I'll be forced to suspend you for the rest of the quarter." He shoves his hands into his pockets and won't look me in the eye.

Shit. Anton is a good guy. Not exactly a friend, but not an asshole either. And I put him in this position. Missing Ruby's review sessions...that was inexcusable. I have more than a hundred papers to grade, and I've been relying on last year's syllabi to make it through my lectures. How much longer before my students start to complain?

Guilt heats my cheeks but leaves the rest of me cold. "I'll take the week off," I say softly. "Please tell Ruby I'm sorry."

WITH NOTHING TO do but go home—the last place I want to be—I turn off all the lights in my office, lock the door, and log on to my computer. I might be "on vacation," but my credentials still work. Every day, I've spent hours searching for some *shred* of information. Every search term has gone into a little notebook, color-coded, with Post-it flags to cross-reference anything interesting. But weeks of research hasn't yielded anything useful.

Seeing my own ghost

Ghostly doppelgänger

Whisper ghost

I glance around, even though I *know* I'm alone. I'm about to break so many rules, I could be fired if anyone finds out what I'm doing. But the internet can't help me, so I open a Tor browser. The dark web is where secrets have secrets, and the unexplained is only the beginning. Maybe there, I'll find something.

Or I'll ruin my entire career.

At this point, do I care? No. I need answers—and a way to make my whisper vanish. For good.

Navigating this hidden—and forbidden—knowledge is like wandering through a labyrinth in the dark. Conspiracy theories abound. Everything from faking the moon landing—really? People are still going on about that one?—to blaming climate change on a vampire opening a rift to Hell.

Nothing about whispers. Or at least *my* whisper. Every search is a dead end. Until I stumble upon someone talking about the world of *The Other*.

ONegLovr: Dude. There are medical clinics that only treat the paranormal! I haven't had a proper dental exam in fifty years. If my maker hadn't been staked through the heart a week after turning me, I'd find a way to end him for not telling me about this!

His maker? Holy shit. This guy thinks he's an actual vampire. With a maker.

He must be a fan of Anne Rice. Or romance novels.

A dozen others pile on. By their screen names, they think

they're witches, vampires, shifters, and even ghosts. I keep digging, even deeper, until I find an honest-to-God list of Other clinics. Including three within the San Francisco city limits.

This can't be real. Can it? If I weren't seeing a ghost every time I turned around—and one who looks just like me—I wouldn't put stock in anything I've just read. But with no other options, maybe I should suspend my disbelief?

By the time I log off, it's well after six, and my stomach feels hollow. But one of the clinics is on my way home. Dinner can wait. I need to see a doctor. Right now.

THE PRETTY RECEPTIONIST at DVS Urgent Care narrows her eyes at me. "Can I help you?"

"Uh...yes. I need to see a doctor." My voice cracks, and I sweep my gaze around the waiting room. Everyone here *looks* normal enough. A mother with two little boys who chase each other around the room, an older man with a cane next to his seat, and a security guard in a boring, tan uniform leaning against the far wall.

The woman pulls out a small, black box, flips a switch, and frowns. "There's another clinic across the street that might be a better fit for you. We...have a very long wait right now."

I turn, staring out the glass doors. The place across the street is affiliated with the local hospital. And they weren't on the list I pulled off the dark web.

"No, I need to see someone here," I insist. "Please." Leaning closer, I lower my voice. "I'm not...I'm...something else. I'm Other."

"You're not, dear." She shakes her head. "Not according to my scans."

"Well, your scanner must be broken." I snatch the device from her hand. "Oh, my God."

Ocular Transmutational Health Existence Reporter
O.T.H.E.R.?

"You have got to be kidding me. This is how you determine if someone should be seen here? This is a joke, right?"

Claws extend from her pale fingers, and she plucks the box from my palm so quickly, I see nothing but a black blur.

"No. It's not. If you were...*other*...this device would tell me. You need to leave. Now. If you don't, I'll have to get George to escort you out and wipe your memory of this entire encounter." She drops the black box back into her pocket, and out of the corner of my eye, George straightens.

"I'm seeing my own ghost!" My voice drops to a whisper, but with too harsh of an edge to hide my words from the others in the waiting room. "All the time. And sometimes, I *am* her! Please. Don't kick me out. Let me see a doctor. I can't sleep I'm going to lose my job if I can't make this stop." Tears well in my eyes, and through the shimmer they lend to the room, I think her expression softens slightly.

The nurse sighs. "All right. I'll get you in with Dr. Nem. But if he doesn't find any evidence of *other* in you, he won't be as kind as George."

I force my shoulders back and meet her gaze. Her eyes aren't a normal human color. They're almost...purple. I wonder what she is. What all of these people are. But most of all, I wonder what I am.

"I don't care. I'll risk it."

DR. NEM WHIRLS around as a tray of medical equipment clatters to the floor. Shaking off the fog that came over me when he grabbed my head, his fingers digging into my temples, I leap off the exam table and dart through the door. I make it out of the clinic two steps ahead of George. The security guard is *definitely* not human. His eyes glow bright red, and are those...wings fluttering along his back? Shit.

The doctor tried to be kind—at first. But when I refused to

believe my whisper was a figment of my imagination, his anger scared the shit out of me.

"You are as human as they come," Dr. Nem says. *"This ghost you're seeing? It's all in your head."*

"It's not! She can...do things. She knocked a book off the shelf in the library this afternoon!"

He narrows his eyes at me. The man is covered with a layer of short, brown fur. His ears stick out from the top of his head, and his flattened nose flares with his huff. "She needs to be disciplined for showing herself to you. After I wipe your memory, I'm calling the Bureau. She's broken at least half a dozen laws."

My whisper floats alongside me as we cross the street. "Is he right? Are you a ghost?"

She shakes her head and points to me.

"What the hell does that mean? God, if you can't talk, the least you could do is learn sign language or something."

With a harsh glare—or as harsh as she can manage since she's mostly translucent—she stamps her foot against the pavement, then disappears completely.

Great. Dr. Nem practically laughed in my face, then threatened me—and my whisper. Do I risk trying another clinic? Or is that a one-way ticket to getting my memory wiped?

I'm so exhausted, each step feels like I'm walking through quicksand. Or...what I always imagined quicksand to feel like.

Is quicksand even real?

That thought occupies me for so long, I almost miss the light and have to run across the street to catch the bus.

But I learned two things today. First, my whisper cares for me. At least a little. She stopped Dr. Nem from wiping my memory.

The second? She's definitely getting stronger.

FIVE

Gabriel

I have tired of the constant *noise* in New York City. The car horns never stop. I attempted to ride the subway—a man selling pretzels from a cart on the street corner assured me this was the ultimate New York experience. But all I find is the stench of too many bodies pressed together with little room to breathe, let alone move.

A hand grabs my ass, and I turn to find a male with a hungry grin and raw lust in his hazel eyes. "Get off at the next stop," he says, "and I'll show you a good time, handsome."

I look into his mind. He wants to get on his knees and suck my cock? The visual is not unpleasant. Though I had no idea such things between strangers were...encouraged in this realm.

I almost agree. After all, I am here to experience *all* of humanity. But then the man pictures three others lying in wait to rob me. I stare down at him, infusing my voice with all of my angelic power. "If you ever proposition someone with the intention of taking their valuables again, *human*, you may very well find yourself trapped on the wrong side of Hell's gates. Do you understand me?"

The stench of urine cuts through the air between us. It stains his light brown pants, and he shrinks back, apologies tumbling from his lips until the train stops, and he flees into the crowd on the platform.

Interesting.

Maddox warned me that humans were often terrible to one another. I have watched over wars, even genocides, but to experience it one-on-one is new.

I move to the end of the platform and wait for the crowds to clear before I hop down onto the tracks and stride deeper into the subway tunnels.

Once I have enough privacy that no one will notice me disappear, I pull out my phone. Killian taught me how to use the internet, and I bring up the browser to search.

Typical small town in the United States

Scrolling through the list, I'm drawn to the beauty of Big Sky, Montana. There are only a little over two thousand people in the entire city. This is a place I should see.

I picture it in my mind, and let my angelic power carry me there.

THE MOTEL'S scratchy sheets offend my skin. Sinclair was not pleased that I charged my stay at a "five-star hotel" in New York City to his credit card, so I chose a place with only one star in Big Sky. This...may have been a mistake.

My body still aches. I abandon the idea of sleep not long after 6:00 a.m. In the center of the small room, I unfurl my wings. Unchecked agony pulls a scream from my lips, but I clap my hand over my mouth to stifle the sound.

It has been four days since I flew into the fires of Hell, and the pain will not fade. Dying, blackened feathers litter the gaudy motel carpet. The mirror over the bed reveals the extent of the devastation. Even the skin on my back has not fully healed, though the blisters are gone.

I stare at my reflection and touch two fingers to my cheek. It is...rough. Dark. Covered in short hair halfway down my neck. What am I supposed to do about this? Is this normal?

Phone in hand, I hide my wings with a groan and stumble for the bathroom. Maddox and Killian would only call me naive again if I ask them for advice. The warlock tried to hide his laughter when I asked him if it was safe to purchase the pretzel from that "food cart" in New York City. So I dial the only other person in this realm who might be willing to talk to me.

"What the fuck do you think you're doing calling this early?" Sinclair growls.

His voice sounds strange. Rough. Then again, his consciousness did dive headfirst into the burning River Phlegethon only days ago. Perhaps there have been lasting effects I had not considered.

"Early?" I cannot stop staring at my reflection. "The sun is up. Is that not when most in this realm wake?"

Sinclair lowers his voice, and his tone changes completely. Gentle. An undercurrent of worry and concern. "Go back to sleep, my love. Gabriel needs a lesson on time zones. And common courtesy."

My huff tugs at the muscles in my back. "I do not know what these *time zones* are, but I seem to have grown hair. On my face. A fair amount of it."

The demon's laughter carries over the small device. He mocks me? This is serious, and I do not know if I like it.

"Gabriel, have you never shaved before?"

"Why the fuck would I need to? This does not happen in the celestial realm. Surely you remember..."

"Watch yourself. I was banished, then consigned to Hell's endless torment for centuries. And you had a hand in it all. No one—not even the Almighty herself—would blame me for hanging up on you."

He is not wrong.

"Sinclair, I do not deserve your forgiveness. So I will not ask for it. But I *am* sorry for my part in what happened to you—and to

Zoe." I sink down onto the edge of the tub and run a hand through my hair. "I will not call you again."

"Wait. Zoe needs sleep, and if I am to teach you how to shave, I require coffee. I will call you back in ten minutes. Do *not* pick up a razor before then lest you sever your carotid artery. Even with your angelic strength, that type of injury could still be fatal."

Willow

It took me two days to work up the courage to try a second *Other* medical clinic. At least this one didn't threaten to wipe my memory. They just laughed at me and gave me a referral to a therapist.

The kindly older woman—Dr. Nolan—balances her tablet on her knee so she can take notes. I'm pretty sure she's a witch of some sort, because she doesn't type a thing. Just waves her hand at the device as I explain everything that's happened in the past three weeks.

"So...I can't be human. Right? If my whisper looked like someone else, then sure. I could believe she was just a ghost who decided to haunt me. Not that she has a reason." I swipe at my damp eyes with a tissue and glare over Dr. Nolan's shoulder. My whisper glares right back at me. "But she's *me*. Right down to what I'm wearing every day."

"Why do you call her your 'whisper'?" the doctor asks.

"Because when I was at the church—when this all started—I heard a voice. It called me the 'whisper keeper.'"

"WILLOW, I'm writing you a prescription for a mild sleeping pill. Chronic insomnia can result in hallucinations, anxiety, and depression—among many other things. Clearly you experienced *something* at the cathedral. Something *other*. But a carbon copy of yourself no one else can see? That the most advanced *Other* technology can't detect? I'm afraid that's simply not possible.

"I suspect after a few nights of solid sleep, this 'whisper' will be nothing but a memory."

"But—"

"Here you go, dear. I'm afraid our time is up for the day. Make an appointment for next week and we can see how you're sleeping then." She passes me the white slip of paper with the neatest handwriting I've ever seen, then snaps her fingers. Her office door opens, and I want to cry.

Why won't anyone believe me?

HOURS LATER, I huddle on the couch wrapped in my weighted blanket. The rains are back, and the water cascading down my windows mirrors my mood.

The bottle of pills sits on the coffee table, mocking me.

"Mild, my ass," I mutter. The pharmacist was shocked at the dosage and advised me to cut the pills in half to start.

My fingers curl around the mug of tea, the warmth reassuring. I haven't seen my whisper since I left Nolan's office and ended up at a bus stop less than half a mile from St. Mary's Cathedral.

She appeared at my elbow. Her gauzy fingers brushed my skin. I sensed—rather than felt—her tug on my arm. But I refused to budge, and she took off at a run toward the old church.

Seeing through her eyes left me so nauseous, I was about to vomit all over my shoes. I couldn't move. Walking—hell, even standing—when you can't see a damn thing around you is a recipe for disaster. The pull to follow her was almost overwhelming.

Seconds after she turned the corner and the cathedral came into view, my vision shrank down to nothing for a heartbeat, and she was gone.

A single tear tumbles down my cheek. I open the prescription bottle and stare at the little white pills inside. What choice do I have? People go mad from lack of sleep.

My whisper is real. I'd bet my life on it. But if she continues to keep me up night after night, it won't be long before Nolan has me committed. Or I commit myself.

Before I can fish out one of the tablets, someone knocks on my apartment door. Struggling out from under the weighted blanket, I swipe my phone from the cushion next to me, then check the peephole.

A man and a woman in matching black suits stand stiffly. I can feel their tension through the door. Slowly, I reach for the pepper spray hanging from a hook on the wall, check the chain, and flip the lock. "Can I help you?"

"Willow Saunders?" the woman asks. "I'm Dr. Hannah Smith and this is Special Agent Isaac Barton." She holds up a badge in a small billfold. "We're with the Agency for Uncovering Rare Anomalies, a branch of the National Security Agency."

The NSA?

"Um, I hope you won't take this the wrong way, but I've never heard of the Agency for Uncovering Rare Anomalies." I adjust my grip on the pepper spray. "And no one from the NSA should know my name."

Special Agent Barton arches a brow. "You've been all over the dark web for weeks while logged into your UCSF staff account. Finding your name wasn't difficult."

Oh, shit.

"I specialize in mythology and the occult. All those queries were for a research paper."

Can they hear the desperation in my tone? Or see the small tube of caustic spray in my hand? I should never have opened the door. Or put down my phone. Government agents carry guns, don't they? And Barton looks like he'd have no problems using one. On me.

"Dr. Saunders—Willow—you don't need to lie to us," Dr. Smith says with a gentle smile. "We're on your side. Perhaps we should talk inside?"

"It's late. I think you should...come in?"

I have my hand on the chain when the words register.

"Wait. No. I'd like you to leave. I'm sorry. I'm really tired, and I can't deal with this now. Good night, Dr. Smith. Mr. Barton."

"Call me Hannah. Please." Her brown eyes radiate compassion. "We believe you, Willow. You're not delusional. Your whisper is very real and very, *very* special."

I look from her to her partner. Barton doesn't smile, but I'm not sure why I ever thought he was threatening. More like an older brother who isn't sure what his sister has gotten herself into.

He clears his throat. "We understand you have concerns. It's only natural. The NSA operates in the shadows. But we have a public phone number anyone can call. Tomorrow, verify our identities with them. Once you've done so," he pulls a business card from his jacket pocket and passes it through the crack in the door, "call us. Our mobile numbers are on the back."

My shoulders start to unglue themselves from my ears. Logic. I can handle logic. "What happens if I decide to call?"

Hannah's brown eyes sparkle, and her smile widens even more. "We can teach you how to control your whisper. How to work *with* her. You could be the most powerful witch the world has ever known, Willow. Together, we could save many, many lives."

SIX

Willow

I pour myself a second cup of coffee and open my laptop. I took one of the pills Dr. Nolan prescribed, but it didn't do spit for me after my visit from the two NSA agents—other than leave me with the world's worst hangover and dangerously low blood pressure. I've almost passed out twice this morning, and I've only been out of bed for an hour.

It's not hard to verify that Dr. Hannah Smith and Special Agent Isaac Barton work for the National Security Agency. The helpful woman on the phone emails me their ID photos and confirms they're assigned to a special project at the moment, but she won't—or can't—tell me what it is.

I wish I could talk to my whisper. Or that she could talk back to me. Heck, I'd settle for *seeing* her right now. What if she doesn't come back?

My laugh hits at the exact wrong time, and I almost choke on a sip of coffee. I finally find people who believe me the same day my whisper disappears forever? I'm not *that* unlucky. Am I?

You're about to be fired from the best job you've ever had because your department chair thinks you're losing your mind. That seems pretty damn unlucky.

Well, shit. My thoughts run wild when I'm sleep deprived, and the marathon they're currently on feels like it's leading me right through the Bermuda Triangle.

I stare at the card Barton left for me until the numbers on the back start to blur. What do I have to lose? If my whisper truly is gone, they'll understand, right? Or they'll know how to bring her back.

Dr. Smith picks up on the first ring. "Willow? It's good to hear from you. I hope you were able to get some rest last night."

"Uh, n-no. Not really. But…I called the NSA. Can we meet?"

"Of course. If you're up to it. We can always wait until you've had a good night's sleep. We want to help you. Not add even more stress to your life." The warmth and concern in her voice raises a lump in my throat. She's not pretending to care like Dr. Nolan did. Not trying to drug me into oblivion rather than *help* me.

"No. I don't want to wait. Where should I meet you?" If I have to go one more day without knowing *why* I now have a whisper, I'm not sure I'll survive it.

"Anywhere you'd like," Hannah says. "We can come to your apartment, I can give you our address, or, if it would make you more comfortable, choose a public location and we'll be there within an hour."

I swallow hard. In for a penny, in for a pound. Or so my dad always says. "I'll come to you."

<hr>

THE ADDRESS HANNAH gave me is less than two miles away. The rains have stopped, so I tuck my pepper spray and phone into my crossbody bag. The walk along the waterfront should calm me. So should the presence of my whisper at my side. She appeared the moment I stepped out of my apartment.

She hasn't pulled me into her head, though. Thank God. Every time she appears, I think she gets a little stronger. I can still see right through her, but from time to time, I catch a flicker of shadow. Not mine. Hers. I wish I could ask her if she *feels* more real. If she's doing this on purpose. But though she has occasionally answered a question with a nod or a shake of her head, she's ignoring me now.

I check my phone outside a plain, almost run-down building two blocks off Market Street. It would look like every other building if not for the fancy security panel next to the heavy metal door.

The screen glows as I approach, and a beam of blue light sweeps across my face.

Welcome, Willow Saunders.

Well, that's not creepy. Though, this is the NSA. They could probably find out what I had for breakfast this morning. Or get my kindergarten report card.

The door swings open, and I step into a brightly lit waiting area, complete with couches, a fancy espresso machine, and plants in every corner.

I beeline for another cup of coffee. I need all the caffeine I can get. The rich scent comforts me, and I wrap the paper cup in both hands, needing its warmth for what I'm about to do.

Part of the wall slides open without a sound, and Hannah steps into the waiting room. "Oh, Willow. You look like you haven't slept at all!" She nudges my chin up gently—she's several inches taller than I am—and stares into my eyes. "This whole ordeal has been hell on you, hasn't it?"

A wave of emotion clogs my throat. Tears lend a watery glow to the room, and I nod. "I just want to understand...why."

"I know. You will. I promise." She's so earnest. So open. She'll explain everything.

"Dr. Smith, I—"

"You must call me Hannah." She leads me through the hidden door, down the hall, and to another security panel where she punches in a long code and swipes a badge clipped to her black jacket.

I gape at the state-of-the-art lab. Glossy white workstations, flat-screen monitors, and half a dozen men and women chatting or fiddling with equipment. In the far corner, in a glass-walled conference room, Barton sits in an ergonomic chair with a cup of coffee at his elbow.

"Can I get you a refill? Or maybe something better?" Hannah asks, pausing at a gourmet beverage station. "The machine in the lobby is good, but this one makes cappuccinos and lattes too. We have the best coffee in the city."

Three cups in a day is plenty. Any more and I risk having a severe POTS episode. But my mouth waters as she makes herself a cappuccino.

"Um...sure? That smells great." I pass her my paper cup, and after a few moments fiddling with the levers and dials on the machine, she offers me a ceramic mug with a perfect layer of foam on top. I take a sip, and the flavor calms my nerves.

She shuts the conference room door, and all the sounds of the lab fall away. It's almost eerie how quiet it is now. I can hear Hannah breathing, and Barton's fingers drumming softly against the arm of his chair.

"Willow," Isaac says, leaning forward and steepling his hands on the polished wood table, "the *manifestation* you've been experiencing is not a figment of your imagination as your therapist believes. Whispers are so rare, only a handful of people outside of this lab know about them—and about Whisper Keepers. How long have you been seeing your whisper? Two weeks? Three?"

I almost drop the mug.

"A little less than three."

Did he guess? Or...?

The dark web. I did more than search. I posted too.

His intense hazel eyes gentle slightly. "That's a long time if you don't know why. I'm assuming—because you're here—you don't."

I shake my head. If I try to speak, I'll end up sobbing. I'm going to get answers. *Real* answers. I can feel it in my bones. In my heart. These people can help me.

"Whisper keepers hold some of the most powerful magic in all the world. You, Willow, are a witch, and the things you can do—that you'll be able to do—"

"I'm not a witch," I protest, my voice cracking. "If I were, wouldn't the Other medical clinic have been able to tell? They did these scans. Some device. The *Ocular Transmutational Health Existence something.*"

"Reporter," Hannah says with a delicate, feminine snort. "I swear, whoever names things in the world of the Other has the oddest sense of humor. Or maybe no sense of humor at all."

I manage a weak chuckle. She's not wrong. Calling an *Other* detector something that anagrams to O.T.H.E.R. is so obvious, it borders on the ridiculous.

She drains the last of her cappuccino and dabs at her lips with a handkerchief. "Most magic has its origins in the elements. Earth, air, fire, water, and aether. Witches tap into these elements, bending them to their will and using their power. They register on the device because the elements flow through them every moment of every day. Your magic is different. Yours is woven so deeply into your DNA, it can't be scanned for."

"I don't understand. How?" I run my fingers over the edge of the mug. An odd scent wafts over me now that the cappuccino is mostly gone. Almost...metallic. But it fades in seconds.

"The magic is your legacy," she says. "It skips generations—from what we've been able to learn. But all the women in your line carry it. *Accessing* it, though...that's a completely different matter."

The women in my line?

I don't know any of the women in "my line." My parents adopted me when I was an infant. I'd been found on a park bench at dawn, wrapped in a pink blanket, only days old.

Isaac clears his throat. "The spells you need to use your gifts come from an ancient book locked away behind so many wards and barriers, only your whisper can get to it."

"I don't understand. I'm thirty-six years old. And I only started seeing my...whisper less than three weeks ago. If I've had this magic in me all my life, why did it choose *now* to manifest?"

Ugh. I should have asked for water instead of a cappuccino. My mouth is suddenly bone dry, and my heart is beating so hard, I can feel it in my cheeks.

"Have you ever been to St. Mary's Cathedral on Gough Street?" Hannah asks.

Shock cools the flames licking up my neck. My body is freezing now. I wrap my arms around myself so I don't start to shiver. "Y-yes. How did you know?"

Isaac leans forward. "The book is in a vault under the cathedral. You must have been close enough for the power to sense you. It created your whisper. Gave you the key to claim your birthright."

"I don't *want* this birthright. Can't I...turn it off? Or give it back?" Tears prick at my eyes.

Hannah and Isaac exchange a glance. Something passes between them, but before I can figure out what it is, Hannah shakes her head. "I'm sorry, Willow. We don't think you can. But you can learn to control it." A large flat screen monitor winks on at the head of the table, and I gasp as Dr. Nolan's session notes come into focus.

"Willow complains that the 'whisper' wakes her up at night. She claims to be able to see through the ghost's eyes and hear what's going on around the ghost, even when they aren't in the same room. Her delusions are quite well thought out, which is remarkable. And suspicious."

"Suspicious?" A harsh sob escapes my lips. "She thinks I made the whole thing up?"

"Shhh." Hannah reaches across the table and covers my hand with hers. "We scrubbed your records from her files, and we'll gently *suggest* that she transfer out of the San Francisco Bay Area. We can be very persuasive when we want to be."

I let that woman drug me. She was so certain I was making the whole thing up, and I let her drug me.

Hannah's fingers are warm, and she gives my hand a gentle squeeze. "We can teach you how to protect yourself from your whisper's...whims," she says. She's so confident. So calm, I can't help but believe her. She gestures between herself and Isaac. "We're both human, Willow. But we've studied magic for our entire careers. Half the techs out there are witches and warlocks. We employ a vampire and a shifter as consultants when we need them. Your talents? They can do so much good in the world."

"I don't understand how my whisper—my magic—can help anyone. She's a ghost. She can't *do* anything but keep me up at night and pull me into her reality."

Hannah shakes her head. "She's not a ghost. She's an extension of you, Willow. Non-corporeal—for now—but we think if you were to work *with* her instead of fighting her all the time, she could one day affect the physical world around her. And if you can activate the full power of your gifts..." Hannah's light brown eyes take on a sparkle, "we think you'll be able to find the Blade of Liminal Transference."

"The...what?" I try—unsuccessfully—to stifle my laugh. "That's...not a thing."

Isaac sits up straighter in his chair, and for a moment, I think he's about to snap at me. But then he blows out a deep breath. "Until three weeks ago, you didn't know anything about the world of the *Other*. How many different types of creatures can you name?"

"Uh...vampires, witches, werewolves, ghosts? Faeries? I have a Ph.D. in Mythology and the Occult. I know a lot about what the rest of the world thinks are...*other* creatures. That doesn't mean they're all...real." He's testing me—baiting me—and frustration prickles over my skin.

"They are. All of them," he says. "But so are centaurs, banshees, hydras, sirens, griffins, unicorns, every type of shifter you can imagine—including werewolves—dragons, even yetis and the Loch Ness monster."

My jaw drops open. Until I remember what we were talking about in the first place. "Fine. But...the Blade of Liminal Transference? The BLT? That's a sandwich."

This was a mistake. I don't care if my whisper keeps me up

every night for the rest of my life. I can't trust anyone who thinks BLT is a good name for some sort of magical artifact.

Hannah reaches for my hand before I can get to my feet. "Willow, the Blade was named centuries ago. Long before anyone decided bacon, lettuce, and tomato made a proper sandwich. And the device the *Other* medical clinic used on you? What was that called again?"

"O.T.H.E.R. Point taken. I guess." I drain the last sip of the now-cool cappuccino, then set the mug aside. "Why do you need *me* to find this thing? Is it a weapon?"

With a tiny cough, Hannah sits back. "The last witch to possess the Blade—that we know of—died in 1879. Her sons built St. Mary's Cathedral and they kept her spell book in the vault under the old church. But after the earthquake and fire in 1906, the vault was sealed shut."

"That still doesn't explain why you need me. You're the NSA. Go down there with some sort of drill and break in." I push my chair away from the table.

"We can't. The vault is warded." Isaac jerks up and starts to pace. "Six stone masons and two witches have died in the last fifty years trying to do just that. But the wards will open for you. *Only* for you."

I stand too quickly. My heart pounds so hard, it's all I can feel. A soft roar fills my ears. Bracing my hands on my thighs, I force slow, deep breaths until Hannah wraps an arm around my waist and eases me back into the fancy chair.

"You're special, Willow," she says. "So is the Blade. Once you come into your full power, you'll work miracles with it."

I scoff. "Miracles? No one can work miracles."

"You can. A hundred and fifty years ago, we didn't have the medical technology we do now. We weren't *this* close to curing cancer. Parkinson's. Dementia. Shifters have a natural immunity to almost all human diseases—and many *Other* illnesses too. The Blade can transfer that immunity to anyone—or everyone. And it's not just the big ones. Cancer. Heart disease. Renal failure.

Vampire blood allergies will be a thing of the past. Wand Rot could be wiped out in a matter of *days*."

This is all too much. Wand Rot. Vampire blood allergies. Miracles.

My head spins. Dark spots float all around me. Hannah sounds like she's underwater. My blood pressure drops like the roller coaster just started its descent. I'm going to pass out. I can't stop it. All I can do is give in.

SEVEN

Willow

I open my eyes to find my whisper staring down at me, concern knitting her brows. Her hand brushes mine, though I feel nothing from the touch.

"Go away. Please."

She doesn't respond. How can she without a voice?

Lying on my couch under my weighted blanket, I stare out the window at the city skyline. Until she glides over and distorts my view.

"This isn't helping. *You're* not helping. I need to think. Hannah's waiting for an answer. She can help me. Us. If I'm stuck with this power, I should use it for something good. Right?"

Her shoulders heave and...is that a tear glistening on her cheek? Shit. I hurt her feelings.

"I didn't mean stuck like *that*. But, geez. You keep me up every night. And I miss my students. Anton won't let me come back if I can't get through a day without being pulled into your..." I wave my hand up and down, "body? Spirit? Can't you stop this? Even for a day or two?"

She shrugs.

"So you don't know how to control this...*thing* between us at all?" I'm so happy we're actually communicating—even if it is just yes and no questions—that when she shakes her head, I only sigh.

I roll onto my back and stare up at the ceiling. It's been three weeks since I've had a solid night's sleep. Since I've felt...sane. Since I've known where my life was going.

My phone buzzes on the coffee table, and I groan as I struggle to get my arm out from under the blanket.

Hannah: How are you feeling? I won't lie to you, Willow. We want—and need—you to work with us. But we also want you to be happy. And healthy. Whatever you decide. If you need to get away for a few days to think, we can put you up in a nice hotel with all the bells and whistles. No strings attached. Just say the word and we'll make it happen.

Tears burn my eyes. I've been on my own since I moved out of my parents' house at nineteen. College, graduate school. Teaching. Getting my Ph.D. I can't remember the last time I took a vacation. Or stayed in a fancy hotel. Self-care isn't a priority when you're trying to make tenure.

Willow: That's really nice of you. But it's too much. I can't accept.

The little reply bubbles dance at the bottom of the screen for a few seconds.

Hannah: We're the United States government. We spent almost $500,000 on a self-cleaning toilet in a D.C. Metro station that's been broken for five years now. If we can do that, we can certainly fund a stay at the Four Seasons for a few days. Let me do this for you. If nothing else, maybe it'll help you sleep.

I shouldn't. But what if it *does* help? I look over to the window, hoping my whisper might be listening, but she's gone, and I'm alone again.

Willow: You can guarantee the no strings part?

I hold my breath as the bubbles return to the screen.

Hannah: I'll have it notarized and in writing. If you want to pack a bag, there will be a car waiting downstairs in an hour.

FROM THE CHAISE lounge in my room at the Four Seasons, I stare out at the bay. This place is amazing. Last night, all I cared about was the big bed with endless pillows, but today, Hannah arranged for an in-room massage and facial, room service for every meal, and a *very* nice bottle of wine to go with dinner.

But the best part is the little zen fountain currently burbling on the table a few feet away. The one with a powerful magic dampener built in.

I haven't seen my whisper since I got here. I slept ten hours last night, uninterrupted, and for the first time in three weeks, my brain doesn't feel like a tub of wet cement.

Totally worth the little pang of guilt I feel at keeping her away. It's only for a couple of days. Just long enough for me to decide what to do. And to remember what it's like to be *me* again.

Gabriel

The last rays of the sun stretch for the alley behind Sinclair's building. The incubus demon leans against a weathered brick wall, hands in the pockets of his long, leather coat.

"I have been waiting for twenty minutes, archangel. Zoe is *alone*." He straightens, looks me up and down, and arches a brow. "Are you—is that—popcorn?"

The red and white striped bag crinkles in my hand. "Kettle Corn. Both sweet and salty. I discovered it at an event called a 'county fair' in Ohio. Have you tried it?"

"There are few foods I have not tried. Or have you forgotten how many years I have passed in this realm?" With a shake of his head, he turns and strides to the end of the narrow alley, only pausing when a bus rumbles by to toss a gaze over his shoulder. "Are you coming?"

His attitude grates. As if my presence is some sort of burden or annoyance to him. Though, perhaps it is.

In truth, I almost did not return to San Francisco. I suspect Sinclair only extended the invitation to this "dinner party" at Zoe's behest. He would likely be happy to never see me again after all the pain I caused them both.

"Zoe would like to have our...friends...over for dinner. Tomorrow at 6:30 p.m. But I swear to you, Gabriel, if you simply appear in the middle of our home, I will throw you off the balcony. Without the use of your wings, you will break many bones. Zoe may have the soul of a celestial, but her human body is fragile—thanks to Seraphiel's meddling ways."

"Well?" He has not moved except to cross his arms over his chest. "I will not stand here all night."

I shake off the memory of his phone call and sigh. "If I must."

"If you must?" Sinclair scoffs. "You have free will, Gabriel. If you do not wish to be here, take your kettle corn and fuck off."

"You invited me. And I have not eaten in two hours."

Sinclair's blue eyes flash a darker shade, and I release the tight hold I keep on my angelic powers for a brief moment. He is... amused with me. Not angry. Baffled, perhaps. Also, worried about Zoe.

"Two hours is hardly enough time for you to starve. And if I'm not mistaken, kettle corn is—technically—food."

I reach for his arm. He stiffens, the muscles tensing under my fingers, and glares at me.

"Zoe *has* recovered, has she not?"

A fresh wave of worry washes over him. Strange. The Sinclair I returned to the earthen realm centuries ago cared for nothing and no one. Mating has changed him in many ways.

"Watch yourself, Gabriel. Physically, she is healing," Sinclair says with a heavy sigh. "But she will bear the scars from those days for eternity." He shoves at his jacket sleeve, then unbuttons the cuff of his black dress shirt and rolls it up to his elbow. A shimmering tattoo of a masked, winged man carrying a whip brands his skin. "As will I."

Sinclair spent more than two hundred years as Thorn's unwilling slave, forced to trap and torture the demon's victims without mercy. He wears his guilt like a second skin. Or perhaps it is so ingrained in him now, he will never be able to shed it.

What is this sour taste in my mouth? The heavy weight on my shoulders? This twisting in my gut?

Emotions. *Human* emotions. I am an archangel. One of the Almighty's chosen. I do not need emotions. But the longer I spend in the earthen realm, the more of them I seem to experience. And the more I find them utterly...addicting.

Wonder. Frustration. Joy. And now...guilt.

"Enough of this," Sin says. He fastens the cuff of his dress shirt once more and gestures to the top of the building. "Zoe has not been alone since..." His words dissolve into a growl.

He has not left her side since he rescued her? "I thought you returned to the Bureau this week."

"We did."

My brows furrow, another foreign sensation. "Surely she did not allow you to accompany her to the bathroom?"

"Fuck. No. Must everything be literal with you?" He shakes his head. "I am going inside. Follow or don't." He stalks around the corner toward the gilded double doors.

I trail after the incubus at a distance. He is still angry. As he should be. My actions—my apathy—allowed Seraphiel to trap Zoe in a prison of her own body for centuries, and could have easily led to her eternal torment had Sin not fallen in love with her—twice—and finally figured out who she had once been.

At the building's front doors, I pause. Perhaps my presence will be too painful.

But if I do not join them for dinner, what else will I do with myself? My wings have not yet healed, and though there is still much of the world for me to experience, Sinclair will certainly tire of funding my education in humanity soon.

When that happens, I will have no choice but to call Azrael and beg him to carry me back to the celestial realm. The very idea of that leaves a sour taste in my mouth. Seraphiel will never let me hear the end of it.

"You opened a portal to Hell and nearly destroyed your wings? You are an idiot, Gabriel. The Almighty will banish you for this!"

Would she? I suppose it *is* possible. Seraphiel has her ear. The rest of us are lucky to garner an audience.

"Gabriel?" The deep voice startles me. Pain ripples across my back as my wings beg to be released. But I cannot let them. An angel on the streets of San Francisco would attract much attention. Especially an angel whose wings look like they have been through a wood chipper.

Turning, I hide my wince, and peer up. At a chin. With white fur. Higher still, I find the yeti's face. Dark eyes, a black nose, and sharp teeth. Dressed in a suit of all things.

Kunchin, one of Sinclair and Zoe's colleagues at the Bureau of the Occult and the Other, peers down at me. "He wasn't sure you'd come."

"It was this or something called a 'cow pie toss' at the Akron County Fair. The stench alone was...off putting." I drop the bag of kettle corn into a trash receptacle and heft my duffel bag higher on my shoulder. "Though I was mildly curious to see how far excrement could fly."

The yeti chuckles, and I wonder what about my response was humorous.

A car pulls up to the curb, the back door opens, and a strikingly beautiful woman alights. Her gaze darts up and down the street, and I can sense her fear.

"Dion. Are you well?" I ask. The panther shifter was abducted with Zoe, starved, beaten, and held for days in old drainage tunnels far below the city. I cannot imagine the pain she must have endured, yet physically, she seems to have recovered.

She flinches and pulls her ankle-length wool coat tighter around her body. "Gabriel. You look...very different without your wings. And robes."

I stare down at the khaki pants, dark blue shirt, and loafers. They do not change my body. Only...*decorate* it in different ways.

Then I realize why she is confused. "It is my facial hair. Shaving is quite annoying. And time consuming. I have decided while I am in the earthen realm, I will grow a beard." I stroke the hair. It changed from scratchy to soft sometime in the past two days, and I discovered a wondrous product called beard oil.

"One of the benefits of being a yeti," Kunchin says. "Though having a Bureau-issued perception filter helps too." He offers Dion his arm. "Let's go inside. Sin and Zoe are waiting for us."

I HANG BACK until Sinclair welcomes the yeti and Dion into his home and takes their coats. Once the warded doors of the penthouse close, the panther shifter shudders. Sleek, black fur ripples over every inch of exposed skin. Her eyes take on a more slanted appearance, and she relaxes with a sigh.

"I *hate* going out in public in my human skin. I feel so exposed, and I haven't been able to get warm since..." Her cheeks pale, and she makes her way into the lavish living room where flames flicker behind a glass panel in the wall. "My heating bill is going to be through the roof this month. Or...for the rest of my life."

"Zoe, my love," Sinclair says as he knocks gently on their bedroom door at the end of the hall. "Dion and Kunchin are here. Gabriel as well. Mad and Killian are on their way with the food."

I can sense Zoe's emotions over all the others in the room. Perhaps because she is a celestial. Or because of the overwhelming guilt I will never be able to escape over my part in what happened to her.

The door opens, and Zoe fits herself to Sinclair's side. He winds one of her red curls around his finger, the gesture so intimate, I think I should perhaps look away.

The two share a glance—a brief moment of connection—and I wonder what it would be like to be so attuned to another being that your souls intertwine. I will never know. Archangels do not... mate. We belong in the celestial realm. Alone. Always alone.

EIGHT

Willow

Only a handful of stars dot the darkened sky above St. Mary's Cathedral. It's almost midnight, and this is my first training exercise with the Agency for Uncovering Rare Anomalies.

My whisper floats along beside me, and I think I can *feel* her excitement. Hannah, Isaac, and the rest of their team believe in us. They think we can do something wonderful. Something to help people.

"Are you sure I have to take a leave of absence from my job?" I ask Hannah as we follow Isaac through the door to the rectory. It's almost completely silent inside the church, only the odd sounds of an old building surrounding us in the dimly lit space.

"Once you've fully realized your power, you'll be able to locate the BLT." Hannah rests her hand at the small of my back and guides me up the aisle between the pews. "But it could be anywhere from Florida to the Arctic Circle. We have no idea if it's protected by more wards or guarded by an army."

"An army?" The words escape on a squeak. "I'm not fighting an army. I'm a college professor!"

Hannah's light laugh doesn't reassure me. Much. It's almost impossible to panic with her at my side.

"I'm so sorry, Willow. That was a terrible joke. I've been looking for the Blade—and the next Whisper Keeper—for so long, I'm a little giddy. We don't truly believe we'll find an army. At worst, perhaps a small coven of witches we'll need to convince of our good intentions."

"But...we're only a month into the quarter. My students need me." For a moment, I wonder who I am if I'm not Dr. Willow Saunders, adjunct professor. Until I realize I could be more. I could be Willow Saunders, the witch. Willow Saunders, the woman who helped cure cancer. Willow Saunders, the Whisper Keeper.

"We'll talk to your department chair," Hannah assures me. "You won't lose your job. Give us a year, and we'll change the world. And how amazing will it be for your students to have an actual *witch* teaching them about the occult?"

A hint of excitement stirs in my belly. Hannah's right. I signed a ten-page NDA this morning. I can't talk about anything I see in the AURA lab, can't reveal anything contained in the book—the book I'm not even sure I believe in yet—and can't tell anyone that I'm the Whisper Keeper. They even want me to move in to a secured apartment over the lab for the next couple of months. But after everything is done—after I've found the Blade and done my part, I can go back to my life.

A wave of relief loosens the knot in my stomach. Until Isaac pulls the dark purple drape aside, and the dank, *old* smell from the antechamber below wafts over me.

"And you're sure the book is here?" I ask, stopping on the first step. My whisper is already down the stairs, probably desperate to get into the old vault. Or heck. Maybe she's already inside.

"It's definitely here," Isaac says, a slight edge to his voice.

"We've been searching for the book for five years," Hannah explains. "But even if we hadn't found journal entries to confirm it, *you're* the proof, Willow. You and your whisper. She appeared for the first time the same day you took a tour of St.

Mary's. Why would that happen if not for the presence of the book?"

She's so certain. Half a dozen times in the past two days, I've come close to bolting. But Hannah has been there with a reassuring word, a cup of coffee, or one of her warm smiles. Every time I talk to her, I feel better. Calmer. And I *know* I'm doing the right thing.

"Willow?" Hannah holds out her hand. "I'll be by your side the whole time. If you start to feel faint, all you have to do is say the word, and we'll stop for the night."

"The last time I went down there...I was terrified." My voice sounds so small. So pitiful. "It was like I wasn't even...*me.*"

Hannah rests her hands on my shoulders. She's only an inch taller than I am, so we're almost eye-to-eye. "You're not alone anymore. You have the support of the entire AURA team. We've got you. You *will* do this, and you'll be fine."

Her confidence frees me from the fear keeping me paralyzed. I'm going to do this. My whisper wants this. *I* want this.

Hannah follows me down the stairs. Isaac is fiddling with a pair of floodlights, transforming the antechamber's vibe from "spooky murder room" to "ancient IKEA."

My whisper paces back and forth in front of the sealed vault door. I thought she'd have already gone inside. But maybe she can't unless I'm with her?

"Is your whisper here?" Hannah asks.

"Yes. She's waiting for me." My stomach twists into a knot. The magic inside calls to me, wrapping its tendrils around my limbs to pull me closer. I can't stop myself until my hands are pressed to the old, scarred metal. "Help—"

A blue glow surrounds me, the air suddenly thick with an ancient, spicy scent. It seeps into my pores. I breathe deeply, desperate to fill my lungs with it, and only then realize I'm no longer in my own body.

Gray stone surrounds me—us—as my whisper stands in the center of the vault. She holds out her hands, still nearly translucent in the flickering light.

We turn in a circle, slowly. Torches stand six feet tall in each corner, tongues of cerulean flames casting the entire room in an eerie light. Writing—etching—marks every single surface. Symbols. Words. Pictures.

Two steps forward, and a stone altar seems to materialize out of thin air. We move as one. I don't fight her any more. She's in control. I have to trust she knows what she's doing.

A leather-bound tome rests on the ancient dais with symbols burned into the cover. Before my eyes, they start to move. Swirling, changing, alive with frenetic energy.

She reaches for the book, but her fingers go right through it. Anger prickles over her skin. Frustration. Pure, raw *need*. Her emotions have never been so clear. She needs to touch it. To open it.

"You've done it before," I try to tell her. But I have no idea if she can hear me. Or sense me. *"Focus."*

Maybe *I'm* the one who needs to focus. But how when I'm trapped in her consciousness? It's not like I can control her.

She tries again and again, stamping her foot against the stone floor when nothing works. My head swims. The incense is too strong. The room starts to spin. The symbols slow until I can *almost* read them. But then I'm falling. Flailing. A weak whimper escapes my lips, and everything goes black.

———

A SOFT RUSTLING ROUSES ME. Followed by a cool cloth draped over my forehead. I force my eyes open. Hannah leans over me, concern in her tired gaze. "Oh, thank goodness. You've been out for over an hour."

With a groan, I try to sit up, but I'm too dizzy.

Nope. Not happening.

The heavy scent of the incense is gone—replaced by fresh linen and something vaguely fruity. Soft lights chase the shadows away, but I don't recognize the room I'm in. I'm still dressed in jeans, a tank top, and my UCSF sweatshirt, but this isn't my bed.

"What...happened? And where are we?" Someone is using the inside of my skull as a drum, and I don't like it. Not one bit.

Hannah slides her arm under my shoulders, lifts me gently, and tucks a pillow behind my back. "You're in the apartment over the lab. We worried we might need one of our healers to take care of you. As for what happened, you'll have to tell me One minute you were standing right up against the vault door, then you let out a scream and collapsed. We couldn't wake you up—not even with smelling salts—but your vitals were all within normal ranges, so we brought you back here."

Oh.

"What did you see inside the vault?" she asks, tucking the soft blanket tighter around my body.

I'm so tired. All I want to do is sleep. But I tell her everything I can remember. The blue flames. The altar. The leather cover, alive with symbols that made no sense to me.

"But my whisper couldn't open it. She wasn't strong enough. I've seen her affect the physical world before, but in that vault... she couldn't." A single tear tumbles down my cheek. Why do I feel like I failed?

"You did so well, Willow," Hannah says, and her smile eases a fraction of my guilt. "The next time, you'll be stronger. You'll *both* be stronger."

"How?" I don't know that I believe her, but she's so confident, she must have some sort of plan.

"We'll talk about that tomorrow. Get some rest. You've earned it." She pats my shoulder, then reaches for the lamp on the bedside table.

My eyes are so heavy. But I reach for her arm. ' I want to go home. Can someone take me home?" Even as I say the words, I know she's going to refuse. I can barely sit up, let alone walk.

"Willow, I don't think you should be alone tonight. Stay here. I'll sleep on the couch in case you need me. Oh, and I turned the magic dampener on. Your whisper won't wake you. She's earned some rest too."

I want to thank her, but the words are simply too hard. So

when she slips out of the room and shuts the door, I let myself drift into oblivion.

Gabriel

I step out into the darkness, shedding my jacket as I do so. Once I am safely hidden in the alley, I release my wings. Followed by a scream. Fortunately, this time of night—or morning—there are few people around to notice.

Blackened feathers fall to the pavement all around me. Why am I not healing?

"Your powers change once you leave the celestial realm. Trust me." Maddox's words have haunted me every day. But he *broke* one of his wings when he came here and it healed within a few hours.

Hellfire is one of the only ways to kill an angel. The last angel who attempted to fly through it made it back to the celestial realm —because the Almighty willed it so—but died screaming. Not even she could save him.

I wrap my wings around my body. They are in no better condition now than they were five days ago. How is this possible?

A single flutter is all I can manage before the pain drives me to my knees. My angelic powers were back to full strength quickly. I cut my finger on the bag of kettle corn this morning, and the skin was unmarked within the hour. But my wings... they could take weeks to heal at this rate. Months even.

I stare at the penthouse windows high above. They're warded to keep prying eyes out, but they hold a subtle glow. The others— Kunchin, Dion, Maddox, and Killian—are still there. Talking. Laughing. Drinking.

I passed the evening in relative silence. I did not belong. Zoe hugged me when I left, and I could have used my gifts to sense her emotions—to determine if she truly was happy to see me, but I did not want to know the answer.

I find a hotel off Market Street, hand over Sinclair's credit card, and get a room for the night.

In the past week, I have tried pretzels, pizza, french fries, tacos, borscht, schnitzel, and kettle corn. I have ridden on a roller coaster, watched the sun rise and set, slept on luxurious sheets and a dirty Greyhound bus. I have talked to hundreds of people around the world. Their joy and pain have fueled me. Given me purpose. But they have also left me hollow.

I need more. Perhaps that is why my wings have not healed. Perhaps in some deep, dark part of my mind, I do not want them to. Because when they do, I will have to go home. I'll return to the celestial realm for all eternity, and I will never feel like this again.

NINE

Willow

A subtle buzzing tickles my throat. The pacemaker-like device implanted below my collarbone sends a tiny electric current up one of the nerves in my neck. It's supposed to increase the blood flow to my brain. And boost my whisper's power.

I refused the WCU—Whisper Control Unit—for two days. But no matter how hard I tried or how angry my whisper got, we still couldn't turn the pages of that damn book.

She also started waking me up at night again. With how much a session at the cathedral takes out of me, it just made sense to stay in AURA's luxury apartment. I pass out almost every time, only waking up once I'm back in the unfamiliar bed with Hannah watching over me.

I run my fingers over the slight swelling under my collarbone. An inch-long incision. Four butterfly bandages. The procedure only took an hour, and while the wound is tender, it's not terribly painful.

With one type of current, the WCU can send my whisper away, and with another, it can give her a kick-ass power boost. Since AURA's magic dampener seems to have failed—my whisper has been waking me up multiple times a night since our first session at the cathedral—I let Hannah send her away before I went to sleep last night. I haven't seen her since.

I think she's angry with me. I suppose I'd be mad too if someone zapped me into oblivion. Hannah swore it wouldn't hurt her, but I won't feel steady until I see her again. Despite turning my life completely upside down, she's not evil. She doesn't *want* to hurt me.

We follow Isaac through the rectory door. As always, it's quiet this time of night. The church is locked up, the votive candles have all burned down to nothing, and only the frescos are still lit. I shiver whenever I see them. It's like they're warning me away from the antechamber below. Or perhaps I'm just afraid that I'll fail—again.

Nausea crawls up my throat. Being here tonight feels wrong. I'd give anything for one of my strawberry candies right now. Or even my crossbody bag. Something to hold onto. Something *normal*.

The closer we get to the antechamber, the more my hands shake.

"Hurry up," Isaac says and pulls the drape aside. He's been tense all day, snapping at some of the techs in the lab and looking over Hannah's shoulder as she calibrated the WCU.

Tonight, he aims both floodlights at the vault door. I'm drawn to it again, though unlike the last few days, I can still breathe when I press my hands to the ancient metal.

A cough catches in my throat. The incision site throbs, and my eyes water. But when I wipe away the tears, my whisper is standing right next to me.

"She's here."

Hannah checks the WCU's screen. "You're at Level Two. Can you touch her?"

I reach for my whisper's hand, but my fingers find only air. "No. She's still...a ghost."

Her glare chills me to the bone.

"Sorry. Still...not corporeal. Is that better?" I ask.

She nods, almost...smiling at me.

The tickle in my throat gets stronger, and I cough again. Is this normal?

None of this is normal. You're talking to a gho—non-corporeal being—in an old cathedral, about to go back into a magically sealed vault to read a grimoire no one but you has seen in over a hundred years.

"We're going to Level Three," Hannah says.

My whisper swivels toward the vault door. She takes two quick steps forward, then seems to almost...bounce off the metal. Anger carries over the fragile bond between us, and she balls her hands into fists.

"Turn it off. She can't get in." I don't know how I know this. I shouldn't. Her feelings have never been this...*clear* to me before. Maybe Hannah was right and the WCU is exactly what I needed to connect with her.

The buzzing in my neck stops.

My whisper stands shoulder to shoulder with me, a gleam in her translucent eyes. I blink, and everything around me blurs. Forces buffet me from all sides. I'm dizzy, but right when I think I can't take another second of this, my whisper bursts into the vault.

The tongues of blue flame flare brighter. Hotter. Incense burns my nose. Or her nose, since I'm reasonably certain my body is still in the antechamber, pressed against the vault door.

Her fingers brush the cover, and I *feel* the leather. The deep grooves of the markings. But she can't open it.

We need more.

I try to focus on the WCU. On my corporeal body out there with Hannah and Isaac. Can I speak? Move of my own free will? Crap. Why didn't I think to ask Hannah what *she* saw every time I've been pulled into my whisper's reality?

Pain lances through us, a razor's edge cutting us open and flooding the small space with pure, white light until every shadow is banished to the depths of some far away Underworld we can't see or touch.

In the next moment, our reality contracts down to a pinprick.

Darkness holds sway for so long, I start to panic. We're trapped in here. *I'm* trapped in here. What if I can't return to *my* body? What if my whisper never escapes? What if—

A blink, and the vault is again what it was. Lit by ever-burning blue flames, filled with perfumed air. But now, a chill bursts over my skin. I can feel everything. Under my feet, the stones are uneven. I run my hands over the book's cover. The marks stop moving, and I gasp.

Power lies within.

The words weren't there a second ago. They weren't words at all.

My whisper ignores the fear twisting my stomach into knots and curls her fingers around the edge of the cover.

The first yellowed page is blank. My heart sinks. There has to be more. Right?

As if the magic infused within the spell book can hear me, ink wells up, soaking into the parchment until the image of an ornate blade with a carved handle is so clear, it looks like it was drawn only yesterday.

The Blade of Liminal Transference

I snort—silently. *"We are so renaming this thing."*

My whisper shakes her head. I want to ask her why she cares. Or how she knows anything about the book and the Blade. She's three weeks old for Pete's sake.

Turning another page, she waits. I think she might even hold her breath. Or...whatever passes for breath when you're a whisper ghost.

Only the purest of heart can see these words.
Love and hate. Light and darkness. Life and death.
The circle begins where the circle ends.
Proceed, and you will be forever transformed.
May the power not stain your soul.

My whisper clutches her throat. I can't breathe. The air is sucked out of the room in a great *whoosh*. Instead of incense and spice, the harsh tang of blood hits the back of my throat.

A scream fills my ears. Mine, I think. Or hers.

I'm flying back. Violently ripped from my whisper and tossed around like I'm about to find myself trapped under a house in Oz.

My body slams into something hard and cold. Every muscle seizes. The pain is like nothing I've ever felt before. It's pulling me under. Somewhere I fear I'll never come back from.

***

LIKE EVERY OTHER NIGHT, I wake back in the apartment over AURA's lab. Hannah sits in a chair next to the bed, her tablet in her hand.

"I failed. Again," I manage, too weak to sit up. The first tear trails over the bridge of my nose. I can't even wipe it away.

"Willow! You didn't." Hannah's voice holds a mixture of pride and awe. "We could see the magic in you tonight. You were... almost glowing. Tell me everything you saw while you were inside."

Despite my exhaustion, I recount every second. How my whisper instinctively knew what to do. How the ink appeared on the pages. Even how it *smelled*. By the time I'm done, my voice is almost gone.

"You did so well, Willow. Better than we ever could have hoped for." She pats my arm, and pride raises a lump in my throat. "We'll try again tomorrow. Tweak some of the settings on the WCU. I think we need to modulate the power. Give you enough to turn the page, but not so much we overwhelm you and your whisper. Now get some rest. You need your strength."

The outer door shuts with a quiet *click* a minute later. Before I can close my eyes, my whisper appears next to the bed. Tears glisten on her gauzy cheeks. She reaches for me, but her fingers find nothing but air.

"I'm okay," I mumble, my words slurring. My lids are suddenly too heavy to hold open. "Promise."

The last thing I see as sleep takes me is another tear running down her cheek.

TEN

Willow

The flickering blue flames are brighter this time. Like they're growing along with my power. My whisper goes right to the book, but her near-translucent fingers can't grasp the pages.

Frustration builds inside her. She balls her hands into fists and pounds them against the stone altar. Once. Twice.

"Ow!"

The third time, impact sings up her arms. So strong, I feel the pain in my own hands. But I don't think Hannah's increased the power of the WCU. Maybe...she doesn't need to? Maybe this is all me? Or us?

Ink slowly fills the next blank page. This writing is bolder. Angrier.

Accept the power of the Blade, and the magic will be yours for the rest of your days. No weapon in this world can destroy it. It is bound to the souls of all who have come before. You have a choice, Whisper Keeper. Continue and you will possess control over magic itself. Leave now, and the Blade will remain hidden until the next in your line is called.

My whisper splays her hands over the ancient parchment. Her indecision weighs heavily on me. Or is she sensing my fear?

I thought the Blade was a tool for good. But these warnings are getting more and more ominous.

She huffs, then continues on. More ink, so many lines they blur in front of our eyes until the last period at the very end of the page is formed.

You will be bound to this place. To this burden. The Blade, the grimoire, and the Whisper Keeper are one. Before you take the final step, heed the warnings of those who came before.

1879 - These are the final words of Frances Rowland, Whisper Keeper.

I go to my death willingly. They have found me, and they will soon force me—

The vault and my whisper are ripped away from me so quickly, my whole world spins. "No!" I shout, back in my own body on the cold, stone floor beneath the cathedral.

Hannah grabs my shoulders, giving me a gentle shake until I focus on the worry in her eyes. Flecks of purple glow in the blue of her irises, and a wave of calm washes over me. "You're okay, Willow. Your two minutes were up, and we pulled you out. We have to increase the length of time we use the WCU slowly so we don't accidentally overwhelm your system. How do you feel?"

"I...I wasn't ready." The last Whisper Keeper's words play on a loop in my head. *"They will soon force me..."*

Force her to do what?

My chest tightens. I scramble to my feet, but start to wheeze. The sensation of my blood pressure bottoming out drives all rational thought from my head. Stumbling for the stairs, I struggle to draw a deep breath. "I need..."

Isaac grabs my arms in a bruising grip. The pain shocks me enough to focus on the anger in his dark eyes. "You're not done for the day."

"Let...go." The words don't sound like me. Tiny. Pleading. Panicked. "I need air."

"You'll get it after you finish with the book. After you find the spell to activate your power. We're not leaving until your whisper reads every page."

Every page? The grimoire has a hundred of them! It'll take me weeks to get through them all.

I try to yank my arms away, but he shoves me toward the vault door. Hannah dials up the WCU, and with a wail, I'm sucked back into my whisper.

Her tears stain the ancient pages. But the ink is still as clear.

They have found me, and they will soon force me to steal the talents—the very lives—of those trapped in the dungeons with me. Witches and werewolves, vampires and fae. The wretched souls howl in pain, knowing what our captors have planned. An unbeatable army, powerful enough to rule the earthen realm. To fight the Almighty. To breach the gates of Heaven.

I cannot fight any longer. Weeks of torture have broken me. I must find a way to die so the world may live. I pray the next Whisper Keeper is strong enough to resist the call. Only then will our ancestors truly be able to rest.

My whisper covers her face with her hands. They're almost solid now, but the haunting blue flames seep around the edges of her fingers.

"What do we do?"

I'd give anything to be able to talk to her. To know what she's thinking beyond these waves of emotion.

Her hands snap back to the grimoire like they're bound to it somehow. She tries to look away. I can feel her resistance. Perfumed air swirls around us. We sway as one, disoriented, until she turns the next page.

Another diary entry. This one from the late 1700s. Darker than the last. A third. A fourth. They all end with the Whisper Keeper taking her own life. With a warning for the future.

Sobs wrack her—our—shoulders. I can feel the finality in the air. The diary entries go all the way back to the 1100s. To the first Whisper Keeper and her coven. To *why* the Blade was created in the first place.

The next words we read...they'll be the end. We'll be bound to the Blade until we die. AURA doesn't want to cure cancer. I know that now. Like a veil has been lifted from my eyes, I can see their true intentions. My only hope is to run.

The page turns. The ink seeps up from somewhere unknown, and the final words appear.

The Blade is mine and mine alone.
It calls me forth to find its home.
Magic has but one true course.
No truth is found in might and force.
I hold it high for all to see.
Let no one set this power free.

A wave of magic hits me—us—in the chest. It seeps into every part of me. Into my pores. My veins. My bones. My whisper throws her head back in a silent scream until her throat is raw.

Pain explodes across my cheek. I'm ripped from her with such force, it feels like I'm flying. Until I hit the very real, very rough wall of the antechamber. Isaac and Hannah stare down at me.

They know. The power is mine now. And I'm theirs.

Gabriel

The old cathedral is utterly silent this time of night. The dim lights do nothing to chase the shadows away. I did not want to come here. But as I lay in bed, staring up at the hotel ceiling, I felt Azrael's call.

Letting him appear in my room would have caused a commotion. At least here, we are alone. I whisper his name, drawing him to me, and a moment later, a punch of power rattles the pews and almost sends me to my knees.

Fuck. I have spent too long in the earthen realm if I cannot withstand the jolt of a single angel appearing before me.

"Gabriel."

His black wings fold against his robes, and a current of jealousy runs through me. Another very *human* emotion I am not accustomed to.

"You called?"

He stares at me, confusion knitting his brows together. "Where are your robes?"

"Robes are not typically worn in the earthen realm. Surely you knew this? Or do you not look at a soul's earthly body when you help them cross over to the afterlife?"

His lips curve into a frown. "I don't pay attention to what they wear. Why should I?"

Two weeks ago, I would not have had an answer for him. Or even asked the question. But now, his apathy grates on me. "Because humans choose their clothing with purpose. They often use it to define who they are."

"That is ridiculous. The Almighty does not care how a soul *dresses*." He shakes his head and scoffs, his wings shifting with every movement. "She *does* care that you have been shirking your duties. As does Seraphiel. I assured him you would return to the celestial realm *very soon*."

Fuck. "I am not ready." Grabbing Azrael's arms, I barely resist the urge to shake him. "There is so much we can learn here, brother. So much we do not understand about how this realm has changed since its creation."

The Angel of Death beats his wings, lifting us both five feet off the ground before he shakes off my hold. I fall, and my head slams into the side of one of the pews. The harsh scent of blood fills my nose. *My* blood.

"Put your hands on me again, *brother*, and you will find yourself with much more than a minor head wound."

I touch the cut on my temple. It is already starting to heal. In five minutes, it will be nothing but a memory. Much like my wings, at the moment.

"Of all our brethren, I thought you would be the one who would understand. I am not staying in this realm for my health, Azrael. We spend our entire existence *watching*. We think we are all knowing, but in truth, we are blind. We need to find a way to see."

Azrael smooths his hands down his pristine, black robes. His silver belt glows with his power. "I can buy you another few days in this realm. Seraphiel is distracted dealing with Lucifer. Hell's guardian is demanding an audience with the Almighty, and you know how well that went the last time. But if you're not back once that mess is sorted, Seraphiel will order you home."

"Seraphiel can fuck off," I mutter. "He is a power-hungry twat, and everyone knows it."

Azrael's chuckle seems to surprise him. He sobers quickly and steps closer to the altar. "That he may be. But he has the Almighty's ear. Do not test him."

His return to the celestial realm ruffles my hair, but I am prepared for the blast of power and maintain my footing.

The frescos behind the altar draw my gaze. Over the past two weeks, I have seen many churches. The ones in Italy were my favorite. Magnificent in every way. Some so ornate, they moved humans to tears. This cathedral is plain by comparison. Yet, there is beauty in its simplicity.

I should return to my hotel. Figure out where to go next. If I only have one more week, I must be...discriminating in my choices. And steel myself for the ridicule I will surely encounter when the other archangels see the ravaged state of my wings.

"Stop! Please!"

The woman's voice carries from somewhere behind the altar. Panicked. In pain. Familiar. I close my eyes and release the hold I keep on my angelic power. Utter hopelessness and despair. Fear. Her emotions are like a thousand razor sharp daggers piercing my soul.

At the distinctive sound of a slap, I stride for a purple drape covering part of the wall. It flutters slightly, though the air in the sanctuary is utterly still.

"I didn't see the last page! You have to believe me!"

"You lie," a man growls. "Tell us where the Blade is, or you'll find out what happens when we turn the WCU up to eleven."

The woman screams in agony. I race down a narrow, twisting set of stairs, and burst into a large antechamber with stone walls. Bright floodlights point at a metal door.

An angry dark-haired man pins a curvy blonde's arms over her head, while another woman—this one decidedly *not* human—twists the knob on a black box in her hand.

Tears stream down the blonde's face. I know her. I met her in this very cathedral, perhaps ten days ago. Dr. Willow Saunders.

"Please," she whimpers, her voice fading as her body shakes violently. "Hurts..."

"Let her go!" I shout, springing for the brute. One well-placed punch to his side sends him flying. Willow crumples to the ground, still crying.

The other woman narrows her gaze at me. "What are you?" she asks with a smile designed to seduce even the hardest of men. Her voice is like ambrosia, sweet and rich and addicting.

"I am—" Fuck, no. I wrap my fingers around her throat, cutting off her air. Was I truly about to answer her? I could snap her neck, but I am no killer. Not unless there is no other choice.

Her eyes roll back in her head. I toss her toward an old, pitted metal door with no handle, then scoop Willow into my arms. A seizure racks her body. I have to get her somewhere safe.

The man stirs with a groan. I run for the stairs, unwilling to let these assholes witness any of my angelic power.

Once I reach the sanctuary, I kick one of the lecterns in front of the passageway. That should slow them down.

Willow gasps for breath. "I will take care of you," I say softly. "You are safe with me."

Closing my eyes, I call upon my talents and picture my hotel room in my mind. The man shouts, "Trap her in the void! Now!"

Her agony washes over me. So much regret and pain. The fine hairs on the back of my neck prickle. With a final wail, her entire consciousness fades into oblivion. I can sense nothing from her. Not even a trace of emotion. Yet...her heart still beats. Her chest stutters with weak breaths. What have they done to her?

A seductive, silken voice wraps around me from the stairs. "Let her go."

"Fuck you," I grit out. With every bit of strength I can muster, I bend the very fabric of the world to my will, and we disappear.

ELEVEN

Gabriel

Willow does not stir. Not when we appear in my hotel room. Not when I lay her on the bed. Not when I brush damp curls from her forehead.

"Trap her in the void."

What void? Is this why I cannot sense her? Her body is here. But her mind is gone. I drop to my knees next to the mattress and cup her cheeks with my hands. Angels have many talents. I was created—not born—at the beginning, and my memory is nearly perfect.

From my post in the celestial realm, I have watched over this world. I have seen cities rise and fall. Seen men and women go to war over the smallest slights and the vilest acts.

I have met witches, vampires, shifters, fae, ghouls, and demons. Only one yeti, but perhaps that will change with time.

The woman with the black box was something new. Part fae, I am certain. No other creature could have even *tried* to influence me. Had she been pure fae, I doubt I would have been able to resist her.

Closing my eyes, I search for a sliver of Willow's consciousness. An odd sensation pulses under the heel of my right hand. Slowly, I stroke my fingers down her cheeks to her neck.

It is stronger here. Tiny vibrations under her skin. Her sweatshirt provides only the barest peek at her collarbone. At the edges of several thin, white bandages.

For the first time in my existence, I am uncertain what to do.

"Can you hear me, Willow? It is Gabriel. We met—briefly. I caught you. Then you ran. Do you remember me? I have thought of you often since that night."

Why am I telling her all of this?

"You must fight your way free of this...void. I cannot find you there and I desperately wish to hear your voice again. And see your smile."

A shift in the air alerts me to a presence in the room behind me. Leaping to my feet in front of Willow, I prepare to do battle with this unknown enemy.

But my gaze locks on a wispy form hovering next to the window. It's *Willow*. Or her twin. "What are you?" I ask. "A ghost? She is still alive. Her heart beats. And the Angel of Death is nowhere to be found. Are you...her? Or something else?"

The being stares at me, her lips parted slightly, waiting.

"Right. I asked too many questions. Are you a ghost?"

She shakes her head.

"Is Willow dying?" I hold my breath, unsure I'm prepared for the answer.

Another no. I glance up at the ceiling and whisper a quick, "Thank you," to the Almighty.

"Do you know how to bring her back from the void?"

The spirit's eyes widen, and in the next second, she vanishes into thin air.

"Well, fuck."

Willow

Darkness surrounds me. Suffocating me. I can't breathe. Can't see. Can't hear.

I hold the power of the Blade. Hannah and Isaac know it. How? Did I read the book's words aloud? Could they *feel* it?

Hannah's eyes changed the moment I tried to resist. The kind-hearted woman who watched *Ghostbusters* with me one night when I couldn't sleep vanished, replaced by something—someone—evil.

My heart shatters into dust. Or...does it? I don't even know if I'm still alive. I can't feel...anything.

Breathe.

Nothing.

Wiggle your fingers and toes.

Nothing.

Open your eyes.

Nothing.

Isaac grabbed me. He ordered me to find the Blade. Then Hannah...she was so angry.

"Tell us where the BLT is, or you'll find out what happens when we turn the WCU up to eleven."

Oh, God. They did it. Each level hurt worse than the last. My whisper screamed. She...*disintegrated* in agony. I felt her pain like it was my own. Or...maybe I'm wrong and it *was* my pain.

"Trap her in the void!"

Is that where I am? The void?

"...Willow...have thought of you often..."

There was a man—is a man. I can hear him now. I think. He saved me. I couldn't see him. I couldn't see anything by then. But he tried to stop Isaac and Hannah.

His voice is familiar. It becomes my anchor in this endless storm of nothingness. If I can hold on to it, maybe I can find my way out of here.

But it too fades away, and I'm alone. I'd cry if I could. But trapped, all I can do is wait and pray.

MY EYES ARE GRITTY. I struggle to open them for a full minute before I realize what I'm doing—and what it means. I'm not dead. I'm out of the void!

But I'm too weak to move or speak. Lying on something soft, I draw a shaky breath.

"Oh, thank the Almighty above," a deep, smooth voice says. That same voice. My anchor. My rescuer. "It has been two hours. I thought...I feared you might never wake up."

Warm hands cover mine. The gentle touch brings tears to my eyes. "Say something, Willow. I do not know how to help you."

I can only manage a weak whimper. If I could, I'd reach for him. Beg him to hold me. Ask him his name. I can't remember.

As if he can read my mind, he gathers me in his arms. My whole body aches, but I feel safe with him. Safe enough to force my heavy lids open.

He's beautiful. Long golden brown hair. A short beard. Perfect skin. Amber eyes that glow with intensity. In his embrace, I feel so tiny. He held me once before.

My cheeks heat. He did more than that. He had me in his lap and...

"Do you remember me?" he asks.

"Gabriel." The single word takes everything I have left. The urge to close my eyes is almost overwhelming.

"Very good, *deliciae*. You're safe here."

"Nuh-huh." I'm not safe anywhere. AURA will come for me. They'll never let me go. They'll force me to find the Blade. To use it. Shit. What if they can track the WCU? They're part of the NSA. Of course they can track the WCU.

Panic lends me the strength to push him away. He backs up until he's almost at the window, his hands raised. "I mean you no harm, Willow. Who—or what—is AURA? The man and woman at the church were hurting you, and I stopped them."

He says it like he didn't just piss off two people who will stop at nothing to get the power coursing through me.

I can feel the Blade's call, even now. It's far away, but the urge to find it—to possess it—is like nothing I've ever known before. Almost...musical. So soft and alluring, I ache for it.

If I stay here, Isaac and Hannah will find me. My only hope is to run.

"Don't...follow me," I manage and stumble for the door.

"Wait!" Gabriel calls after me. "What is the void? Why did they send you there? I can help, Willow!"

For a single heartbeat, I falter. He was so kind when we first met. But so were Hannah and Isaac. If Gabriel figures out what kind of power I can wield, he'll want it too. I can't trust anyone. Not until I find some way to destroy the Blade. And myself along with it.

THE LIGHTS of the Embarcadero blind me as I stumble out of Gabriel's hotel. We're nowhere near the cathedral or AURA's lab. The brief spark of hope keeps me going. But for how much longer? And...where? I can't go to my apartment. That's the first place they'd look. UCSF, maybe? But I don't have my ID, my phone, or any money. Hannah "took care of everything" when I agreed to move into the apartment above the lab. She went everywhere with me. To the coffee shop. The drugstore. Grocery shopping.

I filed for a leave of absence from the university. I told Anton I had to take care of some personal business and wouldn't be reachable for a few months. Even if I had my credentials, they probably wouldn't work.

How could I have been so stupid? I did everything Hannah asked without question. Why didn't I realize what she was doing?

She isolated me from my entire life.

Barefoot, still weak from my time in the void, I fight against my rising panic. Ducking into an alley, I rest my back against the wall and close my eyes. But all I see is Hannah's face.

When I tried to resist at the cathedral, she...*snarled* at me. Her eyes hardened—changed color, even. And her expression... She was so angry. It was like her mask fell away and underneath...was a monster.

Oh, God. "She's not human." But what the fuck is she? A witch?

I'm the worst kind of *Other*. I don't know anything about this world.

My whisper appears before me, frantic. She points to my neck, then hers.

"I know! They'll turn it on again. They'll send me back to the void. But what the hell am I supposed to do about it?" Sinking down until my ass hits the pavement, I start to cry.

She rakes her fingers down her neck, then stares at me expectantly. Can I really tear the WCU out of my body?

I tug off my sweatshirt and stare down at the four butterfly bandages closing the incision above my tank top.

As I pull off the first one, the tickle starts in my throat. "No! Not yet! They can't..."

My whisper is as panicked as I am. Tears swim in her eyes. It's only a dull hum. I still have time.

Except the power ratchets up several levels after I tear through the third bandage. My vision goes glassy. Across from me, my whisper screams silently into the night.

I claw at my skin, unable to wait a moment longer to get this fucking torture device out of my body. Blood wells under my nails. Too much of it. I can't find purchase. It's too slick, and the pain gets worse every second.

"Willow! Fuck me. Thank the Almighty above. You..."

Gabriel's words are lost to my scream. The device is buried under layers of muscle, too deep for me to reach. Pure agony locks my limbs. My throat spasms.

"L-level...s-seven," I stutter. In a few seconds, I'll be back in the void. I can't see my whisper. I can't see anything. But I'm still here, because I can feel Gabriel laying his hand over the destruction I've waged on my skin.

"This is what is causing you pain." It's not a question. The certainty in his voice is my only hope. He'll find a way to turn it off. He has to. Or I'm afraid this time, I won't find my way back again.

***

Gabriel

In my arms, Willow shudders. Her eyes cloud over, pupils blown wide. I only found her because of the strange specter floating at the edge of the alley. When the being saw me, it wrapped its fingers around my arm and pulled me into the darkness between buildings.

But as soon as Willow screamed, it lost its corporeal form, and now...it's gone. Blood streams from the wound below her collarbone. I can sense *something* underneath my palm. But though I have the knowledge of several millennia of existence, I do not know what to do to help her.

Nor do I have time to waste. Her consciousness is fading once more. Whoever controls this device is sending her back into the void. Deeper and deeper with every second that passes.

Pulling her closer, I press my lips to the shell of her ear. "Fight them, *deliciae*. Hold on for me." There is only one place I can go.

At the last moment, I remember my promise to Sinclair and Zoe. I cannot simply appear in the center of the penthouse. So I focus on the hallway outside their door.

My power sends us there in an instant, but the late hour, my aching wings, and the burden of carrying another with me—twice —conspire to send me to my knees. I barely manage to hold on to the precious human in my arms.

"Sinclair!" I roar as I stagger to my feet. "Open the bloody door! Now!" Punctuating my demand with three swift kicks to the reinforced wood, I pray the penthouse is not completely soundproofed.

Willow's keening cry shatters my control. It is so much more than mere pain. She is in agony. Not only her body, but her spirit.

Her soul. She knows what is happening to her. Whatever this void is, she is desperate to never go back there again.

The door swings open. "Gabriel, you bastard—fuck." The incubus is shirtless, wearing only a pair of silk pajama pants. Hundreds of scars criss-cross his chest, a particularly recent one still red and angry at his side.

"Help me." I push past him, striding for the living room and one of the soft leather couches.

"Oh my God!" Zoe rushes down the hall, buttoning one of Sinclair's dress shirts over her naked body. "Who is she? And what—"

"T-t-ten," Willow whimpers. Her muscles seize, and she lets out a weak wail.

"There is something *inside* her. Here." I rip at her tank top, exposing more of the wound. "Whatever it is...if we do not remove it, she will end up in a void—a place she will not be able to escape for God knows how long."

"Move," Sinclair snaps.

He has a thin kitchen knife in his hand, along with a bottle of scotch. Using his teeth, he uncorks the alcohol, then pours some over the blade. "Hold her down, Gabriel. This will hurt her."

"No!" My roar rattles the windows, and a vase of flowers above the fireplace tumbles to the floor and shatters. "I will do it. I *must* do it. Zoe, can you hold her?"

I do not know why, but the idea of Sinclair cutting into Willow angers me. She is mine to protect, and there is nothing I will not do to keep her safe.

"Have it your way, then. I'll call Maddox. Killian may have some knowledge of..."

His words fade away as the sound of my own heartbeat fills my ears. My hands shake.

I must focus.

Having my fingers under a human's skin is not one of the experiences I expected to have in this realm—or ever care to repeat. As gently as I can, I slide the knife into her flesh. She is too far gone to notice the pain.

"She is fading." The words scrape over the lump in my throat. Fear's oily presence slithers along my spine. The tip of the blade hits something metallic. Thank fuck. With a flick of my wrist, a small disc slides out from under her muscle.

Wires snake from the little device. I cannot simply rip them from her body. I could sever something...vital. But I cut them from the little disc with the knife. Her muscles go slack.

Fuck. Was I too slow? Is she trapped in the void? Or merely unconscious? Precious seconds tick by as I search for her spirit—for the smallest spark of her soul. When I find it, it's so faint, I fear she could die at any moment.

"Gabriel?" Zoe touches my arm. "She's still bleeding. We need a healer."

"The wires must be removed as well," Sin adds. "I will call one of the mages. But give me that disc. Something that size...it could have a tracking chip and my wards will only hide us for so long."

I drop the device into his hand. "What can I do for her?"

Zoe passes me a thick, black towel. "Press down on the wound. It'll slow the bleeding. But be careful. You're strong enough, you could snap her bones without even trying."

Fuck. She is right. "Help me. Please. I...I do not want to hurt her."

Shock registers in Zoe's green eyes for a brief moment. "Sit down, then. Hold her. I'll do the rest."

I cradle Willow in my arms, her back pressed to my chest, while Zoe holds the towel to the wound. Sin returns, a small black box in one hand, and more towels in the other.

"Anastasia will be here momentarily. So...who is this woman, Gabriel? And who the fuck is trying to hurt her?"

TWELVE

Willow

Voices. I hear voices somewhere close by. Gabriel's is the only one I recognize. Another man and a woman are with him. Panic surges through my limbs. I don't make a sound. If I didn't need to breathe, I wouldn't. What if Hannah and Isaac found me? What if Hannah turned her charms on Gabriel and he's in her thrall?

"Sinclair, if I had any idea *why* this happened to her, I would tell you," Gabriel says. "I found her in the basement of St. Mary's Cathedral, being tortured. For what purpose, I do not know."

There's a soft beep, followed by a growl. "The Bureau's techs say the disc delivered an electrical charge through the wires to her vagus nerve. Similar devices are used to stop epileptic seizures in humans, but this one had a magical component as well. Whoever did this to her...they are not human."

"Of course they're not," the woman scoffs. "She's a witch. A very powerful one. The healer confirmed as much. She wouldn't have simply *let* someone implant a torture device inside her—" Her voice cracks. "Oh, God. Unless it was a fae."

"Zoe, my love. Breathe."

I risk opening my eyes to slits. I'm lying on a couch in a ritzy apartment. Floor-to-ceiling windows look out over the city. My shoulder throbs, but it's almost like the wound is a distant memory now. And the ache is too.

My tank top is torn, but no one undressed me, thank God. Though where the hell are my shoes?

"Willow?" Gabriel's voice startles me. I try to sit up, but a wave of dizziness sends me crashing back down to the couch cushions. "Fuck. The healer said she would be fine." He kneels next to me, smooths a hand over my hair, and stares down at me with those golden-hued eyes. "Say something, *deliciae*."

"I'm...okay." My voice doesn't sound like mine. My throat is so raw, I'm surprised I can speak at all. "I have a medical condition."

Understanding dawns over his handsome face. "You told me of this. When we met in the church."

"It doesn't go away," I manage. "Help me?" If I try to sit up on my own, I'm just going to topple over again. And I want Gabriel's arms around me for at least a few minutes before I have to run again. I can't stay in this fancy apartment with huge windows that look out over the city. Even though I feel safe here, I can't trust him. Or anyone. Not after Hannah fooled me so thoroughly.

Gabriel slides one arm around my back, managing to cup my head as he lifts me gently.

Wow. His touch is every bit as comforting as it was weeks ago. It's not only his strength, but his essence. He's steady. Reassuring. Confident. "Do you have much pain?" he asks.

"My throat." My fingers flutter over my neck, and I wince. The skin feels burned. Like the world's worst sunburn. I know I screamed, but this is...more.

Gabriel brushes my hair back, rests his palm over my chest, and closes his eyes. A low growl rumbles through him.

The man and woman standing behind Gabriel look at one another. The man nods. "I can try, my love."

"Willow?" The woman lowers herself down to sit on the glass coffee table. "I'm Zoe. This is Sinclair. He's part incubus demon, and he has this...talent. If you let him, he can convince your body to sort of...forget the pain."

"No!" I shove at Gabriel's arms, but he only tightens his hold on me. "I can't. You don't understand. Hannah...she..."

"Hannah? Is that the woman who was hurting you?" His eyes flash a deeper amber. Anger coils in his limbs. "What is she?"

Sinclair claps his hand on Gabriel's shoulder. "Are you *trying* to scare Willow? Or are you simply that terrible at reading human emotions?"

The men glare at one another until Zoe shakes her head. "I don't care how badly the two of you want to punch each other—or this Hannah woman. Stand down." She leans forward and rests her elbows on her knees. "I didn't trust Sin either the first time he offered to take some of my pain away. Granted, I thought I was human back then."

Sinclair chuckles. "My love, 'back then' was only three weeks ago."

With a slight grimace, Zoe rolls her shoulders. "Since I've barely been 'alive' for two years this time, three weeks might as well be ten years."

This time?

I'm so confused. It must show, because Gabriel cups my cheek, his thumb skating gently under my eye. "Zoe is a daughter of Seraphim. Reborn in a human body, but very much celestial. You can trust Sinclair. He is only part incubus. His other half is—" at Sin's cough, Gabriel sighs. "He does not lie."

"Yeah, and I'm sure if I'd asked her, Hannah would have said the same thing. She said she was human, and I believed her. I'm not making that mistake again." This time, Gabriel doesn't stop me when I wriggle out of his arms. The room only spins for a few seconds before I get my bearings. My feet ache. Where the hell are my shoes? Was I wearing them when I ran from his hotel room? I don't remember.

"I believe she is part fae," he says. Zoe stiffens, and a growl escapes Sinclair's clenched jaw. "Her words affected me, but I was able to resist."

Shit. Why does that make things so much worse?

Because if she can influence Gabriel—if it's not just me—she can turn the whole world against me.

My gaze sweeps around the room. A long hallway with several doors to my right. A darkened fireplace to my left. Straight ahead...is that a kitchen? I blink hard. Yes. A large, stainless steel refrigerator stands tall in one corner. The front door must be in that direction. But with three people—beings—in my way, do I have any hope of escape?

"Willow, no one will harm you here." Sinclair takes several steps away from Zoe. "Gabriel can be quite an ass, but neither of us lie. It is not in our nature. I believe I can prove this to you." He shrugs out of his robe to reveal a sculpted chest covered in scars.

Fear steals all the heat from my body. Gabriel doesn't move. A hint of a smile curves Zoe's lips. Sinclair closes his eyes for a brief moment. A rush of air swirls around the room.

Huge, black wings beat softly, lifting him from the ground. "My mother was a succubus demon. But my father was an angel. Zoe is a daughter of the Seraphim. And the man in front of you is none other than one of the first chosen. You were saved by the Archangel Gabriel."

THIRTEEN

Gabriel

If I were not so concerned with frightening Willow even more, I would punch Sinclair in the face.

How dare the demon stop me from revealing his angelic parentage and then do it himself less than two minutes later.

Sin's feet touch the ground. Without ceremony, he hides his wings, shrugs back into his robe, and belts it tightly.

Willow's full lips form an *o*. She darts a glance toward the front door. "This...isn't real. I'm still stuck in the void. Or.. dead. Or..."

I take a step closer. She calmed when she was in my arms, and I suspect she is dangerously close to hyperventilating. "If you were still in the void, I would not be able to sense your emotions, and I feel them all. You are scared. Confused. In pain. We cannot fix the first two, but Sinclair can ease your physical discomfort without affecting your mind."

"Don't incubi feed off of *sex*?" she asks.

Sin takes Zoe's hand. "I do. If I were desperate, I could also feed off fear, though I would rather drink battery acid. But Zoe is my mate. I do not take from anyone but her, nor will I for the rest of our very long lives. I swear to you, I would not influence you in any way."

Willow turns to me. "Are you going to 'wing-out' too?"

"Wing...out? No. My wings were recently damaged. No one needs to see the state they are currently in. Also, I promised I would not display my full angelic power inside this penthouse." I meet her light blue eyes. "I could inadvertently...break things."

"Like eardrums," Zoe mutters. "Windows. Furniture."

I offer Willow my hand. Disappointment weighs heavily on me when she does not take it. "*Deliciae*, if we wanted to harm you, we could have done so while you were unconscious. We did not. We removed that cursed device causing you so much pain, and Sinclair called in a healer to treat the wound." I gesture to her shoulder. "See for yourself."

She doesn't move. I take several steps toward the hall—away from the front door—and urge Sin and Zoe to do the same. If she runs, I will follow her. But her fear of being trapped here is almost as strong as her fear of those two assholes in the cathedral.

Slowly, she creeps along the edges of the living space, her gaze darting from me to the door and back again. Only when she is certain she is close enough to escape does she look down at the reddened skin below her collarbone.

"There's no scar," she whispers. "How?"

"Healing magic has been around for centuries," Sin says. "Your wound was not serious. The technology and magic inside the device, however, were. Why would someone want to lock your consciousness away in such a fashion?"

The edge to his voice is too much for her to bear. I sense the exact moment she decides to run. The front door slams shut, and though I could stop her easily—if I broke my promise to Zoe—the elevator ride to the ground floor will take her at least sixty seconds. If not more. I will have time.

"You could have been gentler with her," I say.

Sinclair catches my arm before I can slip into the hall. "Be careful, Gabriel. If there is a fae involved, and she finds out what—who—you are…"

"I know. But as I am currently unable to 'wing-out,' there should be no danger of that. I did think you would know better than to casually reveal exactly who I am." I shake off his hold, step into the hall, and let my power carry me to the lobby.

The dial over the elevator slowly counts down from the thirteenth floor. I lean against the security desk, one ankle crossed over the other. The door slides open with a quiet *ding*. Willow darts out, then skids on the polished marble floor as she sees me. What little color she has in her cheeks drains in a heartbeat.

"Please. You have to let me go. They'll find me." Tears shimmer in her eyes. "Once they have what they want, they'll make me do…terrible things. I can't imagine what they'll do to anyone who tries to get in their way."

"No one will force you to do anything while I am around." I offer her my hand once more. "I can protect you. The woman—Hannah—does not have the same power over me that she does over…others. And while I cannot fly at the moment, I have certain *abilities* that make me a formidable enemy. And a strong protector."

"Your friends don't trust me."

"They are not my—fuck. I suppose they are." I have never had…friends before. It is an odd realization. One I am surprisingly grateful for. "They work for the Bureau of the Occult and the Other. It is their job to be…suspicious."

"The Bureau of the Occult and…oh God. B.O.O.? Their name is B.O.O.? Is *everything* in the Other community a joke?" She hugs herself tightly and shivers.

"The Other community often pokes fun at itself. It is part of their…*charm.* Or so they say. I have never found it all that charming." With a shrug, I push off the desk. "You are only learning of the Bureau now?"

Her cheeks tinge the slightest shade of pink. "I thought I was human until three weeks ago." A wave of goosebumps washes over her bare arms.

Fuck.

"Please, Willow. Come back to the hotel with me. I have your shoes, and I can give you one of my sweaters. Though I'm afraid it will be quite large on you, it will keep you warm."

She stares at me, her emotions so very clear. Disbelief. Offense. A hint of fear. "You seriously expect me to *go to a hotel with you?* I may not know anything about the Other community, but I'm not a complete idiot."

"You were in my hotel room an hour ago. Did I harm you in any way?" I don't understand her resistance. I kept her safe. Cared for her. Tried to bring her back from the void. And she is afraid of me now?

A single tear tumbles over her lashes. "My *body* was in your hotel room. *I* was trapped in the void." Her strangled sob shatters my control. I tried to keep my distance. To give her time to trust me. But I cannot abide her suffering.

In two steps, I have her in my arms. She struggles for a moment, then sinks against me. "I will not let anyone harm you. I swear on my wings."

For several tense moments, she tries to hold back her tears. "Y-you...make me feel safe. But so did they. How can I trust anything after what they did to me?"

I nudge her chin up so I can see her eyes. So much pain. But also...power. Magic gathers within her, swirling like a tornado.

"Let me get you somewhere safe. Then start from the beginning."

The air stirs gently. Willow's ghostly twin hovers just over her shoulder.

I turn us so she can see the apparition. "Perhaps you can also explain who *she* is."

Willow sucks in a sharp breath. "You can see my whisper?"

"Of course. She practically accosted me outside the hotel and led me to the alley. Admittedly, I *had* offended her by calling her a ghost."

Tears brim in Willow's eyes. Her *whisper* glares at me until I incline my head. "I will not make that mistake again. You have my word."

The whisper's expression softens. She turns, her spectral fingers brushing Willow's cheek, then reaching up to mine. Something passes between the two of them. I can sense the connection they share, but not what the whisper is feeling.

Willow meets my gaze, her tears still threatening to fall. "She trusts you. I don't know why, but she does."

"Do you?" I hold my breath—when did I start breathing all the time?—as I wait for her answer.

"I...I think...yes. As much as I can trust anyone—or anything—right now. I do."

"Then close your eyes. This may be shocking. Even a bit painful. But I will protect you as best I can." I cup the back of her head with one hand, the other fused to her hip. "Hold on tight."

Bending space and time around us, I focus on our destination. The trip—my third or fourth of the night—drains much of my remaining strength.

Easing Willow down onto the bed, I stagger back until I find the desk chair, then collapse into it.

"Gabriel?" She lays her hand on my knee, the touch settling me in a way I am not prepared for. "Are you okay?"

"Even angels have limits, love. I may have just found mine."

Willow

Holy-celestial-shit. He really *is* an angel.

Despite studying mythology and the occult for years, I know so little of this *other* world. If I believe Sinclair, demons are real too. And though my own power doesn't match anything my studies have told me about witches, I can't deny that I *am* other.

Gabriel slumps back in the plain hotel desk chair. He's pale, and tiny lines crinkle at the corners of his lids.

For a moment, I wonder if he's asleep. Or maybe he passed

out. But then he opens his eyes, and the molten heat shocks me enough I jerk back.

"Did I hurt you?" he asks.

I'm not prepared for the question. Or for how intensely he's staring at me. "Uh...no?"

"The power an angel can manifest—well, as I said earlier, we have been known to break things. Unintentionally." His smile lights up the entire room. Or maybe I'm delirious. "I have never carried anyone with me before. I feared it would be...uncomfortable for you."

"I felt like I was on a roller coaster. But...sideways instead of down." I scan the room, looking for my whisper, but she either didn't follow us or she's choosing to stay hidden.

Gabriel pushes to his feet with a groan and staggers over to his duffel bag sitting on the dresser. After a minute, he comes away with a black t-shirt and a maroon sweater. "These should keep you warm enough."

They're expensive. Soft. And they smell like him.

I'm not sure I can stand. My legs feel like wet noodles. But he hasn't turned around. Does he expect me to strip down to my bra right in front of him?

"Um, a little privacy?"

"For...?"

Oh, my God. He's genuinely confused. "I'm going to take my shirt off. What's left of it, anyway."

"I watched the earthen realm's creation. I have seen many naked human bodies."

"Not mine! Turn around. Please." With a huff, I cross my arms over my half-exposed chest and wait, challenging him to refuse. Probably not the smartest thing to do, but I'm so very *done* with this day, I'm not backing down now.

"I will get you a glass of water," he says, then heads into the bathroom. "Tell me when you are...clothed."

Every muscle aches. Stripping out of my bloody tank top, I peer down at my bra. Great. It's ruined too.

The clothes are big enough to fit two of me, and I have to roll the sweater's sleeves three times. But the thick weave is so comforting, I don't care.

"Okay. You can come back now." The room only spins a little as I towards the headboard. I could sleep for a week. Maybe a month if I thought I'd be safe. But when the sun comes up, I have to run. I just hope Gabriel will let me go.

FOURTEEN

Gabriel

Willow looks so small wearing my sweater. And exhausted. Her eyelids are bruised and swollen, the skin at her neck tinged with red. She fiddles with the rolled-up sleeves as a weak shiver runs through her body.

The clock ticks over to 4:00 a.m. I set the glass of water on the nightstand, then tuck the blankets around her before I back away. She's still wary of me.

"You should sleep. I will stay awake. If anyone comes for you, I can take us back to Sinclair's. His penthouse is heavily warded."

A delicate snort escapes her lips. "You look like something the cat dragged in, Gabriel. I'm not sure you could take us anywhere right now."

I look around the room. "There are no cats here."

"It's a figure of speech." Willow yawns, her swollen eyes closing for a long moment before she forces them open again. "How can you be an angel and know so little about the world?"

"I did not care to learn." The truth surprises me. As does the ease of admitting it. I run a hand through my thick locks. "In the celestial realm, we want for nothing. We do not hunger or thirst.

We do not need to sleep or eat. But without needs—without desires—it is too easy to become…apathetic."

"So you don't normally spend time…here?" She wriggles until she's lying on her side, her head on the pillow. If she stays awake another five minutes, it will be a miracle.

"In the earthen realm? No." Guilt roils deep in my gut. "I had to right a wrong." If Willow were not so exhausted, I would tell her everything. How I failed Sinclair centuries ago. How my actions led to Zoe's torture. How I lost my wings and fear I will never get them back. She is so easy to talk to, and she has not judged me for my actions. Yet. But I sense she is barely holding on. "This is a conversation for another time. You should rest."

She looks like she wants to protest, but with a sigh, she loses the battle. Her breathing slows, and I reach for my phone. I ignore three messages from Sinclair asking for an update. I am so angry with him for scaring Willow, I would surely say something regrettable. What I need now is one of the most powerful warlocks in all of history.

Gabriel: What do you know about a mostly non-corporeal being called a "whisper"?

Ten minutes pass before my phone screen lights up with a reply.

Killian: Not a bloody thing. But I can look through my spell books. Provided you tell me why you are asking.

Gabriel: I cannot.

Killian: Then fuck off, mate. I'm busy.

His words sting. Though I deserve them. The past ten days have enlightened me about many things. Including how poorly I treated Killian and his mate when they tried to teach me about the earthen realm.

Gabriel: Please. I know I have been an ass. But this could be important.

The three dots at the bottom of the screen bounce for so long, I wonder if he is writing an entire book. Or perhaps cursing me with every profane word he knows. I would deserve that.

Killian: If this turns into another "we could all die" cock up, I am going to be very pissed off.

I slap my hand over my mouth before I laugh and wake Willow. If I did not value my continued existence, I would tell the warlock that he is *always* very pissed off.

———

A SOFT WHIMPER WAKES ME. I leap up, suddenly on full alert. Fuck. Willow is shaking, her face twisted in pain.

"No. Please..." she moans.

I'm at her side in two steps and gather her in my arms. Her eyes flutter behind her lids. A nightmare. A measure of relief washes over me. They haven't found her. She's not in physical danger.

"Willow?" I link our fingers and bring our joined hands to my lips. "Wake up, *deliciae.*"

Darling. This woman is precious to me. The ancient Latin word is instinctual, as is protecting her.

Tears tumble down her cheeks. Her muscles tense. I can feel every sliver of emotion. The power thrumming within her aches to be released.

"Can't..." A strangled cry escapes her lips, and her eyes fly open. Magic bursts over her skin, a million tiny sparks dancing in the darkened room. "Gabriel."

I slide my fingers into her hair, dragging my thumb along the edge of her jaw. She sighs, and my body comes alive. A pure, raw need so intense, if I give in, I will lose all control.

"You are safe. You will always be safe with me." My cock juts painfully against my zipper. This is not the time. Willow needs my protection, not my seed.

"I wish I could believe that. What I have to do...it's not fair. I want..." Trembling fingers skim my cheek. With every word, I lose another part of my soul to her.

"What do you want? Tell me, and if it is within my power to give, it will be yours."

"I want to live. I want...you."

She doesn't speak, but her thoughts are so very clear to me.

Dipping my head, I brush my lips to hers. Barely a touch, but she moans, and I am lost. To her. And I don't know that I will ever be found again.

***

Willow

I can't do this. I shouldn't. But in Gabriel's strong arms, the burden of the Blade eases. I can still feel it calling to me. But I'm able to breathe. To want. To need.

His lips were velvet against mine. One taste. One kiss with my angel and I can go.

My angel?

He's not mine. He belongs to God. Or at least to the celestial realm. And I belong to the Blade until my last breath. A breath I'm terrified will come all too soon.

Every second we spend together, I want more. How much longer until I can't walk away?

"Willow, you do not know what you do to me." His voice rumbles in his chest, deep and smooth.

What I do to him?

He's setting *me* on fire. With every touch, I lose another piece of myself. The first rays of morning's light seep through a crack in the curtains. I have to run soon. Leaving him won't be easy. Getting away will be even harder. But if I don't, AURA won't just come after me. They'll set their sights on him too.

I wrap my arms around Gabriel's neck. It's been so long since anyone's held me. I don't remember the last time I went on a date. Two years? Three? My job was all I cared about. All I needed. God, I was so stupid.

When our lips meet, the world falls away. I ache to get closer, but the blanket traps my legs. His tongue teases mine. Finding the hem of his shirt, I yank it up until I can reach his skin. He's so warm. Hard ridges of muscle flex at my touch.

A low growl builds in his throat. I could live in his scent. Do all angels smell so damn good? Our kisses turn desperate. I find his nipple and skate my nails over the sensitive skin.

I feel *everything*. The goosebumps racing over his abs. His lips trailing down the curve of my neck. His heart beating in time with mine. His hard length pressing against my ass. My fingers close over the button on his pants.

"No!" The word escapes as a snarl, and the haze of desire clears in an instant.

I jerk back. Humiliation crawls up my cheeks. "I'm sorry. I shouldn't have—"

"Fuck." Gabriel eases me back down to the bed so gently, I want to cry. "You did nothing wrong. *Nothing*." He backs away, turns, and adjusts himself with a groan. "I want you, Willow. With all that I am. But if I give in...I could hurt you. Or...worse."

The sting of rejection eases a fraction. Regret pours off him in waves. "You wouldn't hurt me," I whisper. "I'm not sure of anything else in my life right now, Gabriel. But I'm sure of that."

He runs a hand through his hair, pulling on the dark strands. I shove at the blankets and swing my legs over the side of the bed. My blood pressure bottoms out, but I don't care. I have to touch him.

The world goes soft as I get to my feet, but I force a deep breath and stagger over to him. Wrapping my arms around his waist from behind, I press my cheek to his shoulder.

"I'm not asking for forever. Or even a day."

He turns, his hands sliding down my back to cup my ass. His amber eyes hold endless depths of need. "What *are* you asking for, *deliciae*?"

"Just an hour to be...*me*. Or hell. Five minutes. I'm scared, Gabriel. Once I find the Blade—"

He frowns. "What blade?"

Shit.

"Forget you heard that. Please." Even as I say the words, I

know he won't. He can't. He cares about me—despite not knowing a thing about me.

"Willow. What blade?" His warm fingers skim the back of my neck until he tangles them in my hair. "Talk to me. I can help."

"You can't. No one can." I sniffle and swipe at the tears welling in my eyes. "Hannah and Isaac...they'll find me. And when they do, they'll force me to find the Blade. To wield it. I can't let that happen."

Gabriel

I tighten my fingers in Willow's hair. "Angels can sense human emotions. One of our many *gifts*. But today, it is a curse. You are terrified. Whatever you are planning...you do not have to do it alone."

"Yes, I do." She tries to wriggle free, planting her palms against my chest for leverage, but she is no match for my strength —or my determination to protect her. "Let go. Please."

The tremble in her voice—along with her plea—is like a dagger to my heart. I release her, and take two steps back. "You said you trusted me. Is that still true?"

I sense her struggle. A part of her does. Completely. But is it enough?

"I trust *you*. I don't trust myself. I thought Hannah and Isaac wanted to help people. I thought I'd be safe with them. I let them put that *thing* in me. I knew they had witches working with them, but I took them at their word when they said they were human. My whisper knew. She tried to warn me, I think. But I didn't listen. I didn't know how."

"You are not to blame, *deliciae*. The woman is part fae—or vampire, I suppose, as they can also enthrall their prey."

Willow cringes. "Prey. God, that's all I was to them. Prey. A few pretty words, and I was theirs. I'll always *be* theirs."

"You belong to no one," I growl. The room—the entire hotel—

vibrates with a wave of my angelic power. If I am not careful, I will bring the old building down around us. The scant two hours of sleep I managed in the uncomfortable chair were enough to strengthen me, but my control is hanging on by a thread.

Before I can—again—beg Willow to tell me about the Blade, my phone buzzes on the dresser.

Killian: You bloody angelic twat. Maddox and I should be packing for Tahiti. Instead, we're going to Newfoundland to track down a Valkyrie vampire. Get yourself and your witch to the Bureau. Sin and Zoe will be waiting.

"Well, fuck."

FIFTEEN

Willow

Gabriel tucks the phone back into his pocket. "I need to know about your whisper. Right now."

I shake my head. "No. I can't. You're in enough danger as it is."

Shoulders straight, he arches a single brow "I am an archangel. One of the ancients. And immortal. I do not care about danger. I care about you."

Oh.

"I could run..."

The other brow lifts. "And I would follow. I can find you anywhere, Willow."

I snort. "Because *that's* not creepy. Pro tip? Stalking isn't sexy."

"Who said anything about stalking? Archangels can locate any soul they choose." He steps closer and cups my cheek. "I know you, *deliciae*. I have tasted you and, for the first time in my very long existence, I wish I were not...what I am. I wish I could give you all of me."

Releasing a heavy sigh, I sink down onto the edge of the bed.

"I don't know a lot about her—my whisper. She's a part of me. Sort of. But she has her own free will. I can't control her. When she shows up, when she doesn't."

How much do I tell him? His friends work for the paranormal equivalent of the FBI. If they search for "whisper" and "blade," will they find out who I am? What I can do?

Gabriel sits close enough our thighs touch. His warmth seeps into me. "Where does she come from?"

"There's a vault under St. Mary's. It's warded—or so Hannah said—and it's been sealed off since the fire in 1906. I took a couple of students on a tour of the cathedral a month ago, and when the priest took us into the basement, I passed out. That night, I saw my whisper for the first time."

"Was she trapped there?" He sweeps his gaze around the room, but we're alone. I haven't seen my whisper since we left Sinclair and Zoe's building, and I'm starting to worry about her.

"I don't know." The realization brings tears to my eyes. She's been my semi-constant companion for a month now. And yet, she's still a complete mystery to me. "I think...maybe she was 'born' when I got close enough to the grimoire inside the vault for it to sense me."

His eyes narrow, turning molten with flecks of gold churning in the amber depths. "A book *sensed* you? That is not how books work. I may not understand humanity, but I am well-versed in books. Who do you think carved the stones to give to Moses?"

"Y-you...the...T-ten Command-m-ments?" I sputter. "Holy shit."

"Holy, yes. Shit, no. Though I suppose many people have called them that over the centuries." Gabriel stares up at the ceiling for a long moment. "The magic contained in the grimoire... is that what those two assholes want?"

I chew on my lower lip—a nervous habit I thought I'd broken back in college. If he learns the rest, will he try to take the Blade from me? Or worse? Stop me from destroying it?

"Willow." The gentle word is almost too much. But when he

turns, cups my cheeks in his hands, and brushes a kiss to my lips, I break.

"The magic isn't in the grimoire anymore. It's in me. There's an ancient blade out there somewhere that only I can wield. It…I don't even know what all it can do, but I think it can transfer power from one person to another. They told me they wanted to use it to cure disease. To siphon off a little of a shifter's immunity, for example, and transfer it to a human with cancer. But that was all a lie. They want a weapon, and they think…if they have *me* and the Blade…they'll be unstoppable."

I LET the hot water wash over my body. After my admission, I spent a full ten minutes sobbing in Gabriel's arms. When I'd run out of tears, he asked for my trust, and dammit. I agreed.

"Sinclair and Zoe will meet us at the Bureau. If anyone can find out more about the people after you, it will be them. I will call…a friend of theirs…and get you fresh clothing. I suspect if you show up in my sweater, there will be…questions."

Questions. I have so many questions, I could ask them one after another for a year and still not get through them all.

What's going to happen after they start looking into AURA? How can I trust no one at the Bureau is secretly working for AURA? Where has my whisper been for the past six hours? How much longer can I stay in this city before Hannah and Isaac find me?

Why haven't they come after me already? What are they waiting for? Do they know about Gabriel? Or about the incubus demon and his Seraphim mate? God, I don't even know what a Seraphim is. Only that it sounds really damn celestial.

If I keep spiraling like this, I'll shut down. So I close my eyes and focus on the water as it hits my skin. Once my heart rate returns to something *close* to normal, I use Gabriel's shampoo to wash my hair. The idea that I'll smell like him for the rest of the day brings me a small measure of comfort.

Why couldn't I have met him months ago?

Because he wasn't in this realm. Because you never would have believed angels were real. Because meeting a literal demon would probably have sent you over the edge completely.

When I'm done, I wrap myself in a fluffy towel and peek out a crack in the bathroom door. "Gabriel?"

He stares at me, at my bare legs and wet hair, and one of the tendons in his neck strains. "I should...shower as well. Dion brought you several changes of clothes."

"Oh. Okay." He's upset. Tense. Even...angry. I slip out of the bathroom, staying as far from him as I can until he shuts the door between us. Did something happen while I was showering? Or...is it...me?

"It better not be me," I mutter, dumping the shopping bags out onto the bed. Brand new leather boots, a stylish pair of jeans, black yoga pants, a soft, teal sweater with flared sleeves, a purple sweatshirt, several tank tops, thick socks, and three matching sets of lace bras and panties. All in my size. Wow. I guess angels—or at least this angel—isn't hurting for money.

Then again, last night I woke up in a ritzy penthouse where the parking fees alone are probably more than my salary. Is *everyone* in the world of the Other rich?

Going to the Bureau scares the shit out of me. But Gabriel swore no one would hold me against my will or force me to do anything I didn't want to do. Angels don't lie. At least...I hope they don't.

Gabriel

In the hotel's narrow shower, I brace an arm against the wall and wrap my free hand around my cock. Seeing Willow in nothing but a towel stoked the near constant state of arousal I have been battling since our kiss. One taste, and I will never be the same again.

Giving my shaft one, firm stroke, I groan. In all my millennia of existence, no human has ever affected me like this. I have been with half a dozen women—and two men—but never felt more than a passing affection for any of them.

I close my eyes, picturing the way the towel clung to her curves. The part of her lips. The need in her beautiful eyes when she touched me. My hips start to move of their own accord. My hand is a poor substitute, but if I do not slake this need, I fear it will destroy me.

She needs me focused. If those bastards come for her, I cannot be distracted.

"Willow." I let her name spill from my lips as I thrust harder. Faster. My balls tighten. Pressure builds. My breath saws in and out of my chest, ragged. I can almost taste her. The water running down my back should be soothing, but I imagine her short nails scraping my skin instead. She wanted me. And I hurt her.

With one final stroke, I let go. The scent of my release mixes with the steam and the hint of Willow remaining in the room.

This is as close as I can ever get to fucking her. To loving her. But in my heart, she is already forever mine.

THE BUREAU of the Occult and the Other hides in plain sight. I kept Willow tucked against my side for the twenty-minute ride across town. I could have carried us there instantly, but the strain of exhaustion still weighs on me. Two hours of sleep is not enough, and we do not know what threats we will face today.

"This is it?" Willow peers up at the building. "I thought it would be...more in line with their name."

"Laughable?"

"Official. Like with warning signs. Or at least a security guard." She presses closer to me. "Anyone could walk right in."

"They'd have to be able to see the place first," a rough voice says.

Willow yelps, then darts behind me as Kunchin ambles over

from his SUV, a travel mug in one massive hand and a box of doughnuts in the other.

"Gabriel..."

I open my senses. Her fear washes over me. Fuck. She is not prepared for this. Any of it.

"Willow, this is Kunchin," I say. "The yeti works here. He is... a friend."

"A yeti?" She slaps her hand over her mouth. Her cheeks flush bright red. "Oh, God. I'm sorry. I'm just...I've never..."

Kunchin frowns. "You're clearly *other* as my perception filter doesn't work on you. But you've never seen one of us before? Or a gorilla shifter? They're everywhere down by the Embarcadero. Though I'm *much* more elegant." He brushes the hand with his coffee mug down his blue silk tie. "And taller."

"Her powers only manifested a few weeks ago." This was a mistake. I should have insisted we meet at Sinclair's penthouse. If Willow is frightened by the yeti, I do not want to know what she will think of the vampires. Or the ghouls.

"Oh. Well, the entire building is warded," Kunchin explains. "Humans see an empty lot, and if they get too close, they'll feel an irresistible urge to suddenly be anywhere else." He takes a long sip from his mug. "Lieutenant Eve's morning briefing is in half an hour, and I need to check my email first. Good to see you again, Gabriel. Willow." With a nod, he strides for the double doors.

"A yeti. In a suit." Willow's voice cracks. She turns to me, resting her forehead against my shoulder. "And I insulted him."

"This was never your world, *deliciae*." I rub her back in long, slow strokes. "But when we go inside, I suggest you avoid staring at the ghouls. They have been known to hold grudges for centuries."

"Or...you could just forget everything I told you," she says softly. "I know you're immortal. But that doesn't mean you can't be killed. Right? AURA will never stop hunting me. I have to find the Blade before they do and destroy it."

"And you expect me to let you do that alone?" The words are too loud and carry so much power, a car alarm goes off at the edge of the parking lot. Willow shies away from me, cringing, with her hands over her ears.

"Gabriel, get the fuck inside." Sinclair holds the front door open while Zoe hurries over to Willow and takes her arm. "The Lieutenant is already angry that I will not tell her what this case is about. If you insist on bringing down the building, you will learn just how quickly an eagle shifter can claw your eyes out."

SIXTEEN

Willow

Zoe keeps her arm around my shoulders as she leads me through a sea of desks to a set of stairs at the back of the building. "Don't stare at the shifters," she says softly. "They don't like it."

I keep my gaze pinned to the floor. Safer that way. I don't want to be ripped apart. Or haunted for the rest of my life. All around me, conversations stop or drop to whispers until we're at the top of the stairs.

"Okay. No one else is around. You can breathe now." She swipes a plastic badge over a sensor along the wall, and a metal door slides open. The conference room looks like something out of *Star Trek*. Huge, glowing blue screens line one entire wall, with terminals spaced around a glossy black conference table. In one corner, a fancy beverage machine sits on a small cabinet, surrounded by a handful of cups. "We got lucky," she says. "This is the only room with its own coffee machine. The sludge downstairs will eat a hole in your stomach. Well, unless you're a shifter or a vampire. They can heal so quickly, they could be drinking battery acid all day and be fine. Do you want a cup?"

"God, yes. I feel like a zombie."

Zoe cringes. "Um, some of the ghouls identify as zombie cryptids. Don't let them hear you say that."

I can feel the blood drain from my cheeks. The Blade might not get a chance to kill me. The wrong word or sideways glance in this building and one of the other agents could tear me apart.

"Sinclair and Gabriel will be up in a couple of minutes." She slides a steaming cup in front of me. "They have to smooth things over with our Lieutenant. How does your neck feel?"

My fingers skim my throat. "Better. I'm...um...sorry about last night. If I offended you. Or Sinclair."

"You didn't." She peers at me over the rim of her mug. "Ask."

I almost choke on a sip of coffee. "Ask...what?"

"Anything." Her smile is reassuring. Warm. "I was you a few weeks ago, Willow. This world is still new to me too."

"But Gabriel said you were...a Seraphim. This *is* your world, right?" I'm so confused.

Zoe's cheeks tinge with color. "Do you know what a Seraphim is?"

"No." The coffee warms my hands but does nothing to steady my nerves.

"I'm a *daughter* of Seraphim. The highest of the angels. The watchers. My body's human. It's only my soul that's celestial. I was sent to this realm centuries ago to trap a demon's consciousness in Hell. But I failed. One of the other angels was...well... really fucking pissed."

"Not Gabriel?" The way she talks, this isn't a good story. What if Gabriel isn't the man—angel—I think he is?

"No. Not Gabriel. Long story short, he trapped me in a prison of my own body until I had 'learned my lesson.' Then eventually sent me back here a second time—to do the same damn thing—with no idea who or what I was. If I hadn't been partnered with Sin...I might not have remembered until it was too late." She shudders, a shadow passing over her face for a brief moment.

Something hits the door behind us, and we both jerk. A little of my coffee spills onto the table.

Zoe rolls her eyes. "Gabriel, I know you can hear me. Tell Sin to let you go and get in here. We need to call Mad and Killian."

I don't know who Mad and Killian are or how Gabriel can hear us through the heavy metal door, but a moment later, the two men walk in, breathing heavily. A drop of blood stains Gabriel's lip. Sinclair pulls a handkerchief from his pocket and wipes his knuckles.

"Men," Zoe mutters. "What was it this time?"

"The archangel called me an ass," Sin says, his tone so mild he might as well be ordering a turkey sandwich. "I was merely earning the title."

Gabriel sinks into the chair next to me and takes my hand. "You are tired, *deliciae*. I wish you had slept more."

His touch calms me like nothing else can. "You keep calling me that. What does it mean?"

"*Deliciae*?" He stares down at our joined hands. 'It is ancient Latin for...well, darling would be the closest translation. If the word makes you uncomfortable...I will not use it again."

I try to force the lump in my throat away, but the damn thing won't budge. We've known each other less than a day—unless you count the few moments we spent at the cathedral weeks ago—but we're connected in a way I've never experienced before.

Do all angels have this effect on humans? Or...witches?

"Willow?" Gabriel skims a knuckle along my cheek. I blink hard, then meet his concerned gaze. "You were somewhere else."

"This...this isn't real." My eyes burn, the first hint of tears pricking at the corners. "None of this. Angels, demons, my whisper...it can't be. I'm in a coma. Or dead. Or—"

Gabriel's lips crash against mine. His tongue demands entrance, and I part for him. The kiss sets me on fire. I grip his arms, my fingers digging into the firm muscles as if he can ground me in this reality I so desperately want to believe in.

"Ahem." Sinclair clears his throat. "If the two of you would prefer to be alone..."

Gabriel breaks off the kiss, but keeps me caged in his arms. "This is real, Willow. All of it," he whispers in my ear. Turning to

Sinclair, he levels the demon with a withering gaze. "I thought a sex demon would be more comfortable with public displays of affection."

Sin straightens his shoulders, one hand curled protectively around Zoe's waist. His deep blue eyes are ringed with red. "The amount of energy you sent into the room just now was... disorienting."

Oh, my God. This isn't happening. I stare into the coffee mug to hide my embarrassment.

"My apologies," Gabriel says, his tone subdued as he scoots his chair a few inches away. "I did not think of that."

"Can we focus on the real problem?" Zoe holds out her hand for Sin's phone, then connects it to the conference room system. "Mad and Killian are waiting for us."

With a few taps to the screen, Sinclair launches a video call.

Greatest Warlock of All Time

Gabriel snorts. "You cannot be serious."

"He spelled my phone," Sin mutters. "Every time I attempt to change it, the title gets more and more ridiculous. If try again...I fear he could end up calling himself '*God.*'"

Gabriel brushes his hair over his shoulder. "And piss off the Almighty? Not even Killian is that stupid."

"I heard that." On screen, a dark-haired man, exhausted, wearing a thick, wool fisherman's sweater, stares back at us. Next to him, a shorter man with features so much like Sin's, they have to be related, crowds closer. "We tracked down the Valkyrie, Kàra. But she's a bloody vampire, so we only had an hour with her before she had to go to ground."

"Well?" Sinclair asks.

Killian stifles his yawn. "The last time Kàra heard anyone talk about a whisper was 1756. She only heard rumors. But not long after they started, her sire—he's dead now—started hunting for the whisper's keeper. This Keeper could apparently wield an ancient weapon with so much power, every vampire, witch, and shifter was pissing themselves, convinced the world was going to end."

The other man, the one related to Sin, leans closer to the

camera. "If the weapon is in play," he says, "the whisper—and the whisper keeper—will know where it is."

"Any idea what this weapon is called?" Sinclair asks.

I clear my throat, and everyone in the room turns to me. "The Blade of Liminal Transference. It..." Can I really tell them? If I do, I lose any chance to run. Or worse. Sinclair or Killian—or anyone else at the Bureau—could decide they want the power for themselves.

"Willow, you can trust them," Gabriel says softly. "I can sense your fear, but Sinclair is one of the most honorable men I know. And despite his hubris, Killian is utterly devoted to protecting this world. Maddox—his mate—is half angel. You could not have found better allies in this realm."

I force a deep breath. Gabriel's conviction infuses his every word. I want to trust him. I want to trust all of them.

With a soft stirring of the air, my whisper appears across the table.

Oh, God.

I've never been so relieved to see her and know she's okay. Gabriel inclines his head, and she responds in kind.

"I do not believe she will steer you wrong, *deliciae*." He strokes his hand up and down my back. Some of the tension I've carried since walking in here fades away.

"Uh, Willow?" Zoe asks. "What's going on?"

"My whisper is here. Gabriel can see her. You can't?" I gesture across the table, but Zoe and Sin shake their heads.

Sinclair frowns. "The Bureau is heavily warded. *Appearing* in the middle of one of the conference rooms should not be possible."

"Oh, really?" Gabriel scoffs. "Must I remind you how I first met Zoe?"

"You're a fucking archangel. The rules simply do not apply to you. Nor do you care about them." The tension in Sin's voice sends a shiver down my spine. "But that is a discussion for another time. What does this *whisper* want?"

She glides over to me, her shimmering eyes never leaving my face. A light brush of her hand sends warmth racing up my arm.

"I think...she wants me to trust you." Her nod is the last bit of encouragement I need. I've cursed her more than once. Wished she'd disappear and never come back. Wondered what terrible thing I'd done in the past to be burdened by this power.

But in this moment, I *know* she's on my side. I needed her, and she came.

I sit up a little straighter and face the screen. "There's a lot I don't know. But the Blade of Liminal Transference can siphon an *Other's* power and...well...transfer it to someone else. I'm the only one alive who can wield it. The device Gabriel cut out of me last night? That belongs to an organization called AURA – the Agency for Uncovering Rare Anomalies. They're supposedly part of the NSA, but that could be a lie for all I know. The two in charge—Isaac and Hannah—won't stop until they have me again. Unless I can find a way to destroy the Blade, they'll use it—and me —until they have the entire *Other* community in their thrall."

***

Gabriel

It's well after noon now, and Willow is still talking. Every time she mentions Hannah—and how the woman influenced her every decision—I wish I had done much more than throw the fae across the room.

She used her *talents* on a woman with no knowledge of the Other world. She cut her off from her friends, her coworkers, her very life. Then convinced Willow it would be best if AURA implanted a *torture device* into her body.

"Fuck!" Sinclair growls. The demon stalks over to one of the workstations built into the conference table. Each keystroke is louder and harder than the last. "I had Kunchin run a GHOST search for Willow's name."

"A GHOST search?" she asks.

Zoe leans closer. "Global Habitant Optical Scanning and Tracking. Basically, it's our version of facial recognition."

"And you called it GHOST." Willow shakes her head. "This day—this *world*—keeps getting stranger every minute."

"Well, we are at B.O.O.," Zoe says with a little smile. "But I promise you, the system itself is very real and very effective. Sin? What did you find?"

The demon mutters an oath under his breath. "This was filed five days ago."

The center screen flickers to life, and I reach for Willow's hand. "Is that...her *death certificate?*"

Her horror slams into me—a physical force that almost knocks me out of my chair. With every hour—every touch—our connection grows, and I fear what will happen when my heart is no longer mine, but hers. Completely.

"Yes. It's fake," Sin adds. "Not even a good one. Sloppy."

Time of Death: 12:30 *a.m.*

Cause of death: Blunt force trauma to the head

Location: Fisherman's Wharf

"Why would they do this?" Willow's voice cracks. She stifles a sob. I wrap my arm around her and pull her closer.

"You said you'd taken a leave of absence from your job," Zoe says. "But you didn't officially move out of your apartment. And, presumably, you have friends?"

Willow nods against my chest. "A few. But...they're not local, mostly. From my graduate program."

Zoe sinks down into her chair and holds Willow's gaze. "They were covering their bases. Making sure that if anyone *did* come to check on you or report you missing, there would be a plausible explanation. They faked your death so no one would look for you."

"Or," Sinclair adds with a quick glance in my direction, "as leverage. A display of their power. They had no way of knowing how long it would take you to read that grimoire. They could not take the chance you would try to return to your life."

With every word, Willow shrinks into herself further. She shakes against me, trying to hold back the tears glistening on her lashes. "So that's it? I don't exist anymore?"

"Enough!" My outburst rattles the coffee mugs on the table. Zoe claps her hands over her ears and glares at me.

Fuck.

I cannot continue to sit here and do nothing while the woman in my arms—the woman I care so deeply for—loses everything she holds dear.

"Watch yourself, Gabriel," Sin says. Red rims his eyes, glowing so brightly, I expect his wings to burst forth any second. "You know we will not stand for this. It will take some time to straighten things out with the medical examiner and City Hall, but we will take care of it. *After* we put an end to these bastards and find a way to destroy the Blade."

"The other Whisper Keepers couldn't ...*unmake* it." Willow shakes off my hold, scoots her chair a few inches away, and starts fiddling with the hem of her shirt. "That's why they all...chose to die. Because there was no other way."

"You will *not* sacrifice yourself for this thing." I spin her chair until she faces me. "I won't allow it."

"It's not your choice, Gabriel. It's mine." Her tears spill over, glistening on her pale cheeks. "It *wants* to be found. It's calling to me. Last night it was this tiny presence in the back of my mind. Like music playing in another room. But it's so much stronger now. In another day or two, I won't be able to resist it."

"But you will die, *deliciae*. There has to be another way." I hold her face in my hands. She's so beautiful. I memorize everything about her. The tiny scar on the bridge of her nose. The curve of her dark blond brows. The flecks of green and silver in her blue eyes.

She leans in, resting her forehead against mine. "There's no weapon in this world powerful enough to destroy the Blade. This is the only way."

How cruel is fate? To lead me to Willow, then rip her away from me within days?

Crueler than all of Lucifer's Hellions put together.

I jerk to my feet so quickly, Willow almost topples out of her chair. "No weapon *in this world*. That is what the other Whisper Keepers said? Those were the exact words?"

"Y-yes." Her brows knit together, a tiny wrinkle between them begging to be smoothed away. "Why?"

"There is one world more vast and powerful than this one, Willow. Its guardian is an expert with weapons. And he owes me a favor."

SEVENTEEN

Gabriel

"You are out of your goddamn mind," Sinclair growls.

I straighten my shoulders and level him with my most powerful stare. "The Almighty may very well damn me in the near future, but she has not done so yet."

"Lucifer will break you, Gabriel. Or worse. If he tosses you through the gates of Hell, you would be trapped there for all eternity. Without your wings, you would have no hope of escape."

I shrug, which pisses him off even more. Not that I care. "If one of Lucifer's weapons is our best chance of destroying the Blade, that is a risk I am willing to take."

He stalks over to me, but before he can grab me, I take hold of his arms, spin, and slam him against the wall.

His eyes start to glow. "Remove your hands. Now."

The deadly calm to his tone should concern me. He suffered in Hell for centuries. I did not send him there, but I am still to blame.

"Oh, for fuck's sake." Zoe stalks over, slaps a hand on each of our chests, and attempts to separate us. "If you can't play nicely together, one of you needs to leave. You're scaring Willow."

I flinch. Zoe is right. Willow's fear is a bitter taste in my mouth. One I cannot abide. I step back and smooth my hands down my white dress shirt.

"Asshole," Sinclair mutters.

"Hey. You're not blameless here either, partner." Despite her words, Zoe reaches up to touch Sin's cheek. My heart aches at the simple, tender gesture.

"Partner? I am much more than your partner." He puffs out his chest, a hint of his power swirling around the room.

"I love you too," she says.

Willow dashes a few tears from her eyes. "You're really going to Hell? How is that even possible?"

I drop to one knee next to her. "I am going to Hell's gates. Lucifer can come to me."

"But...if you get trapped there—"

I squeeze her hand, then rise to meet Sinclair's frosty gaze. "If I am not back by sunset, call Azrael. He can *retrieve* me."

"I am not waiting until sunset," Sin says. "Five hours in the earthen realm is a quarter century in the Underworld. You have ninety minutes. Use it wisely."

THE UNDERWORLD HAS A SMELL. It seeps into my clothes. Into my lungs. The last time I made this trip and found out the Devil had *lost* Thorn and his concubine, I could not rid myself of the gritty, burnt stench for two days.

My wings still reek of it. It is the scent of decay. Of endless torment and despair.

"Lucifer, you pompous twat, show yourself!"

I pace the rocks outside the black gates, waiting for Beelzebub to grace me with his presence. He owes me for his carelessness.

"If you force me to break in, you will not like the consequences!"

A great rumble starts beneath my feet. The oppressive darkness, broken only by the glow of the flames from the other side of the gates, lifts, and Lucifer appears before me.

Hell's Keeper is not the monster those in the earthen realm imagine him to be. After all, he is—or was—an angel until the Almighty cast him out and shackled him to the Underworld. Black hair, a chiseled jaw, and piercing green eyes give him a magnetism few humans can ignore. At least until they are trapped in his domain and suffering for all eternity.

"Gabriel. To what do I owe the displeasure?" His silken voice twists my frustration and rage into something softer. Until I shake off the glamour he is so fond of using and step back.

"You owe me for your carelessness with the demon, Thorn. I have come to collect on that debt."

Lucifer chuckles. "I have paid in full, brother. Or did you forget while your wings were burning? The daughter of Seraphim and her lover are free, and Thorn has gone mad from some of my more...*creative* methods of torment."

I grab the lapels of his bespoke black suit jacket and haul him up to his toes. "You have not even begun to clear your ledger. The demon killed close to a hundred after you *let him go*. If it were not for Sinclair and Zoe, he would still be killing. You are skilled in torture, Samael, but not even *you* are as cruel as he was to his victims."

"I take that as an insult." Despite his words, a hint of fear churns in his eyes.

Ash floats through the air, staining my white shirt. Rude.

"Take it however you like. I don't give a fuck."

The devil waves his hand, and I fly back, landing on my ass so hard, the breath I'd drawn leaves my lungs in a *whoosh*.

"This is my realm, Gabriel. Or have you forgotten? And I did not let the demon and his concubine go. I do not let anyone go. Especially not two souls with their particular brand of sins." His eyes flicker with an emotion I do not believe I have ever seen before—and cannot name—and the arrogance ingrained in his very being disappears in an instant. "What do you want?"

"A weapon. One forged in the fires of Hell and capable of destroying a blade crafted when magic began."

The Devil laughs in my face.

I lunge for him once more, slamming him against the supposedly impenetrable gates of his domain. With a great metallic screech, the lock shatters.

We tumble into the oppressive heat, but this close to the entrance, the flames are nothing more than an illusion. Lucifer does not fight me. Not even when I land a punch that snaps his head to the side and splits his lip.

"Do you think I am joking? That I would willingly come down here and banter with you?" Another punch, and his right eye starts to swell. "Give me what I need, or I will tell the Almighty about your little security *problem*." I get to my feet and stalk back through the gates. The flames may not be real, but my memories are. My wings demand to be set free. I dig my nails into my palms, wrestling for control. For a moment, I think I have won, but pure agony forces a scream from my lips. Half-burned feathers flutter to the rocks at my feet.

"Gabriel." The Devil stares at me, all hubris gone from his tone. "You are not healing."

"Thank you for that brilliant insight. Did you think I had not noticed?" I try to extend my wings to their fullest, but the pain is too much.

"I think," he says and plucks a single mangled feather from the stone, "you are trapped in a Hell of your own making. One I would gladly free you from if I knew how."

His concern brings a lump to my throat. We were close once. Long before he was banished to the Underworld. He has not cared for anyone since. Or so I'd thought. Perhaps I was wrong.

With a snap of his fingers, he summons a gleaming black axe. The weapon is only as long as his forearm, but the power contained within could level cities.

"Hell's weapons do not belong in the earthen realm. If it falls into the wrong hands, you will be the one to blame."

I feel the weight of the burden as soon as I wrap my fingers around the handle. "I will guard it with my very existence, brother. Thank you."

"Gabriel?" His call stops me before I can picture the Bureau's conference room in my mind. "My Hellions are investigating the breach that freed Thorn and his concubine. I will find those responsible and consign them to an eternity of torment so vile, no one has ever experienced its equal."

Lucifer is many things. An ass, a prankster, and a terrible poker player, among others. But he does not lie. It goes against his very nature.

"Being banished to the depths of Hell was the Almighty's punishment for a crime the likes of which you cannot fathom," he says. "If she finds out I failed, my existence is over. Even *you* cannot hate me that much."

"I do not hate you at all. I never have." With the axe tucked under my arm, I hold his gaze. "The Almighty does not hold grudges, Lucifer."

He shakes his head. "No, she doesn't. But Seraphiel does."

***

Willow

No matter how many times Sinclair and Zoe assure me the Bureau is warded, I can't shake the feeling someone's watching me. It crawls up and down my spine, simmering in my blood like something frigid and evil is about to escape.

My whisper comes and goes. I wish we could talk. She hasn't pulled me into her consciousness since we absorbed the power of the Blade, and I'm starting to wonder if she ever will again.

"I should not have let him go," Sinclair mutters. "Lucifer cannot be trusted."

Zoe looks up from her notebook and narrows her eyes at her partner. "You're not helping. Why don't you go grab us some tacos? Willow is probably starving. I know I am."

I don't think I could eat if my life depended on it. But Zoe's stomach growls loudly.

"You swear you will not leave the building?" Sin asks. The tremor of fear in his voice is jarring. I know I only met him last night, but this doesn't seem like him at all.

Zoe frames his face with her hands. "Dion is home. Behind wards so strong, even Gabriel would have a hard time bypassing them. I won't go anywhere. I promise."

"I will be back in twenty minutes. Call me if you hear from Mad and Killian."

A private moment passes between them, and I look away. This isn't just love. It's something more. Something so beautiful and perfect, it makes me ache.

The door shuts with a quiet click. "Sorry about that," Zoe says. "He still thinks what happened to me—to us—was his fault."

I must look as confused as I feel, because the color drains from Zoe's cheeks.

"You don't know. Shit. I didn't even think... Of course you don't know." She goes to the little coffee station and brews two fresh cups, then sinks down into the chair next to me. "Several weeks ago, I was kidnapped by a full-blood incubus and his fae lover. They used my friend, Dion, as bait to get to me. I'd promised Sin I wouldn't leave BOO without him, but when Dion called...I didn't have a choice."

The exhaustion in her eyes mirrors my own. But behind it, there's something more. Sorrow so deep, it goes on forever. "They went after her to get to me. Fae..." She cups her mug in both hands, and even then it wobbles a little. "A fae's command is impossible to resist. Thorn would torture his victims until their minds were nearly gone, then Regina would bring them—us—back so he could break us completely."

Turning, she gathers her red curls into one hand and sweeps them off her neck. A tattoo of a fairy bound in chains glows on her skin. "That mark gave him complete control of us. Body and mind. It's spelled, and there's nothing I can do to remove it."

"Oh, God. I'm sorry…" If I knew Zoe better, I'd hug her. The regret and pain in her voice breaks my heart.

"Sin is so overprotective because he wasn't here to protect me that night. I don't think he'll *ever* forgive himself, even though it wasn't his fault. If he had been here, Thorn could have taken us both, and we might not have survived at all." She shakes off the haunted look in her eyes and forces a smile. "I'm sorry for dumping all that on you at once. But you need to know how serious BOO is about security. And why."

"Dion is the one Gabriel called to bring me these clothes." I run my hands up and down my thighs, wishing I had a friend who cared for me as much as Zoe obviously cares for Dion

"She's a panther shifter. When this is all over, I'll introduce you. You'll love her."

I don't tell her that when this is all over, I won't be meeting anyone. I'll die before I let AURA get a hold of the Blade, and even if Gabriel does return from Hell with a weapon, we have no idea if it'll do a damn bit of good against the Blade.

The floor under us shakes. Zoe sighs, rolls her head around until her neck cracks, and returns to her workstation "That," she says, "will be Gabriel."

***

Gabriel

I stagger back into the conference room and drop the Devil's axe onto the table.

"Holy shit." Willow gets to her feet. "Is that…?"

"Do not touch it. There are only a few in this realm powerful enough to wield it. I have no idea what it will do to someone who is not…celestial." I capture her hand in mine and bring it to my lips. Being away from her felt *wrong*.

"If the lieutenant asks," Zoe says, "Sin and I knew nothing about your plans to bring a Hell-forged weapon into this building. Got it?"

I incline my head, then glance around the room. "Where is Sinclair?"

"On a taco run. He should be back in ten minutes. Maybe less." Zoe picks up her phone, and her eyes widen. "Shit. Kàra is awake. I'm calling Mad and Killian now. They say they have news."

If it were not for my desperate need to protect Willow, I would find Sinclair right this second and beat him bloody. He was supposed to protect them while I was gone, and he *left*.

He left Zoe as well.

As Zoe plugs her phone into the video system, Willow's fingers trail over my bicep. "Are you okay?" she asks. "You're tense."

Fuck. I need to get a tighter hold on my emotions. "Dealing with Lucifer is tiring. He used to be a friend. But I do not know him at all anymore." With a sigh, I drape my arm around her shoulder.

Killian picks up on the first ring. He and Maddox sit side by side, with another couple next to them. The woman is tall, blond, and beautiful. The man is slightly shorter. They're both so pale, their skin is almost pure white.

"Kàra and Ewan, meet Zoe, Willow, and Gabriel," Killian says. "Are we waiting for Sin?"

"No," Zoe says. "He'll catch up. Kàra? We need to know everything you can tell us about the Blade and how we can destroy it."

EIGHTEEN

Willow

Kára frightens me, despite being all the way in Newfoundland. She's preternaturally still, so utterly focused, and lethal in every way.

"Understand these are only rumors," she says. Her fingers twine with Ewan's. Do they tremble a little? Shit. That's not good. "My sire...he would talk while he *worked on* me and my sisters. The rumors of the Blade started hundreds of years ago. He thought them folly at the start, but after a few months, he changed his mind. Obtaining the weapon was *all* he spoke of.

"There have been many powerful covens in history. But none so powerful as the first." She turns her gaze to Gabriel. "You were present at the beginning, angel. You should understand."

My celestial protector inclines his head. "Present, yes. But I regret to say I concerned myself little with the goings on in this realm beyond my duties."

"Your duties?" I ask.

He straightens his shoulders. "I am the bringer of justice, the revealer of truth, and the interpreter of the Almighty's plan."

"Huh?"

Gabriel's amber eyes narrow. "Excuse me?"

His confusion is almost adorable. "Oh, come on. That's the world's worst canned answer ever. Right up there with 'Your call is important to us' and 'Turn it off and back on again.' What do you actually *do*?"

Kàra clears her throat. "We do not have time for distractions. May I continue? If the Blade is in play, I need to contact my sisters. No one is safe while its magic is in the world. You of all people, Whisper Keeper, should know this."

Her rebuke stings, and a low growl rumbles in Gabriel's chest.

"She's right." I rest my hand on his arm. "I won't be able to resist the Blade's pull much longer. We can talk about this later. But we *will* talk about it."

I hope.

"We do not know what first brought magic to this world," the vampire says. "And all beings fear what they cannot understand. I believe this is why the first coven created the Blade. They feared their magic would die with them. They sought to preserve it. Their intentions could even be called noble, I suppose."

My stomach twists in on itself. The Blade's song grows louder. My whisper hovers in the corner of the conference room. She presses her hands to her heart, and a tear glistens on her cheek. She feels it too.

The urge to move is so strong, my muscles tense. I dig my fingers into the arms of the chair to keep myself grounded. Kàra is still talking. Shit. I lost all focus.

"...power has been passed down through so many generations, it long ago became impossible to trace. Many have tried. Witches —even women without magic who were suspected to be related to the first Whisper Keeper—have been imprisoned and tortured, only to be killed when they could not call upon the Blade's power. You did not know this magic was in your line?"

"I was abandoned as an infant," I say softly. "My parents adopted me when I was a month old."

"Interesting," Kàra says. "Though with the advances in medicine and the sciences, perhaps your lineage could be traced? It might help you narrow down the Blade's location."

"Won't it be with whoever last tried to take its power?" Zoe leans back in her chair, lines of strain tightening around her eyes.

"Perhaps. But artifacts of power tend to find their way... home." The vampire shrugs one shoulder. "And those with ill intentions often get their comeuppance...in the end."

Gabriel runs a hand through his dark locks. "The last entry in the grimoire was from 1879. If this power is passed down from generation to generation, why has there not been another until now?"

"This world has many protectors, angel. You, of all beings, should know this," Kàra says. "My sire went up against several of the Blade's guardians in his time. It is hidden behind powerful magic, and only the Whisper Keeper can find it. This organization you say is after it—and Willow—will hunt her until her last breath. But those of us sworn to keep this realm safe will do what we can to stop them."

———

HOURS LATER, I'm so exhausted, I can barely keep my tears from spilling over. My skin crawls with the need to run.

"You cannot be serious!" Gabriel leaps to his feet and stalks over to Sinclair. "We are not putting Willow in that kind of danger!"

"Do you have a better idea?" Sin keeps his tone level, but his eyes glow with power. "If you merely *appear* with her at the Blade's location, we will have nothing on these bastards."

"I gave you their address," I say softly. "You couldn't—?"

Zoe shakes her head. "Sin sent the ghouls to check it out. It's empty. Completely. They found a few faint traces of magic, but that's it."

Despair steals the last of my control. A single sob catches in my throat. "It's hopeless, then."

Gabriel and Sinclair face off. Zoe attempts to get between

them, but they're almost chest-to-chest in some sort of epic celestial pissing contest. The idea would be comical if it weren't my life—and the fate of the entire world—hanging in the balance.

I don't know who throws the first punch. Or who slams whom into the wall so hard, a crack appears in the plaster. All I can do is drop my face into my hands and cry.

"Enough!" Zoe shouts. I lift my gaze to find her standing on top of the conference table holding the Devil's axe. "You're both *angels,* for fuck's sake. Get yourselves under control. We have work to do."

"Zoe. Give me the weapon," Sinclair says, worry lending a rough edge to his voice. "It could...damage you."

Her gaze pings from her mate to the axe and back again. "I have a celestial's soul, remember? Besides, it's not even heavy." She returns it to the table and lets Sin help her down and into his arms. "Are we sure Lucifer didn't play the Underworld's worst prank on Gabriel?"

My whisper appears out of nowhere, panic in her translucent eyes. Before I can get to my feet, the room starts to spin. Whatever Gabriel says fades into nothingness. With dizzying speed, she carries me—us—through the building and into the last rays of sun streaking from the horizon.

"Stop! This...something's wrong!"

Either she can't hear me or she doesn't care. I don't know which is worse. Oh, God. We're heading for the cathedral.

"No, no, no!"

What if AURA is watching? They've never been able to see my whisper before, but...she's so much stronger now.

The antechamber is dark, but inside the vault, the blue flames banish the shadows to the corners of the room. My whisper splays her fingers over the grimoire, staring intently at the pages like she's expecting something to happen.

"Why are we here?"

She shakes her head, and her hands sink into the book, all the way down to the altar. This is new. I can *feel* the cool stone.

"You need more power. I don't know how to help you. The WCU is gone."

With a roar, the blue flames glow so bright, I can't see a thing. The air swirls around us. Gently at first, then faster and faster until my cheeks sting. How is this possible? It's like *I'm* here. Not just her.

Tears prick at my eyes. I have to close them to slits before the book comes back into focus. Those are *my* hands. Solid and shaking.

I turn the page, pressing my fingers to the edges of the parchment so the wind doesn't blow the entire grimoire to bits. The ink flows, each letter coming faster than the last.

Refuse the call and your life ends here.
Stop the search and your soul will sheer.
Threads from the past can bind or break.
The future is only what you make.
When all is lost will come a choice.
Love...

I can *feel* the grimoire resisting. It doesn't want to finish the last line. But why?

"Tell me the rest!" I beg. Ink wells up, drowning the words until the entire page is pitch black.

Pain—as sharp as an ice pick—drives into my skull. I grab my head in both hands. My scream echoes off the walls.

I only stop when my lungs have nothing left to give. The flames are dying. Every second is darker than the last. My chest tightens. It's hard to breathe. I'm dizzy.

My knees hit the rough stone. I'm too weak to get up. I could die here. No one would ever find me.

Maybe it's better this way.

The magic of the Blade would die with me. AURA would never get their hands on it. On me.

From somewhere far away, I hear Gabriel calling my name. He's desperate.

"Please, Willow. Open your eyes for me. You cannot leave this world. Not yet."

I want to live. I want to see him again. My whisper's panic is a physical weight. "Let...me...go," I beg. "Or we both die."

My consciousness snaps back to my body in a single heartbeat. The bottom drops out of my stomach. I roll onto my side and retch. I'm so cold. I can't feel my hands. Or...anything at all.

Gabriel

In Sinclair's guest suite, I cradle Willow against my chest. She has not stirred in over an hour. I can still sense her, thank fuck. She is not in the void. If they had found a way to send her there again, I do not know what I would have done.

Or, perhaps I do. I would have hunted them. Mercilessly.

Her eyelids flutter. I drag my thumb along her cheek, watching for any signs of distress.

"Come back to me, *deliciae*."

She blinks up at me, her blue eyes unfocused. "Gabriel? Where...are we?"

"I brought you to Sinclair's. His penthouse is protected by more wards than the Bureau could ever hope for. He and Zoe are still coordinating with Lieutenant Eve."

Willow snuggles closer with a sigh. I ache to know why she passed out. But in this moment, her comfort with me—her trust— is all that matters.

"Do you believe in fate?" she asks, her voice heavy and thick with exhaustion.

"As in the Almighty's preordained plan for every soul throughout all of creation?"

"Yeah. That." She peers up at me, slightly more alert now as she waits for my answer.

"Complete and utter bullshit."

Her shoulders jerk, and her brows shoot up. "What?"

Chuckling, I press my lips to her forehead. "Humans have always had free will. The Almighty's plans fell apart the moment

Adam invited that snake into the Garden of Eden. Why do you ask?"

She chews on her lower lip for a moment. I would kiss all that worry away if I did not think I would lose my whole heart to her in an instant. Gently, I ease her up so her back is against the head-board, then take her hands.

"Whatever it is, you can tell me." I have never been so desperate to know another's thoughts before. Or to share my own. In my travels amongst humans the past two weeks, I talked to many of them. But I offered up nothing of myself. For Willow, I would lay my soul bare.

"My whisper took me back to the cathedral," she says, her gaze pinned to our joined hands. "There was another page in the grimoire." A single tear tumbles down her cheek.

"'*Refuse the call and your life ends here. Stop the search and your soul will sheer. Threads from the past can bind or break. The future is only what you make. When all is lost will come a choice.*' There was at least one more line, but my whisper kicked me out of her head before I could read it."

"Witches," I mutter. "Always speaking in circles and rhymes. It has been this way since time began."

"I have to find the Blade. If I don't, the magic will kill me." She's crying now, tiny sniffles and hiccups, each one another cut to my battered heart. "But the rest of it... I don't want to die."

"Willow, look at me." I nudge her chin up and use my thumbs to wipe away her tears. "If there is a way for you to take back your life, we *will* find it. Sinclair and Zoe have a plan. You said the Blade is somewhere to the east. There is a train to Chicago that leaves in the morning. We will take it, but we will not be alone. Maddox and Killian are on their way with Kàra and Ewan. Kàra's sister, Mist is coming from New Orleans. Kunchin will be with us as well."

"They'll come after me," she whispers.

"Let them come." I straighten my shoulders, anger prickling over my skin. "We will end them *and* destroy the Blade. There is no weapon in this realm more powerful than Lucifer's axe. This plan will work. I believe so with all that I am."

She holds my gaze, searching for something. Deceit? Uncertainty? Determination? Whatever it is, she must find it because she nods, and her shoulders relax slightly.

"What time do we leave?"

"The train departs at 7:00 a.m. If you cannot wait that long, we will make the first part of the trip by car."

She blows out a slow breath. "I think I'll be okay." As if her body agrees, her stomach growls loudly.

"You need to eat. I have Sinclair's credit card. What can I get for you?"

A hint of light returns to her eyes, though sadness quickly chases it away. "Pizza from Papa Balducci's. Pepperoni, sausage, and extra cheese."

For a moment, I struggle to understand her emotions. Equal parts joy and pain. Excitement and sorrow.

The truth hits me so hard, I cannot breathe. This is her favorite food in the city. And she's certain that after tonight, she will never taste it again.

THE EVENING PASSES TOO QUICKLY. I order three extra large pizzas. Sin and Zoe join us not long after they arrive, Killian and Maddox a few hours later.

Willow peppers Killian with questions about magic until she's so tired, she can barely keep her eyes open. I pluck her from the couch, ignoring her slurred protests, and carry her to the guest suite.

I pull back the blankets, but she wriggles out of my arms. "I have to brush my teeth and change out of these clothes."

"I...will say good night, then. I asked Sinclair to leave a blanket and pillow for me on the couch."

She stops me before I reach the door. "Gabriel? Stay with me. I don't want to be alone."

I want nothing more than to hold her in my arms all night. But the closer I get to her, the more of my heart I lose. It doesn't matter. Not truly. I would gladly surrender it all to keep her safe.

Quickly, I shed my pants and dress shirt, slide under the duvet, then wonder if I am doing the right thing. Should I sleep in my clothes? Or ask Sinclair for a pair of pajamas? Fuck. The last thing I want to do is knock on the demon's bedroom door wearing nothing but a pair of boxer briefs.

Before I can make a decision, Willow emerges from the bathroom. Fuck. She's wearing nothing but a t-shirt that barely reaches her thighs. Her cheeks turn bright red as she hurries across the room and practically dives under the covers.

I turn off the light. Willow snuggles closer and settles her hand over my chest. "Is this all right?" I ask.

"It would be better if you were holding me," she says softly.

Anything she wants, I will give her. Especially when she's touching me. Wrapping my arm around her, I press a kiss to her hair. "It has been a very long time since I have shared a bed with anyone."

Willow yawns, the sound so utterly content, I expect her to fall asleep within seconds. But before I can drift off myself, she jerks up with a little gasp.

"Wait. Earlier, when you were talking about the Garden of Eden, you said *Adam* started the whole thing? Did he really?"

I chuckle. "Yes. Yes, he did."

NINETEEN

Willow

Every time I turn around, I expect to see Hannah. I woke with her voice in my head more than once last night. All those pretty words, the smooth tone...it was like she was right there. Next to me. But every time, Gabriel was there. His warmth chased her away.

My exhaustion and fear leave me jumpy. The train platform is too crowded. Too loud.

Gabriel carries our suitcase in one hand but keeps the other arm around my waist. Probably smart, as I've thought about running away more than once since we left Sinclair and Zoe's apartment well before sunrise.

I can see Kunchin ahead of us. The yeti is almost seven feet tall and very hard to miss with his snow white fur. Though supposedly, his perception filter keeps humans from seeing his true nature. Sin and Zoe are driving across the country in one of Sin's many cars. He refused to risk Zoe coming face-to-face with another member of the Fae ever again.

They'll stay close. If any of AURA's people come for me, either my compliment of protectors will stop them, or Gabriel will do his amazing travel *thing* and bring me back to Sinclair's penthouse immediately.

Somewhere behind us, Maddox and Killian keep an eye out for anyone suspicious.

A strange sensation settles over me. My skin tingles lightly. "What's happening?" I hiss under my breath.

"Just a spell," Killian says over the small Bluetooth earbud. "Anyone using Fae glamor is about to have a very bad hair day."

I almost laugh. Sinclair's brother-in-law has a great sense of humor. Then again, I think a lot of jokes sound better when delivered in a British accent. Gabriel wasn't amused at my observation, though. His shoulders have been hiked up close to his ears all morning.

I don't know why he's jealous. We can't have a future together—he's an angel and I'm...cursed—but I care for him. I think he feels the same. He keeps calling me *deliciae*. Darling. But he refuses to kiss me again. In this moment, that's all I want. One kiss to make me feel *alive* again. To make me feel like...me.

The Blade's call is getting stronger. Yesterday's soft song, the gentle tug on my soul, has turned into a vise, getting tighter and tighter. It fills my ears, filtering through the sounds of conversation, of traffic on the freeway, of travel. If we don't get moving soon, I'm afraid what will happen next.

My whisper floats close by. Not close enough to touch, but close enough both Gabriel and I can see her. Her emotions are so clear over our fragile bond. Fear. Resignation. A hint of excitement. She wants this, even though she's still terrified.

"Willow?" Mad says over the call. "There's something beyond your right shoulder. Ahead of you. What is it?"

"That's my whisper. You can see her?" I glance up at Gabriel. He doesn't seem surprised.

"Only a shimmer of light," he says. "Nothing more."

"Fuck me. *You* can see ghosts?" Killian asks. "Why are *you* so bloody lucky?"

"Because he is part angel," Gabriel says. "At least that is my assumption. And she does not like being referred to as a ghost. I made that mistake once. I will not make it again."

My whisper gives him a nod and moves a little closer to us.

"Sinclair can't see her," Mad says.

Gabriel scans the crowd for threats as we approach the sleeping car. "Sinclair is part demon. That cancels out his angelic side."

"It does not work that way," Sin mutters. "I *used* to be welcome in the celestial realm. I still would be if not for Seraphiel."

His tone holds a lifetime of pain. There's so much about this world I don't know. Did another angel have anything to do with what happened to Zoe?

A uniformed attendant scans our tickets and points down a narrow hallway. "Your room is at the very end of the car. Instructions for the door lock are posted on the wall. Thank you for riding the United Express."

Despite the tension in Gabriel's body, his eyes hold a hint of excitement too. Even wonder as he takes in the compartment Sinclair booked for us and the instructions for turning the seats into a bed.

"Humans are very inventive," he says, running his hand over the second, smaller bed currently folded up against the wall.

"You're just learning that now? I thought you were responsible for watching over all of creation?" I settle onto one of the bench seats and stare out the window. The platform is almost empty now, only a few late travelers rushing to board.

His amber eyes darken. "I was—no, I am—not a very good angel." My eyes start to burn.

Oh, my God. *I'm* not sad. He is. Yet, I'm the one about to cry. Is this another of his talents? He said he could sense my emotions, but can he broadcast his own?

"I'm sure that's not true." I reach for his hand, but he grabs our suitcase and shoves it into the closet. "Talk to me, Gabriel."

With a heavy sigh, he sits across from me, his elbows on his knees. The train's whistle sounds, and with a lurch, we're moving.

In seconds, the constant song in my ears changes pitch. It's softer now. More soothing. Like the Blade knows I'm coming.

Killian pipes up in my ear. "We are two rooms away. Kunchin is in the next car."

"We require...privacy," Gabriel says. "Call if you see anything suspicious." He tosses his earbud onto the window sill, and waits for me to do the same. As soon as we're completely alone, he pulls the privacy shade over the glass. The world outside takes on a gray tint, but I can still see the city in the distance.

His voice drops to a whisper. "Willow, it is time for you to see my wings."

<hr>

Gabriel

She is not ready. Or perhaps I am merely projecting my own insecurities onto her. Removing my leather jacket, I start to pace the small suite, but quickly give up when I almost run into the door on my second step.

Fuck. I wish the window opened. The walls are oppressively close.

"You are trapped in a Hell of your own making."

The Devil's words echo in my head. Is he right?

Even if he is, I will never admit it. Lucifer would mock me for all eternity.

I am at the door before I realize I have even moved. Only her sharp inhale stops me from escaping into the hall. "Fuck."

"Gabriel? You're scaring me." Willow presses herself to my back, her arms winding around my waist. "You said your wings were damaged. If you don't want me to see them, I understand."

"You need to know." I can barely force the words over the lump in my throat. "I should have called Azrael. Or Sariel. Even Lucifer. You would be safer with them."

"I don't want another angel. I trust *you.*"

I spin around so quickly, Willow stumbles, off balance. My back starts to burn. Yanking the Henley over my head, I let out a groan.

Feathers tumble to the faded carpet. My wings tremble, only half extended in the cramped room.

Willow gasps. Tears shimmer in her eyes. Fuck me. This was a mistake. She will never look at me the same way again. If I could turn away, I would. But then she would see even more, and I cannot let that happen.

Pain racks my body as I struggle to fold my wings against my back. My legs shake. I brace my hand on the wall, gritting my teeth.

Willow takes a step forward. Then another. Her fingers settle on my shoulders. "Turn around," she says softly.

"Do not ask that of me."

"Too late." Her soft smile lights up the room. Opening my senses, I let her emotions wash over me. Worry. Sorrow. Need. Acceptance. "Please, Gabriel. Stop hiding from me."

I do not want to deny her anything. Not even this. Taking a deep breath, I brace myself. If the full extent of the devastation drives her away, will I survive it?

The tips of my wings brush the walls of the train car. I rest my forehead against the door. My heart pounds hard enough, I feel it in my temples.

"Can I touch you? Or will that be too painful?"

She's close enough, her body heat warms my mangled wings. "It would hurt more if you did not, I think."

Her fingers trail over the burnt feathers. Her acceptance tames the worst of the agony. One breath. Then another. Each easier than the last. She spends long moments tracing the base of my wings along my back. Blisters start to heal under her gentle strokes.

"How did it happen?" With her hands on my waist, she urges me to turn and face her. Her eyes hold no judgement. Only understanding.

I lead her back to the couches, force my wings away, and tug my shirt over my head like a shield. "Each of the archangels has a different role. Azrael helps souls cross over after death. Michael is a defender. Raphael is a healer. I am the great communicator. Or...I was supposed to be."

Staring out the window, I let my eyes unfocus. Tall trees blur into a sea of green. Much like history has blurred in my memories. Years, decades, even centuries blended together, and I cared so little about any of them.

"I performed my tasks—when required. Handing the stone tablets to Moses? The look on his face is one I will never forget. I believe his exact words were—translation issues aside—'What in God's name am I supposed to do with these? They are huge.'"

Willow's laughter is a balm to my soul. I even find myself chuckling along with her.

"What did you say to him?" she asks.

"Something along the lines of, 'Start a library,' I believe." Her brows shoot up. It feels so good to smile back at her. To share this pleasant memory. "He did not consider that an appropriate response. But then the burning bush threatened to start a wildfire, and I had to divert a river to put it out. Not my finest hour. Lucifer is much better with flames than I am."

Willow is silent for a moment, then shakes her head. "You're talking about the Devil like he's...a friend."

"He was. Once. A brother, even. He was not always Hell's keeper. Before that, he was a guardian." I lean back against the well-worn cushions and return my gaze to the scenery. "Zoe told you some of what happened to her, yes?"

"That she was kidnapped by a demon, tortured, and branded. Yes." Willow shudders. "Her friend Dion too."

Guilt twists in my gut. The panther shifter did not leave her apartment for almost a week after her ordeal, and unlike Zoe, she was mostly alone. Kunchin checked on her, but the Bureau was in chaos for a time, and he had...duties.

"There is so much more you need to know." I rest my elbows

on my knees, unable to look at her as I confess my sins. How I did not stand up to Seraphiel when he sent Zoe's soul—in another body with another name—to the earthen realm the first time, knowing if she was successful in trapping Thorn's consciousness in Hell, she would spend eternity suffering the Underworld's endless torment alongside him.

How I failed to protest Sinclair's *punishment* for loving her. "Sin was forced to do many terrible things while he was Thorn's prisoner. But he had no choice. Genevieve—Zoe—gave him the strength to fight back. It was he who carried the incubus and his fae lover to Hell, *knowing* he would be trapped there with them. Seraphiel could have freed him. Instead, he imprisoned Zoe in her own body, forbidding even the simple act of breathing. She remembers those centuries. Every moment longer than the last. And I said nothing."

"Why not?" Willow touches my arm, but I pull away.

"The Seraphim are revered. They came before all of us, and do not let us forget our place. Seraphiel, in particular, is a complete dick. But that is no excuse. I could have restored Sinclair's memories at any time. If he had recognized Zoe from the start, perhaps Thorn never would have taken her. If I had bothered to visit my brother—my *friend*—in the Underworld even once, Lucifer might have told me of the breach that allowed Thorn and Regina to escape."

My tears fall silently, dripping down my chin, hitting my hands clasped between my knees, soaking into the carpet at my feet.

"I failed them. All of them. Zoe will live with those terrible memories for the rest of her life. She is a celestial. I damned her to centuries of nightmares. Dion barely survived. Thorn killed hundreds. If losing my wings is to be penance for my crimes, it is not even close to what I deserve."

My chest tightens, and a lump swells in my throat. For a moment, I don't understand. Until the first sob escapes my lips. Shame tears me apart, rending my soul into shreds.

Willow wraps her arms around me, comfort I do not deserve, and I bury my face in her hair.

"Shhh. I've got you, Gabriel."

For the first time in all of my existence, I break, not caring if I am ever able to put myself back together again.

TWENTY

Willow

I don't know what I expected when I demanded Gabriel talk to me. Definitely not this. He's been so confident—full of himself, really—since the first night I met him at the cathedral. But now, he's shaking in my arms.

His anguish is a physical presence in the room. I wouldn't be surprised to find it standing over his shoulder trying to strangle him.

We stay locked together until his sobs fade. "I understand now why so many humans hate to cry," he says and sniffles loudly. He won't look at me, pinning his gaze to the floor.

"Oh my God. You've never cried before?" I grab tissues from the small bathroom and wipe his cheeks. "I know you said the celestial realm is..." I wave my hand vaguely, "paradise, but people cry because they're happy too."

"It is far from paradise." He takes the tissues from me, blows his nose, and disappears into the bathroom. Water runs in the sink. He returns with a fraction more composure. "The longer I spend in this realm, the less I want to return."

"So stay. Zoe said her lieutenant wanted you to join the

Bureau." For a brief moment, I can almost picture a future where I'm still alive. Where Gabriel kisses me like I'm his oxygen and the Blade is nothing but a painful memory.

"Seraphiel will never allow it."

Those five words send me crashing back to reality so fast, I'm surprised I don't break a bone. Or three.

"You can't...I don't know. Protest? Appeal? Go to Celestial Resources and tell them Seraphiel has no business managing anyone?"

With a wry laugh, he shakes his head. "There is no HR Department for angels. The Almighty does not concern herself with our petty disagreements."

"But this isn't petty. This is Seraphiel abusing his power." I'm on my feet again, my mind spinning with outrage. I don't know why I think I can fix this. How does that saying go? Do not meddle in the affairs of dragons because you're crunchy and taste good with ketchup? Me trying to outwit one of the Seraphim is like an ant going up against a dragon. Still, I can't let it go. Not when Gabriel looks at me like he can't quite believe I'm real.

"You said humans have free will. That fate was...well..."

"I believe my exact words were 'complete and utter bullshit.'" He smiles, and though his eyes are still sad, the beauty it brings to his entire being is almost enough to render me speechless.

Almost.

"If we can choose our own path, why can't an angel? Sin and Maddox live here. So there's precedence." I plant my hands on my hips, daring him to challenge my logic.

"Sinclair and Maddox are not archangels. Mad was only allowed to stay because Azrael did not want to admit he'd fucked up and allowed a vial of celestial sand to fall into the hands of a coven of witches determined to live forever."

"Well...shit. What about the other archangels? You said...one of them was a defender. Could he—wait. Celestial sand? There's sand up there?"

When Gabriel laughs, he does so with his whole being. He braces his hands on his thighs, almost gasping for breath. Fresh tears gather at the outer corners of his eyes. "Fuck me. I am crying. Again."

"But I bet it feels a lot better this time." Winding my arms around his waist, I rest my cheek against his chest. I have to remember this moment. How strong and steady he is. The sound of his heartbeat. The way he holds me—like I'm precious, but not fragile. His scent.

Fate might be complete and utter bullshit, but magic is very real. Generations and generations of whisper keepers have all chosen to end their lives. If none of them could find a way to destroy the Blade, my chances are about as good as the chance of finding a four-leaf clover in the middle of the desert.

"I wish I could stay," he says, his lips skimming over my hair. "Leaving you...will destroy me."

KUNCHIN IS in the dining car when we venture out for food. We're somewhere in the Sierra Nevada mountains, and a light dusting of snow makes the trees sparkle.

The yeti holds a delicate cup of coffee in his massive fingers. His three-piece suit is slightly rumpled, and I wonder what he looks like to everyone else. Probably some sort of stockbroker. Or a basketball coach.

"How do the perception filters work?" Most of the lunch rush is gone by now, and I keep my voice just above a whisper.

Gabriel runs a hand through his dark locks. "It is a form of disguising magic. Killian is quite good at those types of spells. I am certain he would love to explain. In great detail."

"What if it fails? How would he know?" The server drops off menus and two bottles of water. I take a healthy swig from mine as Gabriel levels me with his stare.

"There would be screaming."

Water shoots up my nose, and I start to choke. He's out of his chair in an instant. With one hand on my back, the other pressed to my heart, he closes his eyes. Warmth spreads through my entire body, and after more than a few decidedly unfeminine grunts and one awful snort, I can breathe again.

"Warn me next time," I rasp.

He arches a brow. "About what? You asked me a question, and I answered."

He's still holding me when the server returns. "I'm all right now, Gabriel. You can...uh...let go."

The loss of his warmth is shocking. So is the confused look on his face. But it's also cute. He has no idea how funny he can be. Or what an effect he has on me.

We order—a grilled cheese sandwich for me and a veggie burger for him—and then the awkward silence sets in.

Even Kunchin—at the bar across the room—notices. He mouths, "*Are you okay?*" over Gabriel's shoulder.

I incline my head once, then turn to stare out the window again. "We're getting closer."

"How close?" Gabriel sits up a little straighter. "Do we need to contact Sinclair and arrange for cars at the next stop?"

"No. Not yet." Awareness prickles along the back of my neck. "She's here, isn't she?"

"In the corner behind you. She appears fascinated by Kunchin."

"Of course she is. But shouldn't she know what I know?"

"To follow that logic, you would also know what she knows," Gabriel points out. "And she seems to know quite a bit about the grimoire and the Blade that we do not. "

He has a point.

My whisper glides over to us. Her gauzy hand brushes my shoulder. A swirling vortex of emotion threatens to pull me under. My eyes burn. No. This isn't the time.

"Willow." Gabriel takes my hand. "What is it?"

I nod at my whisper. "She's sad. *Really* sad. *Distractingly* sad." To keep myself from sinking into the depths of her despair, I start peeling the label off my water bottle in long strips.

Gabriel crosses his arms and glares at her. "I will not allow you to keep hurting her. You have done enough."

She huffs, blowing one of the strips of damp paper onto the floor.

Anger prickles over my skin. This emotion is all mine. "Do you even know what you're doing to me? How powerless it makes me feel when you rip me out of my own body? I was happy. I had a job I loved, great students...a whole *life*. Now, I'm about to lose it all. So unless you can figure out a way we can communicate—*really* communicate—leave me alone until we find the Blade. I'm done. Just...done."

Dropping my head into my hands, I squeeze my eyes shut. I won't cry. I can't mourn everything I'm about to lose in the middle of the dining car.

Her regret stings the back of my throat, and I can feel her retreating, slowly. "And stop staring at Kunchin," I add before our tenuous connection fades into nothing. "It's rude."

***

Gabriel

I have been so fucking selfish. Willow held me for an hour after I confessed my sins. Yet even though I can sense her emotions as if they were my own, I did not truly understand until now.

My phone buzzes on the table. I would crush it into dust if I could. But until we know we are safe, it is a necessary evil.

Kunchin: What was that all about? Everything okay?

We are not supposed to know one another in case AURA has eyes on this train. I return my gaze to Willow, nod once, and shove the phone into my pocket.

The uniformed server sets plates of food in front of us. Willow is so mired in her grief, I am not sure she notices. With a single, withering glance, I send the man running for the kitchen. "You must eat something, *deliciae*."

Her shoulders heave in a heavy sigh, and she lifts her gaze to the sandwich in front of her. "My mom always says there isn't a single thing a grilled cheese can't cure."

I frown. That makes no sense. "I do very much enjoy cheese, but it cannot work miracles."

She laughs, and though I have no idea what I said that was so funny, I don't care. I will say it a hundred times if I must. "Cheese cannot work—"

"Just try a bite." She slides the plate across the table. The scent is delicious. Perhaps better than pizza. Buttery, almost glistening, with the perfect crunch as my teeth sink into the bread.

"Fuck. This is..." I have no words. Of all the foods I have tried in the earthen realm, grilled cheese is my new favorite.

"Give it back," she teases. "You have your own lunch."

Her earlier sorrow is fading quickly now. Maybe her mother is right. If so, I will order a grilled cheese for every meal until she is safe and I must return to the celestial realm.

For now, I pick up my burger. The first taste is strange. "There is something wrong with this. Meat should not have this...texture."

Another laugh, and her cheeks tinge pink. "You didn't pay much attention to the menu, did you? That's the veggie burger."

"I thought that meant it came *with* vegetables." Every day I spend in this realm I discover something new. How will I survive the rest of eternity without this...excitement?

Or without Willow?

"Here," she says. "Take mine—"

"Absolutely not. What kind of angel would I be if I stole something so precious, it can work miracles?"

Her smile is worth a thousand *veggie* burgers. And a thousand grilled cheese sandwiches. For the first time in my existence, I feel a sense of peace. I thought I knew happiness. Or at least, contentment. Satisfaction. I was wrong.

This moment is greater than the sum of every single second that came before. Elegant in its simplicity. Sharing a meal with Willow, seeing her smile, despite the darkest of threats...

I would do anything to stop time for an hour—even a minute. But if I could, that might make what I feel now less precious. So I pick up my burger and take another bite, savoring the unique flavors. Even the texture I found so off-putting at first is palatable now. Pleasant, even.

"Oh!" Willow's eyes light up, and she plucks several potato chips from her plate and dumps them on mine. "Try another one of my mom's brilliant ideas. Put the chips between the burger and the bun."

I arch a brow. "Why?"

"Trust me, Gabriel. Or...trust my mom. You won't regret it."

"YOUR MOTHER IS A GENIUS."

The food is long gone, and we found two seats on the upper deck of one of the train's viewing cars. The domed, glass ceiling lets us see for miles, and though I wish we could hide safely in our room, remaining in public might help draw out the bastards hunting her.

Willow chuckles and settles closer to me. We hold hands, and though she's tense, the overwhelming sorrow she felt earlier is still at bay. "Mom was a physicist. Dad worked for the CDC. They're both retired now."

After a beat, the sadness returns.

"I wish I'd been able to see them one last time."

Turning to her, I cup her cheek. "I can take you to them right now."

"Gabriel, no. They're on safari in the Serengeti. I can't just... magically appear in the middle of their tent—with an *angel*—tell them I love them, and vanish again. Either they'll drop dead from shock or spend the rest of the trip thinking they're in the first stages of dementia." Her expression softens, the silver flecks in her blue eyes catching the light in a way I never want to forget. "It's better like this. The last time we talked was right before...*every-thing*. They were about to leave for Africa, and they were so excited. I told them I loved them. I know they love me It's okay."

"It is far from 'okay.'" The words are harsher than I intend, but Willow only offers me a sad smile.

"You're right. None of this is okay. Or fair. It's completely fucked up. I should be grading papers or working on my lecture about the rise of paganism in the nineteenth century."

I feel the exact moment her sadness turns into outrage. "This magic I had no idea existed a month ago is going to take everything from me. I shouldn't have to choose between dying and being a pawn in some sick plot to kill millions."

My shoulders stiffen, and I ball my hands into fists. "You will not have to make that choice."

"You're right. Because if you can't destroy the Blade, there *is* no choice. We won't find it tonight. We're too far away. But it's still calling to me. It knows I'm coming. I'm terrified we'll get there—wherever *there* is—and AURA will be waiting. I can't let them take me again. I won't."

A single tear trails down her cheek before she swipes it away. My heart breaks for her. I have never felt so helpless in all of my existence.

I take her hands in mine. "What do you need? Tell me. I cannot sit here and do nothing."

"I need *you*." Her anger is gone—replaced by something new. "I don't want to waste what little time I have left. I'm here. Now. With a handsome, protective angel I want to strip naked and do *very* sinful things to."

Shock steals my ability to speak for so long, the hope in Willow's eyes starts to fade.

Do something. Now!

"Fuck it." I haul her into my arms and claim her lips. Her taste, the way her tongue tangles with mine, and her low, throaty moan shatter my control. This woman is mine, and I am hers. Damn the consequences.

TWENTY-ONE

Oh my God. The air around us crackles for a split second, and then my back hits the window.

Of our room.

He carried us here in an instant. And now he's doing things to my mouth that are probably illegal in a dozen states.

I don't know what came over me. One moment I was mad at the entire world, and the next...I *propositioned an angel.* I'm going to Hell.

Gabriel tears his lips from mine with a growl. "Be sure, Willow. Be very sure."

His tone should scare me, but I've never been more sure of something in my life. "I want this," I manage. My body is on fire. "I want you."

He spins me around, pressing me to the door with another searing kiss. "Do. Not. Move."

Like I could. I'm so turned on, I can't think straight. My nipples ache against the lace of my bra.

Gabriel slams the bench seats down flat, grabs the mattress

from the top shelf, and tosses it onto the platform in a flutter of sheets, blankets, and pillows before turning back to me.

His amber eyes melt into liquid gold. A muscle in his jaw ticks as he stares at me with an intensity bordering on feral.

My gaze travels down his body to the bulge straining against his zipper. We slept in the same bed last night, but I was so exhausted, I don't even know if he wears boxers or briefs.

"Willow—"

I bristle at the edge to his tone. "Don't you dare ask me if I'm sure again."

He's on me in a heartbeat. His fingers sift through my hair, while his body pins me to the door. Rational thought runs for the hills. He kisses my neck, and his lips, tongue, and teeth—oh God, his teeth—set every nerve ending ablaze.

Down to my collarbone. Across my throat. Up to my other ear.

"You taste like the sun," he whispers. "My sun. My light. My world."

His beard scrapes over my skin, leaving the most delicious burn everywhere he kisses.

"More," I beg. My fingers are trembling so badly, I can't work the button on his pants. "Gabriel. Please..."

"*Deliciae. Cor. Vita.* Mine." He grabs my wrists, pinning them over my head with one hand, while the other palms my breast through my sweater.

I struggle against his hold, desperate to touch him, but he's too strong. How can I feel so much when we're still fully clothed? My core is dripping.

"I am going to savor you, Willow. All of you." His lips feather along my ear. "What will it take to make you come?"

"Not...much," I gasp. "But...you have...to get my shirt off... first."

"Do I?" He wedges his thigh between my legs. "That sounds like a challenge."

"Oh, God." Jeans have never been a religious experience. Until now. The thick seam scrapes against my clit. Gabriel pinches my nipple through my sweater, so hard I yelp. But the pain turns to pleasure in an instant. Stars explode in front of my eyes.

I can't move. Pinned by his hand above and his leg below, I'm helpless to do anything but feel. His teeth scrape along the pulse point at my neck. He finds the other nipple, rolling it between two fingers, and I fly apart.

Gabriel seals his mouth to mine, swallowing my scream. My core pulses in endless waves. His scent wraps around me. My fingers tangle in his hair. When did he let go of my wrists? I force my eyes open, shocked to find my sweater gone and his hungry gaze pinned to the lace covering my breasts.

"You are exquisite when you come." His tongue flicks over his lips. "I could pleasure you endlessly—for the rest of my existence—and never get enough of you."

I open my mouth, but can't find my words. *Any* words. After-shocks roll through my core, and it's a good thing he still has me pinned in place. I don't trust my legs to hold me.

"Talk to me, *deliciae.*" Concern knits his brows together. Tightening my fingers in his dark locks, I pour all I wish I could say into my kiss. This moment is everything I wanted and more.

Gabriel tucks his hands under my thighs, lifting me so I can wrap my legs around his waist. We don't come up for air until he lowers me onto the bed.

He cages me with his arms, rolling his hips so his hard length rocks against my core. "I could make you come again like this. Or...I could taste you."

"Please..." I don't know what I'm asking for. Just...*him*. In every way.

Slowly, like he's an animal on the prowl, he inches toward the foot of the bed. His hands stroke along my thighs, to my knees, my calves. I'm whimpering now. Even through my jeans, I can feel the heat of him.

He tugs off my boots, then his, before he finally, blessedly, slides my jeans down my hips. They land on the floor next to my sweater, followed closely by his shirt.

The muscles of his arms cord as he positions himself between my thighs and runs his nose over the lace covering my mound. A growl rumbles in his throat.

One finger traces the edge of my panties. It's too much and not enough at the same time. "You are dripping for me." He brings his finger to his lips, and—holy God—sucks it into his mouth.

His eyes darken. "I knew you would be delicious." Dipping his head, he kisses from my knee almost to my mound, but stops just short. "These have to go."

I agree, but the sound that escapes my lips isn't a word so much as a desperate whimper. Gabriel works the lace over my ass and down my legs. My bra is next, and he sits back on his heels, drinking me in. No man has ever made me feel this sexy. This *wanted.*

He parts my thighs wider, leans down, and runs his tongue through my folds. The feather-light touch threatens to undo me. I moan, and he rears up and kisses me so hard, I feel it all the way down to my clit. My taste lingers on his tongue.

"Fuck me, Gabriel." I'm not above begging. "Please."

His low chuckle holds the promise of more, but he shakes his head. "I am not done with you yet, Willow. Not by a long shot."

<hr>

Gabriel

The naked woman in front of me is my sun. My moon. My stars and my sky. Now that I have tasted her, I do not know how I will ever go back to the celestial realm and leave her alone.

You will not have a choice.

I push those dark thoughts away. For this moment, we belong only to each other.

Her sex weeps for me. Positioning myself between her creamy thighs, I savor every little moan. Each time her breath catches in her throat. The tremble of her muscles. The look in her eyes.

My second taste is better than the first. She's so wet, her arousal glistens over her thighs. I kiss each of her lower lips in turn, then slide a finger into her channel. "You are so tight, *deliciae*."

"Been...a long time," she pants.

I find her clit with my tongue, tracing patterns over the hard nub. She starts to writhe. "No. Not yet." I press one arm over her thighs, pinning her in place. A second finger joins the first, working her channel as I continue to suck on her clit.

Her stomach trembles, her heels dig into the thin mattress. She grabs for my shoulders, my hair.

"Hold onto me," I say, letting my words vibrate against her sex.

A cry spills from her lips. Arching her back, she thrusts her hips up to meet my tongue. I add a third finger, stretching her, curling them until I find her G-spot. At the same time, I score my teeth along her hard nub.

"Come for me, Willow. I need...all of you."

Her entire body stills a second before she shatters into pieces. Another scream—my sun and star is far from quiet when she comes—and I gather her into my arms.

Sweat beads between her breasts. I kiss a path from her navel to her throat, savoring the way each part of her body has its own unique flavor. Her nipple is sweet. The underside of her breast salty. Her sex are like the ocean after a storm. Her shoulder tastes of my soap. Her neck, my shampoo. Her lips...for now, her own arousal. Soon...maybe more.

I pull the blanket over us, holding Willow close. I love how she turns to me. How she tangles our legs together. Smoothing my hand over her hair, I breathe in her scent. I could live in it.

One taste, and I will never be the same again. Going back to the celestial realm after this and surviving? Impossible.

WILLOW'S HAND trails up my chest to toy with my nipple. "Careful, *deliciae*. Do not start something you are not ready to finish."

"I'm ready." She pushes onto an elbow to peer down at me. "It's my turn now."

"That sounds like another challenge." My lips curve, and I arch a brow. "I very much enjoyed the last one."

She shivers, despite the heat building between us. "So did I."

I roll her on top of me, savoring the scrape of her nipples against my chest. The luscious curves of her ass under my hands. Her scent. It's the sea after a storm, a hint of spice touched by the sun, and so much more.

Her first kiss is hesitant. Gentle. Slowly, she teases the seam of my lips with her tongue. I give her time to explore my mouth. To run her hands up and down my arms, over my lats, along the hard planes of my chest.

"I've never kissed a man with a beard before," she says, brushing two fingers to her mouth as she pulls away.

The idea of her with another man—*any* other man—is enough to wrench a growl from my throat.

"Easy, tiger." Willow braces herself on her hands, studying me. "You're not...jealous?"

"You are mine, Willow. No other man will ever—" Fuck. How can I stake my claim to her when I *know* we can never be more than this? When I know one day soon, I will have to leave her?

I run my thumb over one of her nipples. The dusky nub hardens under my touch. A fresh wave of her delicious scent fills my nose.

My gaze pins to her swollen lips. The tip of her tongue darts between them. What would it feel like to have her lick my cock? To see her gorgeous mouth full of me?

"Take my pants off," I command. They are too tight, and I curse the invention of zippers with every foul word I know. Also, underwear. Robes are so much easier.

Willow loosens the button, moving with agonizing slowness.

I narrow my eyes at her. "You are teasing me. And enjoying it."

"Maybe. Payback is a bitch, Gabriel."

With all of my angelic speed and strength, I flip her onto her back, my hand cupping her head so I do not slam her into the mattress. "Yes. Yes, it is."

I slide two fingers into her channel.

"Oh, God," she moans. Her hips buck against me

"Not God. Just your angel." I could make her come with my fingers alone, but I ache to be inside her. Two thrusts, and I suck my fingers into my mouth. Fuuuuuuck.

She shoves my pants halfway down my thighs. "A little help?" Her frustration spills over, her mouth bowing into a pout.

"With pleasure." The trousers land on the floor next to the rest of our clothing, followed by my boxer briefs.

Willow's breath catches in her throat. My cock stands at attention, precum beading from the tip.

"Touch me."

She hesitates for only a moment before her fingers stroke along my shaft. A drop of my essence coats her palm. Her eyelids flutter. My slit is leaking now, weeping only for her.

Willow brings her fingers to her lips. Nothing in all my millennia of existence has ever been sexier than watching her taste me. Her low moan. The heady mix of arousal filling the air.

"Come here," she says softly and grabs my hips, pulling me closer. But uncertainty churns in her gaze. "I've never done this before."

"Fuck, Willow. You do not need—"

Her lips still glisten, and she fists me down to the root. "Yes. I do. I want this, Gabriel. With all that I am. Help me."

I can refuse her nothing. Gently, I cup the back of her head with one hand and brace the other on the wall. "Take me in your mouth, love. Slowly."

Fuck me. Her wet heat is the most delicious reward. Brows lifted in question, she hollows her cheeks once, pulling me deeper.

"Yes, fuck yes. You are perfection, Willow. Let your body tell you what to do. What it needs."

The first stroke of her tongue along my thick vein threatens to send me over the edge. Gritting my teeth, I fight for control. My hips thrust. Willow gags and chokes, but quickly recovers. Light dances in her blue eyes.

Her short nails rake over my ass. The slight burn shoots straight to my balls. "If you do not wish me to come down your throat, you will release me. Right now."

Her lips curve into a smile—as much as they can while wrapped around my cock. Another thrust, this one deeper. She flattens her tongue, working to take more of me.

For a moment, I think I can hold on. But she hums as I hit the back of her throat, and I lose myself to my own pleasure.

TWENTY-TWO

Willow

Too much. It's all…too much. Gabriel's release hits the back of my throat, salty and rich, and I swallow him down. He slows his thrusts, his expression pure and utter bliss.

I had no idea I could feel so needy and so powerful at the same time. That I could *want* so desperately.

He pulls out of my mouth with a quiet *pop* and seals his lips to mine. A low growl rumbles in his chest. This man is sex personified. Dominant. Completely in control. Confident in his every move. And I just…went down on him.

The combination of our tastes stokes my desire. There's an emptiness inside me only *he* can fill. I've never come more than once with a man, but with Gabriel…I've already lost count and I don't think we're done. Not by a long shot.

"Did I hurt you?" he asks, trailing kisses back to my ear.

I shift my hips against him, subtly asking for more. "Not at all. You couldn't even if you tried."

He stiffens, tension in the set of his shoulders. "I could." The sheets rustle under us, and I almost think he whispers, "I will."

"Gabriel?"

Drawing back, he lets his gaze trail over my face. "You are so beautiful, *deliciae.* So perfect. You should be worshipped every day for the rest of your life."

I don't have the heart to tell him the rest of my life will be over soon. Instead, I skim my fingers along his jaw. He leans into the touch for a moment, eyes closed. Goosebumps race over his skin. He's half hard again—or is that still?—and a fresh drop of arousal glistens on his crown.

"Will you...?" I don't know how to ask for what I need. This isn't me. I've always been happy with my vibrator and a fantasy or two—only on the rarest occasions.

Gabriel has ruined me for other men, and I'm here for it.

"I do not have protection. I never expected this—you." Sorrow roughens his tone. "Angels...we can sire children."

My cheeks catch fire. I lower my eyes, pinning my gaze to his lips. "I'm...safe. I can't...ever..."

"Look at me, Willow." His molten irises draw me in. An eternity of love, desire, and pain fill their depths. "Are you certain?"

"Yes. Completely." For the first time in my memory, I don't hate my broken body. Gabriel makes me feel...whole.

Slowly—gently at first—he rolls his hips against mine. The underside of his shaft slides over my folds. I let my legs fall open.

"Fuuuuck," he groans. "You will undo me."

"Oh? I'd like to see that. I didn't get a great view last time. Y'know, with your cock down my throat?"

He laughs, the sound filling the room and bringing a lightness to him I've never seen before. "Then it is a good thing angels have nearly endless stamina."

"You...oh, God...endless?" My eyes threaten to roll back in my head as he swivels his hips against me. "Remember...I'm... human."

"I know, my love." Surging forward, he claims my mouth in a kiss so hard and fast, I can barely breathe.

The head of his cock nudges at my folds.

"More," I demand.

He pushes in deeper. "You are so very tight. Like you were

made for me. Only for me." Two fingers pinch one of my nipples. Pleasure shoots straight to my clit.

"Touch yourself, Willow. Now."

The command pulls a moan from my throat. I slide my hands down my stomach. Anything more than the lightest pressure could send me flying too soon. I want—no, *need*—him inside me when I come.

Circling my clit with my thumb, I draw in a long slow breath. On my exhale, he sinks deeper. Again. And again. My thighs tremble. I'm wound tight, so full, we're practically one.

He groans and starts to thrust. My thumb keeps pace with his strokes. The intensity in his eyes is so beautiful. So very...*him,* but somehow more.

"I will not last long," he grits out, still playing with my nipples, tugging, pinching, drawing me closer and closer to the edge.

My ability to speak is so far gone, I'm not sure I'll ever get it back. Nor do I care.

"Willow! Fuck!" He jerks, liquid heat filling my core. The sight of him coming apart is enough to send me flying right to the edge. I arch my back. My heels dig into the mattress, and I let myself go.

***

Gabriel

Outside the window, the late afternoon sunlight hits the trees, casting long shadows over the landscape.

Willow lies in my arms, at peace—perhaps for the first time since we met only—what?—two weeks ago?

When did *I* last feel this way? I cannot remember. This realm has changed me. I belong here. Living among humans—with *this* human.

I count the days since I last saw Azrael. Fuck. He will return for me soon. Will he see reason? Leave me be until Willow is safe? Of course he will.

Seraphiel will complain, but that is nothing new. Seraphiel can find fault in a sunset.

"What are you thinking about?" Willow shifts, her soft curves molding perfectly to my body. "You're tense."

Lying is not in my nature. In truth, I am not certain I am even able to. But she does not need to know the depths of my sorrow. Or be reminded that leaving her will destroy me.

"Tomorrow will be dangerous," I say, staring up at the ceiling.

"Gabriel, don't take this the wrong way, but... No shit." Her delicate snort is only one of the things I am growing to love about her.

Fuck. Angels do not...fall in love. Not like this.

Willow pushes up on an elbow. Her lips are still swollen, her cheeks pink with the flush that only comes from being thoroughly ravaged. But in her eyes, sadness holds sway.

"AURA could find me at any time. We don't know what powers they have—beyond Hannah's eerily persuasive voice and the magic they put into the WCU. And half of the people here to help us are almost literally *dead to the world* when the sun is up."

"Killian is the most fearsome warlock of his age. Maddox can fly. Kunchin—is very large," I offer.

"Large?" She shakes her head. "He's massive. But unless size gives you some sort of immunity to magic, his height—and all that fur—won't help much."

"You have never seen vampires in battle. They are lethal beyond measure. Kàra and Mist are two of the Valkyrie—goddesses, if the legends are to be believed."

Her frustration pushes into my mind.

"I am not allaying your fears. What if I made you come again?" My brows lift, but Willow laughs in my face.

"Did I say something humorous? I was quite serious."

Another snort, and she plants her palm against my chest.

"If you make me come again—right now—we'll miss dinner completely. And *one* of us needs food to function." She wriggles to the edge of the bed and scoops the pile of clothes from the floor. "I assume—since you'd never had a grilled cheese before—you don't?"

"An angel's powers change in the earthen realm." I catch my boxer briefs when she tosses them to me. Now where are my socks? "My time here has been full of new experiences. Eating, sleeping, breathing..."

"Breathing?" Willow loses her balance trying to step into her jeans. "Shit—"

I catch her before her perfect ass hits the floor. "Careful there, *deliciae*."

She sags against me and tips her head up to meet my gaze. "You don't breathe in the celestial realm?"

I shrug. "We do when speaking. But other times...it is not common."

She runs her hands down my arms. "What else is different? What did you learn when you came here besides...how to care?"

Her question gives me pause. As does her body. Willow is every bit as hot half dressed and flustered as she is naked. I could take her again right now. My cock strains against the boxer briefs. Putting my pants on will be...difficult.

I need a distraction.

"The celestial realm is quiet. No leaf blowers. No...motorcycles or car horns. It has no scent—good or bad." Carefully, I ease my pants over the bulge of my cock. "Very little color at all beyond that of each angel's skin."

"Oh, God. Why would anyone want to live—exist—like that?" she asks.

I shrug. "Because until you leave, you know nothing else. I thought I was happy there. Or...at least content. I was not." My shoulders heave. The urge to confess my feelings for her is almost overwhelming. I want to tell her that going back will be the hardest thing I have ever done, but that would be a lie.

Leaving *Willow*...that will be the hardest thing I will ever do.

My phone buzzes from somewhere in the corner of the room. Willow finds it under my Henley and checks the screen. Her cheeks tinge bright red. "Um. It's Killian. I think he heard us."

I snatch the phone from her hand.

Killian: Are you and Willow ever leaving your room again?

We should have arranged for room service. Then I could ignore the bastard. But as I plan on making Willow come at least another three times before morning, I suppose we must eat.

Gabriel: We are going to the dining car in a few minutes.

Killian: We'll join you. Sinclair has news.

With a sigh, I pull my long hair back and secure it with a band. "I would rather have you all to myself for dinner, but we are —apparently—going on a double date."

Willow

The fine hairs on the back of my neck prickle as my angel protector leads me down the train car's narrow hallway. I cast a glance over my shoulder, convinced there's *someone* there, but we're alone.

Gabriel stops at the door to the next car, turns, and rests his hands on my shoulders. "What's wrong?"

"I don't know."

He searches my face. "That is not an answer."

My lips twist into a frown. "Yes, it is. It's just not a good one. Don't worry. Mad and Killian are waiting for us, and I'm hungry."

For a moment, I think he might argue with me. But all he does is sigh and press a kiss to my forehead. "You will survive this, Willow. I promise."

My thoughts race a thousand miles an hour. I know he thinks he can save me, but he didn't read the last words of generations of whisper keepers. Their pain didn't seep into his fingers through the spelled ink.

When I close my eyes at night, I can almost *hear* them. Their screams. Their sobs. Their overwhelming sadness and despair.

I'd give anything to have a real conversation with even one of them. Anger twists in my chest. The first coven should have done more to protect those who came after.

My ancestors abandoned me.

TWENTY-THREE

Maddox and Killian wave us over to a table in the corner of the dining car. The warlock can see both doors from his seat, but that leaves me with my back to the room. I roll my head from side to side, and my neck cracks loudly.

Gabriel drapes his hand over my thigh under the table and gives it a reassuring squeeze, but I don't think I'll be able to relax until we're safely back in our room.

And naked.

A low sound rumbles in my angel's throat. Leaning closer, he whispers in my ear, "Keep teasing me like that, *deliciae*, and I will make you come at this table."

I swallow hard. He wouldn't.

His fingers press between my legs. Oh, God. He absolutely would.

"So what is Sinclair's news?" he asks, his tone so mild, he might as well be asking about the weather.

Killian pinches a thumb and forefinger together and draws a small symbol in the air. Pale, blue sparks burst over us for a brief moment, and the sounds of the other diners quiet slightly.

"There were seventeen matches to Willow's DNA across three different ancestry databases," the warlock says. "The Bureau is working on tracking them down. Eight are in the United States, three in Canada, and the rest in Western Europe."

"We—" My voice cracks. I squeeze my legs together and clear my throat. "We're getting closer. I don't think the Blade is in Europe or Canada."

Gabriel's fingers still long enough for him to pour me a glass of ice water from a tall carafe in the center of the table. "How close? Will we need to disembark tonight?"

I down half the water before I'm steady enough to answer him. "No. At least, probably not."

The server comes to take our order and drop off a bottle of red wine, but once she's hurried away, Killian checks his phone. "Sin and Zoe have stopped for the night, but they're almost a hundred miles ahead of us. The way my brother-in-law drives, that's less than an hour."

"The Bureau has learned nothing more about the Fae doctor or her accomplice?" Gabriel pinches my inner thigh through my jeans. I'd tell him to stop, but the constant state of arousal might be the only thing keeping me sane.

Maddox fills all of our glasses with the deep red cabernet. "I've been thinking about that. She might not be Fae. Druids have been known to cast spells inducing temporary insanity. Vampires can enthrall almost anyone. Sirens routinely lure victims to their deaths."

"I do not care what she is," Gabriel says sharply. "She is dangerous. We should have sent one of the vampires to the NSA. I am certain they could have found some way to access the agency's personnel files."

"What good would that have done us?" Maddox throws up his hands in frustration. "Knowing her social security number, date of birth, and home address won't help us save Willow. Three lethal vampires will."

The air around the table crackles with tension. Gabriel and Mad glare at one another, while Killian slaps a palm to his mate's chest. "Enough. Both of you. We're all knackered. Can we simply enjoy the rest of the meal together as if the world weren't about to end?"

Gabriel shifts so he can drape his arm around my shoulders. Drawing a shaky breath, I peer up at him. "I'd like that. Can we? Please?"

His gaze softens, and he presses a kiss to my temple. "There is nothing I would not do for you."

A blush creeps up my cheeks. I'm about to reach for my wine when I hear his voice in my head, so soft, it's barely there. *"For you, I would even give up my wings."*

BY THE TIME we finish dessert, I feel almost...normal. The Blade's call has faded to the lightest of melodies. I've even managed to ignore the memory of Hannah's voice and my fear of having my back to the room.

Maddox and Killian bicker like an old married couple. It's adorable. The warlock has a wicked sense of humor, and I could listen to him all day. His sexy British accent doesn't hurt either.

Gabriel polishes off his second glass of wine. His fingers trace patterns on the back of my neck. "It is late. We should turn in."

An odd chill settles over my skin. Killian stiffens. "Shite. The vampires are awake. And...here. We should go to the bar. It will be easier to blend in there."

I glance over my shoulder to find Kàra, Ewan, and Mist staring at us. The women are so preternaturally still, I'm not sure they'll blend in anywhere. But Ewan offers me a smile. He's only been a vampire for a little over a year, I think.

Too quickly, I jerk to my feet. My cheeks prickle as my blood pressure plummets, and darkness shrinks my field of vision down to almost nothing. Gabriel hauls me into his arms. "Breathe for me," he demands.

Trying.

"What's wrong with her?" a woman asks, her voice shockingly close.

My vision clears enough for me to make out blond hair and pale skin. Glowing golden eyes. Scars marring her cheek.

"Step back, vampire." Gabriel practically vibrates with anger as he turns so his back is to Mist, protecting me. "Willow has a medical condition."

"I'm fine," I protest. "Stood up too fast, that's all."

Mist frowns. "I meant no harm, angel. I'm here to protect her."

"Bar. Now," Killian snaps. He grabs Gabriel's arm. "And don't even *think* about just 'popping' over there using your particular talents. Your little stunt after lunch was bloody reckless."

"It was necessary." Gabriel slides his hand down my back and gives my ass a squeeze. "We had somewhere to be."

THE VAMPIRES ORDER shots of bourbon, and Mist passes the bartender a generous tip to leave the bottle.

"What?" she asks when Killian gives her the side eye.

"Do you regularly drink on patrol?"

Ewan throws back his first drink in a single swallow. "Vampires cannae get drunk. One of the few things I miss. That and sunsets."

"If we live through this," Mist says, "come visit me in New Orleans." She pulls a small, fabric pouch from under her flowery peasant top. "I can day walk for up to ten minutes with this."

"Ten minutes?" Kàra chokes on her own drink. "I cannot even stay awake for that long after sunrise. Tell me of this dark—or is it light?—magic, sister."

I know so little about the world of the *Other*, but one thing is very clear. Vampires, witches, and angels might be terrifyingly powerful, but family is still family.

Kàra and Ewan touch one another constantly. As do Killian

and Maddox. The sisters laugh and rib one another as if they've never been apart.

Until the bourbon is gone, and Mist sinks onto one of the stools and fixes her golden-eyed gaze on me. "Rumors about the ancient evil have been swirling for years," she says. "Our sire used to talk about the Blade while he tortured us." She shivers and asks the bartender for a cup of strong coffee. When Gabriel and Maddox start talking about the other archangels, she lowers her voice to a whisper. "I know what you mean to do, Willow. I can see it in your eyes."

"You're not going to try to talk me out of it, are you?"

"I would, if I thought it would do any good." Mist rests her cool fingers on my arm. "I read Tarot, and I pulled cards as soon as I got out of my sleeping trunk tonight."

"This isn't going to be good, is it?"

Mist smiles sadly. "Tarot isn't inherently good or bad. There are many ways to interpret each card. Even more when you consider the relationships between cards within a reading."

"Well, let's hear it, then." My gaze darts to Gabriel for a brief moment, but he's in the middle of an argument with Mad and Killian over someone called Sariel.

"The spread I use most often—and the one I pulled this evening—is a linear one. It relies on three cards. The first is the current situation. I drew the Devil in the reversed position. There are several interpretations, but the most common involves feeling trapped by forces you can't control."

I snort. "Well, that's fitting."

"It could be. If that's the interpretation you choose. But the Devil also suggests that the chains binding you can be broken if you're willing to accept that what you believe may not be what is actually true."

I'd tell her that I don't know what to believe right now, but she's already moved on to the second card.

"The center of the spread focuses on your challenges. For this, I pulled the Nine of Swords. Usually this represents an extreme situation. Hopelessness, anxiety, and pain. Nine is a number of completion while swords represent suffering, alienation, and great obstacles. There is something in your way." She nods in Gabriel's general direction. "My money says it has to do with him."

Shit. She's right. "He's determined to save me."

"Of course he is. He's in love with you."

I choke on my water. "He's going back to the celestial realm as soon as this is all over."

Mist's blond brows shoot up. "If he goes back to the celestial realm, I will pierce my nose with a silver stud."

"But...that's fatal, isn't it?" She's wrong. I know Gabriel cares for me, he's an *angel*. He can't stay.

"Not fatal. Just very, *very* painful." She brushes her blond hair away from her face, revealing three deep scars running from just below her eye to her jawline. "The last card I pulled—the one in the position to give advice—was Death."

"Well, that's fitting." Hearing my fate spelled out so plainly is almost reassuring.

But Mist shakes her head softly. "Death is a card of transition. It doesn't mean a literal death. Death counsels you to embrace this transition. Take the chaos within you. Use it. Don't be afraid of it, Willow. If there is a way to survive, you'll only find it by risking everything."

TWENTY-FOUR

Gabriel

Willow is quiet as we return to our room. I can sense her uncertainty. Whatever she and Mist spoke of weighs heavily on her.

Should I press her? Human emotions are messy and unpredictable. I want to know everything she is feeling, but will the knowledge help *her* in anyway? Or only me?

I flip the lock and rest my back against the door while she disappears into the tiny bathroom. Water runs in the sink. I take the time to strip down to my boxer briefs. Human clothing is so… restrictive. I miss my robes and sandals.

Shockingly, those are the *only* things I miss from the celestial realm. The Sea of Tranquility is beautiful—breathtaking, even—if we needed to breathe at all. An earthen sunset can be just as stunning. Willow's face as she comes even more so.

I will not survive an eternity without her. Yet, if I stay in this realm, I will eventually become mortal. Am I willing to die for a chance at a life with her?

Yes.

The answer does not surprise me. Not truly. I think I have known since our very first kiss.

"All yours," Willow says as she emerges from the bathroom. She smells of mint and soap, her skin pinked and glowing.

I close myself in what is little more than a closet with a sink and toilet, splash water on my face, and brush my teeth—another human custom I had to learn. The mirror reveals tiny lines around my eyes. Those are a surprise. Maddox has them. As does Killian.

Every day brings new experiences. But none more beautiful and perfect than making love to Willow.

I find her huddled on the bed, legs drawn up to her chest and arms around her knees. Her t-shirt clings to her breasts, revealing the hard points of her nipples through the thin fabric.

"*Sol mea*, what's wrong?" Cupping her cheek, I drag my thumb gently under her right eye. Exhaustion shadows her gaze. "Mist upset you. I will speak to her. Right now."

"Gabriel, no." She curls her fingers around my wrist. "You can't protect me from every single thing in this world."

"I absolutely can." Anger bristles over my skin. "Or have you forgotten that I am an archangel?"

She chuckles. "No one could forget that, stud."

"Stud? I am not a breeding stallion." My response has the desired effect. Willow's laughter eases much of the strain in her muscles. "Though, I do like it when you call me that."

Leaning closer, I breathe in her scent. Fresh, clean, but with undercurrents of arousal and my seed lingering on her skin. My cock juts firmly against my boxer briefs. "How many times can I make you come before you beg me to stop?"

Heat floods her cheeks, and she squirms under my gaze. "*Beg* you?"

I answer her whispered question with a searing kiss. She opens for me, and I sweep my tongue along hers. Easing her onto her back, I angle my body so she can feel how hard I am for her.

She moans, swiveling her hips under me. "Gabriel. I need... God. Touch me."

Peeling off her t-shirt, I dip my head to lave my tongue over one of her peaked nipples. The hard nub rises, and goosebumps race over her skin. Her panties are soaked with her desire.

"You were made for me, *deliciae*. Your body. Your heart. Your mind." I turn my attention to her other breast, kissing, nipping, and sucking until she is panting for more.

Desperate to taste her, I tug her panties down her hips with too much force, and they rip into shreds. Her sex weeps for me. My first long, slow stroke through her folds leaves her trembling.

I settle between her legs, my hands stroking up and down the creamy skin. With two fingers thrust deep inside her, I trace circles over and around her clit, using my free arm to stop her from wriggling right off the bed.

My desire for her knows no bounds. I could feast on her forever. Watch her fly apart for the rest of my days. Listen to the sounds of her pleasure for all eternity. It still would not be enough.

Her words dissolve into helpless mewls. She winds her fingers through my hair, tugging me closer as her body implodes and her release bursts over my tongue.

When the sun rises, we will have to face reality. My celestial duties, the threat to Willow's very existence, even the expectations of our friends. But tonight, she is mine. Utterly and completely mine.

WILLOW SLEEPS EASILY. I made her come three times before she begged for my cock, then another two while inside her. Watching her drift off was one of those perfect moments I will hold in my memories forever. I wish I could join her, but with Azrael's deadline looming ever closer, I have been staring at the darkened ceiling for almost an hour now.

Enough.

I swing my legs over the side of the bed, elbows on my knees, and pick up my phone to text the one person who might have answers for me.

Gabriel: I need to speak to you.

It takes five minutes before Mad answers me, each one longer than the last.

Maddox: It's the middle of the night. This can't wait until morning?

Gabriel: No.

Maddox: Fine. Hallway. Five minutes.

I ease myself off the bed, careful not to disturb Willow, and pull on the black boxer briefs. Nakedness does not concern me, but the first time I visited a hotel vending machine in the middle of the night—a very odd experience—I discovered it makes many humans uncomfortable.

Maddox slips out of the room he shares with Killian.

"This better be important," he snaps, then frowns. "Fuck, Gabriel. Have you ever heard of pajamas?" He waves his hand up and down, presumably gesturing to his white t-shirt and a loose pair of pants with...cats on them.

"I do not have time to discuss my clothing choices with you. I need to know how you convinced Seraphiel to let you leave the celestial realm."

Mad runs a hand through his tousled hair. "*That's* what this is about? It's a damn good thing Killian is a sound sleeper or he'd kick your ass. Short answer? I didn't. Azrael sent me to retrieve the celestial sand. I'm not sure *where* Seraphiel was, but based on the timing... shit." His blue eyes darken. "He might have been preparing to send Zoe to earth."

"Even if he was...otherwise occupied, he would have noticed eventually. You must have done something to convince him." I ball my hands into fists, frustrated with this conversation already, but unable to walk away.

"Nothing. My guess? Azrael didn't want Seraphiel to know he lost the sand in the first place. If I'd gone back, there would have been questions. Azrael saw my 'falling in love' as the perfect way to cover his ass and hide his colossal fuck up." Mad shrugs, then narrows his eyes, studying me. "You're going to stay. Holy shit. You're falling in love with Willow."

I would protest, but lying is not in my nature. "I am expected back tomorrow. Azrael will understand a short delay. He does not *like* ferrying souls to the afterlife prematurely. But..."

"The Almighty won't like losing her great communicator," Maddox says, finishing the thought for me. "I don't know what to tell you, Gabriel." He pauses, searching my gaze. "But know this... If Seraphiel decides to be his usual dickish self, you could lose everything. Your angelic strength, your powers, your immortality... even your wings. You're the only one who can decide if Willow is worth that sacrifice."

He returns to his room, the door closing softly behind him.

"She is," I say to no one. "She is worth everything "

TWENTY-FIVE

Gabriel

I cannot sit still. My shoulders ache with tension. Willow has not said more than a few words to me since we woke this morning. Breakfast was utterly silent save for the scrape of silverware and the low din of others dining around us.

Now, we are safely ensconced in our room once more. My phone rings, Sinclair's name flashing across the screen. I snatch the device from the table and put it on speaker.

"Tell me you know where the Blade is," I snap before he can say a word.

Zoe murmurs something that might be, "Calm down," and Sinclair clears his throat.

"We have *leads*. Nothing definitive yet. Of the eight DNA matches in the United States, only four are east of your current location. Two of them were dead ends. The Bureau coordinated with local human law enforcement to investigate. One was a young man with zero interest in family heirlooms, and the other perished in a fire last year."

"Fuck." I run my hands through my hair, tugging on the long strands to the point of pain. "And the other two?"

"It takes time—and tact—to convince a small-town police department to question one of their citizens, Gabriel. Lieutenant Eve is doing her best. After everything she—and the rest of the Bureau—have dealt with of late, we're lucky she has not taken to the sky, never to return."

Regret creeps up the back of my neck. "I suppose since I directly contributed to those...issues, I cannot complain."

"For fuck's sake," Sinclair grits out. "Yes, you were an ass. Yes, you should have restored my memories *long* before you deigned to do so. But despite all the pain Zoe and I have endured, we are together. We survived. Stop blaming yourself so we can all move on."

I am about to tell him I will *never* escape my guilt when Zoe says his name.

"Sin, we got addresses for the other two DNA matches. One of them isn't far from McCook, Nebraska. The other one is in the middle of nowhere, Arkansas."

I check the train schedule tacked to the wall next to the door. "We will not reach McCook until after dinner. Willow, how strong is the Blade's call?"

She rubs her hands up and down her arms. I woke to find her shivering against me this morning, and no amount of coffee or blankets have been able to warm her.

"Very. But...it changed this morning. Like it's actually in pain now." The stress in her voice worsens every hour. "Or...maybe that's just me." Tears shimmer in the corners of her eyes.

The air in the room stirs, and her whisper floats through the wall to hover in front of her.

"She feels it too."

"Arkansas is much further away, yes?" My knowledge of the geography of the United States is minimal, at best.

"About a thousand miles," Zoe says. "A little more than the distance from where you are now to San Francisco."

"I can't take much more of this." Willow shudders, and a single tear tumbles down her pale cheek. "It can't be all the way in Arkansas. It just...can't be."

"Then Nebraska it is. We will disembark there." Scanning the schedule, I nod. "The vampires should be awake by then. You and Zoe will meet us there?"

"We are one stop ahead of you at the moment," Sinclair says. "We'll keep that pace. Update Mad, Killian, and Kunchin. Zoe needs to eat, and I see a diner up ahead. Stay safe."

Willow

Gabriel tucks his phone back into his pocket, turns, and arches a brow at my whisper. "She is freezing. Move so I can hold her."

She does, floating to the window and peering out at the snowy landscape. We're headed high into the mountains today, and though the sun is so bright, it hurts my eyes, the temperature isn't much above freezing.

Sinking down next to me, Gabriel settles back against the cushions. "Come here. Please?"

I let him wrap his arm around me and arrange the blanket over my lap.

"Something isn't right," I say, my head tucked under his chin. "When I woke up this morning, it wasn't this...painful. But right before breakfast, it changed."

"How?" He rubs slow circles over my back and presses kisses to my hair.

I shrug, too tired—and confused—to find the right words.

"I have been told that 'talking it out' can often help solve difficult problems, *deliciae*. Try?"

His fingers move to my neck, kneading gently. Well, I guess if he's going to give me a massage...

"After the grimoire gave me its oh-so-generous magical gift, I could...*hear* the Blade. Have you ever had an earworm?" I ask, peering up at him.

His eyes widen, a look of disgust twisting his features. "Are they common? If so, how do I avoid them? Forever."

My snort kicks off a laughing fit. Tears roll down my cheeks, and I struggle to catch my breath. "Oh, my God. You're hopeless, you know that? An earworm isn't an *actual* worm. It's a song that gets stuck in your head. You can't help singing it or humming it or just *hearing* it over and over and over again. Nothing you do makes it go away."

"And this is what the Blade's call was like?" he asks, the furrow between his brows easing.

"Yes. It was part of me. Mine. As much as my heartbeat or the sound of my own voice. It got louder when I didn't immediately leave to find it. Sadder too. But still comforting. Like a flute or maybe a violin."

"I wish I could have heard it through your ears," he murmurs. "Or taken this burden from you entirely."

Regret roughens his tone, but he heaves a deep breath and returns his fingers to my neck.

"Once the train started moving, the Blade knew. The tone changed. It was happy. Excited. Every hour or so, I'd feel this little tug on my heart. Always east."

He digs his knuckle into a hard knot of tension between my neck and shoulder. The pressure is too much and not enough at the same time. I let out a tiny moan.

"And now?"

I don't want to tell him. Saying the words makes them real. But Gabriel hasn't left my side since he rescued me from the cathedral, and after yesterday...what I feel for him is so strong—so much more than I ever thought possible—I won't hide from him.

"The Blade is scared. And Gabriel?" I tip my head back to meet his gaze. "So am I."

THE NEXT FEW hours are some of the longest of my life. Gabriel tries to distract me, telling me about the celestial realm, about some of the pranks he and Lucifer used to play on the other archangels before the devil was banished to Hell, and about his travels across the world these past few weeks.

"I visited towns that were dying, and others so prosperous, the buildings were adorned with gold. Everywhere, I found men talked the most, but it was the women who had the most to say. I think the men enjoyed the sound of their own voices too much."

I lie in his arms under a pile of blankets, but I'm still shivering. He hasn't stopped touching me for even a minute. I wish he'd strip me naked and ravage me, but with the Blade's fear a constant, bitter taste in my mouth, sex probably isn't the best idea.

"You're tense," I say, wriggling until I can get a hand free to touch his cheek. His beard is getting softer. With his long, wavy hair, he'd look like Tarzan—if it weren't for how precisely he dresses. He seems to favor button down shirts and khakis, and I wonder. What would he look like in jeans and a t-shirt? A sweater vest. Or...naked. In my bed back in San Francisco.

His sigh isn't reassuring. He stares out the window at the snow-covered trees. "I wish we had more time."

I close my eyes so he can't see how close I am to crying—again. "I've lived more in the past two days than I have in years."

"So have I, love. I am not ready to give this new *life* of mine up."

Craning my neck so I can meet his gaze, I put the pieces together. "Are—shit—are you being like...summoned or something?"

He shakes his head with a soft chuckle. "No. Not yet. Though I expect it will happen soon."

My stomach twists itself into a pretzel. "What if we haven't found the Blade by then? I can't do this without you, Gabriel." My hands start to go numb as my heart races and I fight to get my breathing under control. "I don't...I can't...shit..."

"Shhh, love." He pulls me close, his fingers threading through my hair, and seals his lips to mine. Kissing Gabriel is a religious experience—and not just because he's an angel. The man has the most talented mouth I've ever seen. Or felt. In many different ways. But this is the kiss I want to remember at the end. Because in this moment, I fall in love with him.

Gabriel

The air crackles with electricity, and I wrap my arms around Willow, putting my body between her and the window a split second before Azrael appears in the center of the room, his black wings on full display.

"Gabriel. It's time."

"Wh-what's...happening?" Willow sways on her feet. If I had been any slower, Azrael's appearance could have caused her serious harm.

"Willow? Do not be alarmed." I steady her with my arm around her waist. "Azrael does not understand how his *presence* can affect humans. When he visits this realm, it is usually to carry a soul to the afterlife. The dead do not care if their eardrums burst."

"The...oh, God. The *Angel of Death?* Is...are you here for me?" Her voice is little more than a squeak, and I kick myself for not thinking how my words would sound to her.

"No, *deliciae.* Azrael is hoping I see reason and allow him to take me back to the celestial realm."

Azrael snorts. "See reason? You wouldn't know reason if it punched you in the face, Gabriel. And you don't have a choice. You're coming home with me. Now."

"Fuck you."

I ease Willow down to the couch and take her hands in mine. "I gave you my word that I would not leave until we destroyed the Blade. Azrael will honor my promise. But the discussion we need to have first...it will not be pleasant."

She huffs out a breath. One corner of her mouth twitches into what might be a weak smile. "Is that angel-speak for 'you're going to knock him on his ass'?"

"Yes. Perhaps more than once. Stay here and keep the door locked. We will not be long." I press my lips to her forehead and inhale her scent, then drop my voice to a whisper. "When I get back, I will strip you naked and worship your body until you cannot remember your own name."

She shivers, then casts a quick glance over my shoulder at Azrael. "He looks pretty pissed. Be careful."

"Always. Cover your ears and turn toward the window. I am taking him somewhere...private."

"I am not going anywhere—" Azrael loses his words as I tackle him, focusing my thoughts on the train's luggage car.

We appear amid racks of suitcases, duffel bags, and cardboard boxes. "You piece of shit. *Appearing* in front of humans can cause them serious harm. You could have hurt Willow." Shoving him with all my strength, I send him flying halfway across the car.

"Your time is up." He smooths his hands down his bespoke black suit, then plucks a speck of dust from his sleeve. Did he find a soul to give him fashion lessons since we last spoke?

"Seraphiel is on a rampage," he says. "If you don't come with me right now, I'm afraid he'll go to the Almighty and demand she take your wings."

For two days, so many of my thoughts have been consumed by one question. Would I give up all I have ever known for the chance to be with Willow?

Facing off with my brother, I find my answer.

Yes.

I straighten my shoulders and look Azrael in the eyes. "Let Seraphiel do his worst. This is where I belong."

"Gabriel, the earthen realm is exciting. I don't blame you for wanting to stay. But you have responsibilities to fulfill. We all do."

"My *responsibilities* have always been to the people of this realm. But I cannot fulfill them from," I wave my hand toward the ceiling, "up there."

"You have to." Azrael advances on me, his eyes glowing with power. Frigid air races through the car as the train speeds around a curve. "Celestials do not walk among humans."

I punch the Angel of Death in his smug, perfect face. "This one does."

A suitcase tumbles off one of the racks and lands between us. The momentary distraction is all Azrael needs to tackle me. We hit the ground, trading punches until I taste blood and his left eye is starting to swell.

"Why will you not see reason?" he growls and throws me onto the top rack. My head hits the ceiling. Stars glitter at the edges of my vision.

"Reason? There is no reason archangels should be confined to the celestial realm. There is no reason we cannot accomplish our duties while living *among* humans. But most of all, there is no reason for Seraphiel to be such a complete and total twat, yet here we are."

My back aches, the telltale prickle I only feel when my wings demand to be freed spreading out from my spine.

"Fuck. Not now," I mutter. Blood spatters my blue dress shirt, and several of the buttons popped off as we battled. I jump down and pull the stained material over my head.

Deep bruises mar my torso. Azrael is leaner than I am, but the full strength of the celestial realm clings to him, while I have been on earth for weeks.

"Seraphiel is a dick," Azrael says. "But he is one of the Seraphim. He has the right to call you home. As you are unable to return on your own, you will come with me. Now."

My wings burst forth, the light reflecting off them blinding in this dimly lit train car. Pure white, with hundreds of new feathers no longer burned, blistered, or broken.

I turn sideways, extending them to their fullest—and whacking Azrael in the face. No pain. Nothing but raw power that begs to be unleashed. Only yesterday, they were so ruined, I feared they would never be whole again. That I did not deserve to call myself an angel. That when Azrael came for me, I would need to beg for his indulgence.

"I am the Archangel Gabriel. The bringer of justice, the revealer of truth, and the interpreter of the Almighty's plan," I roar so loudly, I would not be surprised if even the vampires woke from the sound. "I have free will—as do all in this realm—and I am exercising it now."

Folding my wings against my back, I stalk over to the Angel of Death, grab his lapels, and get right in his face.

"Tell Seraphiel—and the Almighty—that I quit."

TWENTY-SIX

Willow

I just met the Angel of Death. Well, kind of. He stood there like some black-winged Reaper, staring at Gabriel like he didn't even recognize him.

What if they don't come back? I trust Killian and Maddox. Kunchin. The vampires. Sin and Zoe. But Gabriel...I love him, and I can't do this—any of this—without him.

"Stop it," I mutter to myself. "Loving him isn't going to save you."

My whisper glides over to the window next to me. Her gauzy fingers brush my cheek—solid enough for me to feel the lightest stirring of the air.

"When I die, do you die too?" I ask.

She nods, translucent tears swimming in her eyes. God, I have so many questions I wish she could answer. If she could talk... maybe I wouldn't feel so terribly alone.

We watch the trees pass by for several minutes, and then she starts to pace, wringing her hands every few steps until she's making me dizzy.

"Can you stop? I've been nauseous for an hour and this isn't helping." At her flinch, I sigh. "Sorry. I didn't mean to yell at you, but...you feel the Blade too, right? You can tell it's...in pain?"

She nods and presses her hands to her heart. This is the most expressive she's been in days. Like she *wants* to talk to me but doesn't know how.

"Why don't you pull me in so I can see through your eyes anymore? Is it because we've read all the pages in the book?"

She gives me the saddest look and shakes her head softly. Her hair, almost an exact mirror of mine, falls into her eyes, and she brushes it away.

"If you wanted to, *could* you?"

Another shake of her head, but this time, she floats closer and rests her hand over my heart.

God, I wish I could understand her. But I feel like we're finally about to get somewhere.

"Were you *ever* in control of it?" I shiver, though we took a curve a few minutes ago, and sunlight streams into the compartment.

Another no. "Not even outside the vault? Holy crap. You're really as helpless here as I am."

Finally, a nod.

"Okay. This is ridiculous. I have a damn doctorate degree in the Occult. We should be able to figure this out." I rummage in the suitcase for a small notebook and pen, sit down, and start to write. My entire life, I've relied on long hand whenever I've needed to figure out a complicated problem. It calms me, and I can see patterns that no one else notices.

The grimoire holds the power of the Blade. It's been in the vault for more than a century. Waiting? For what? Me—or any one in my line—to get close?

It needs more than me though. Because only a whisper can get into the vault.

Every time we got close to the vault, she pulled me into her reality. But she wasn't in control. So maybe the grimoire is?

When we were "one," we could turn the grimoire's pages, read the warnings, and take on the power of the Blade.

She hears the call like I do. It's impossible to ignore, but it's not malicious. It felt comforting. Natural. Like it's always been a part of me.

I frown at the words on the page. Shit. Why didn't I think of this before? On the next page, I continue to write.

The Blade isn't evil. It doesn't know why it was created. It's a pawn—just like I am.

My whisper sidles up beside me, points to the word "pawn" and then points to herself.

So I cross the last few words out and add, *"just like we are."*

Drawing a line across the page, I start in on the questions.

Why don't any of the past whisper keepers warn future generations to stay far away?

How does the grimoire get the whisper keepers' last words?

Why is the Blade in pain?

Why did AURA need to give me the WCU when I'm obviously strong enough to make my whisper solid on my own?

My whisper jabs the last question repeatedly, almost frantically. She knows something. I circle the words half a dozen times, desperate for an answer.

"The WCU could send you away and trap me in the void. Were they afraid of me? Of what the two of us could do together?"

I start to capture that thought, but my hand jerks, and the pen scratches across the page in a jagged line. My throat seizes. Clutching my chest, I stagger to my feet, bumping into the table and knocking the notebook to the floor.

What's happening to me? I need Gabriel. Killian. *Someone.*

Only the thinnest stream of air makes it into my lungs. The compartment door slams open. "Gabriel," I croak. "Help…"

But a tall, pale woman with sleek black hair steps inside, her hand lifted toward me. Blood-red nails, sharpened to deadly points, flutter. I'm lifted off the ground, then slammed back against the window. I can't move. Can't breathe. Can't scream.

"Don't fight, Willow dear," a lilting, hauntingly familiar voice calls.

My body relaxes immediately, and the woman lowers her hand, sending me crashing to the floor.

Hannah strides into the room, a placid smile curving her lips. For a moment, I believe everything will finally be okay. She'll take care of me. But then I blink, and those perfect white teeth yellow and sharpen. Her brown eyes darken until they're nearly black.

She's not human. You can't trust her.

"Calista, take care of her. Quickly. We don't know how strong the warlock and his mate are. We might only have a few minutes before they realize they've been spelled.."

The young woman kneels in front of me, grabs my hands, and traces circles around them with a finger. Red ropes appear out of thin air, binding my wrists and tightening to the point of pain.

With a sharp nail, she traces an X over my lips, then stands. I try to scream, but I can't open my mouth, and a thin whimper dies in my throat.

"I *was* hoping to find your handsome protector in here as well," Hannah says. "He resisted me back in San Francisco, and I'm dying to know how. But this is easier, I suppose. You'll tell me all about him soon."

I shake my head. I'll never tell Hannah anything about Gabriel. If she finds out he's an angel, she'll want his power—and she'll use me to take it.

"You don't have a choice, Willow dear. I'm *very* persuasive. After all, I had you in my thrall for two weeks, and you never suspected a thing." She crouches down and drags her knuckle along my jaw. I jerk away from her touch, and her eyes harden. "Clearly I've stayed away too long. My control is slipping. Let's remedy that, shall we?"

I whimper my protest, but Hannah curls her lips back. Pressing her index finger against one sharp tooth, she pierces the tip and a generous drop of blood wells on her skin.

No, no, no.

She's a vampire? But...it's daylight. And we went out in the sun more than once. Didn't we? The few times she hugged me, she was warm. Not like Mist and Kàra and Ewan.

"I can see your confusion, my dear. It's adorable. Truly. Don't fight this. You'll only cause yourself an endless amount of pain." She grabs my chin hard enough to bruise.

My gaze zeros in on the blood. I'm screaming inside, but I can't move. Can't turn my head.

"The Fae power running through my veins lets me sway anyone's thoughts with only my voice. Courtesy of my mother. But it was my vampire father who gave me the most precious gift. Have you ever heard the term 'blood bound'?"

She doesn't wait for an answer. "Once you have tasted even a few drops of a vampire's blood, you will do *anything* they command. The more blood you consume, the longer the bond lasts." Hannah sweeps her finger into my mouth and laughs. "I dosed your coffee every morning, Willow. You hold such power, yet you're helpless to fight me."

The taste of her blood on my tongue turns my stomach. I'd retch if I could move at all. Tears well in my eyes. I turn my gaze to Calista, silently begging her to do something—anything—but she bows her head, staring at the floor.

"Calista cannot help you," Hannah says. "She was my father's blood slave until he met the sun. She has belonged to me for centuries now. The one time she even *thought* about disobeying me, I cut out her tongue. She knows the next time, I'll take an eye. Very slowly."

How could I have ever thought Hannah was a good person?

Somewhere deep down, I know I need to keep fighting. To find some way to escape. But my head feels like it's full of cotton. I can't think straight.

What's happening to me?

"I've been hunting the Blade for my entire life, Willow. Four hundred and thirty-two years. I've had kings, presidents, and dictators worship at my feet, but never a whisper keeper. With you in my thrall, I'll be unstoppable."

Thrall. Whisper. Blade.

The words mean something to me. I know they do. Hannah

rises, and the motion stirs the air, bringing the most delicious scent to my nose.

Gabriel. I was with Gabriel. I love Gabriel.

It takes all of my focus to hold his name in my head for even a minute. But as soon as Hannah snaps her fingers, I forget what I was trying so hard to remember.

"Calista, bring her."

The witch points at me, then lifts her hand in the air. My body obeys her silent command, following Hannah out the door and to the left. We slip between the train cars, the three of us crowding on the tiny platform, exposed to the bitter, biting wind of the Colorado mountains.

Tears sting my cheeks, turning to ice on my skin.

Hannah peers over the edge of the waist-high railing, staring at the landscape ahead of us as we take another turn. "Ah. Right on time," she says brightly.

I strain to see what she's looking at, but held by Calista's spell, I only get a quick glimpse of a steep, snow-covered hill below us. The witch twirls her fingers in a circle, forcing my back to the barrier.

What is she doing? Panic twists my heart in a vise. My chest stutters with each desperate breath.

Calista flings her arm toward the sky, and I rise up and over the railing.

Oh, God. She's not... She can't.

The world around me blurs into endless white as my body flies through the air. A pile of fresh snow cushions my fall, but then I start to tumble down the slope. Branches and twigs slash at my clothes. Each cut burns with a searing pain before going completely numb.

Hannah keeps pace with me, skipping along like she doesn't have a care in the world while I roll and bounce and scream behind my sealed lips. How is she moving so fast?

Vampire. She's a vampire. Remember!

Calista floats behind her, serene, yet haunted at the same time. Is she...flying?

At the bottom of the hill, I slam into an invisible wall. The impact drives the air from my lungs. A van idles along the side of the road. The side door slides open, and Isaac jumps out.

"About damn time," he snaps.

"Watch your tone." Hannah climbs into the back of the vehicle. Isaac flinches and mutters a quick apology.

Calista's spell tosses me into one of the bucket seats. More ropes wind around my torso and legs, binding me in place so tightly, I can barely breathe. The witch takes the seat next to me.

The driver's side door slams—Isaac behind the wheel, I think —and the van lurches into motion.

My clothes are drenched and torn. I'm so cold, I can't feel my hands. Even my legs are starting to go numb. Hannah leans forward, her thin lips curving into a gleeful smile. "We thought we'd have to wait for you to find the Blade. But then the Bureau of the Occult and the Other uploaded your DNA online, and that made everything so much easier."

I strain against Calista's control, trying to force my numb lips to part. At my moan, Hannah rolls her eyes. "Let her speak."

Drawing her nail over my mouth, the witch severs the spell.

"Y-you c-can't touch...the Blade," I manage through my shivers. "Only...I c-can."

"You're the only one who can *use* the Blade," Hannah says. "Anyone can touch it. Don't you think it would have been discovered long ago if it killed anyone who laid a hand on it? We found it in a barn in Nebraska, stuffed inside a box with old photographs, some jewelry, and a set of bone china."

Reaching under her seat, she withdraws a long, leather case. The Blade's strident song rises to a crescendo, so loud, it *hurts*.

I can feel its fear. Its pain. Or...is that mine?

Hannah lifts the lid. The silence is so sudden, so complete, it's dizzying.

Dozens of symbols cover the weapon from the ornate, bronzed handle all the way to the tip. As long as my forearm and deathly sharp, it's aching to be used. But I can't let that happen. If I do, Hannah will kill anyone who gets in her way.

"You want to touch it," Hannah says.

I do. Don't I?

No. Fight her!

I shake my head. "I'll die first."

Her serene, beautiful mask falls away again, and she snarls at me, baring her sharp teeth. "Stop fighting my blood, you little bitch. You belong to me for the rest of your days. You'll wish for death a thousand times before I even *consider* granting you eternal rest."

My stomach twists into knots. I can feel her rooting around in my thoughts, seeking my greatest fears, stealing any last shred of hope I might have.

Wrapping her hand around my neck, she squeezes until I can barely breathe. "We have a long drive to reach our destination. I've been planning this for years. Hunting down the strongest of every creature. Shifters, fae, witches, succubi, Druids... Tonight, I'll finally be able to take their powers as my own."

Trying to shake off her hold only makes her angrier. "I could force feed you more of my blood—I probably will soon anyway—but it's so...*messy*. Not as fun, either. A few hours in the void, and you'll be too weak to resist."

"You can't," I wheeze. "The WCU is gone..."

"Oh, Willow. Your naiveté is adorable." She releases me, and I suck in huge lungfuls of air. So quickly I can barely track the movement, she dips her hand into her pocket, then loops a chain around my throat. It starts to vibrate, the sensation eerily familiar. "So pretty," she says as she traces the links with her finger. "The power chain was one of Calista's greatest creations. It stimulates *both* vagus nerves at the same time. I could have used it from the beginning, but I had to keep up appearances. Most of the others you met at AURA's lab really did believe we were going to cure the world's diseases. Now that I don't have to worry about them any longer, I can do things the easy way."

"But..."

Calista draws a symbol in the air. Pain steals my words. I

thrash against the ropes, but it's no use. They're too tight. My body is trapped, and in minutes, my mind will be too.

"Do you know the best thing about the void?" Hannah sits back in her chair and runs a hand through her dark brown hair. I can only glare at her through my tears. "With your consciousness trapped there, the warlock can't scry for you. It's like you don't even exist."

Calista draws another symbol, and the edges of my vision dim. With the last of my strength, I scream. Every nerve ending in my body explodes in white-hot agony.

I'm slipping away. Fading. *"Please,"* I beg the Universe, the Almighty...anyone. *"Let me die!"*

No one can hear me. No one can save me.

"Gabriel. I'm so sorry. I should have fought harder"

I slip into the void, and the overwhelming *nothingness* consumes me.

TWENTY-SEVEN

Gabriel

The Angel of Death straightens his tie and smooths his hands down the sleeves of his suit. "You're willing to give up your birthright—everything you were *created* to do—for a human?"

My answer comes so easily. "Yes. I would rather spend a single lifetime with Willow than the rest of eternity alone. I love her."

"When I show up without you, Seraphiel is going to lose his shit." Azrael tucks a lock of his hair back into place. "His retribution will be swift."

Fuck me. If the twat takes my powers before we destroy the Blade, all my efforts to keep her safe could be for naught.

I hide my wings and tug the shirt back over my head. "I have no right to ask anything else of you, brother. But I am afraid I must."

The disbelief in his eyes does not surprise me. His resigned sigh does. "If it is within my power, I will give it."

A lump swells in my throat, and I clasp his arm. "Willow is in grave danger." I explain everything as quickly as I can. The creation of the Blade by the first coven, the power it can command, and the lengths the two government agents—if that is even what they were —have already gone to control her. "Lucifer gave me his axe, but only a celestial can wield it. I *must* retain my angelic strength long enough to destroy the Blade. After that...Seraphiel can fuck off."

Azrael sinks down onto a pile of suitcases. "If I return to the celestial realm without you, he will know."

"You could stay here for a time. There is so much *good* in this realm, Azrael. Coffee. Kettle corn. Pizza." I take a seat at his side, resting my elbows on my knees. "Spend a week as I did. *Living.* I promise, you will be a better angel for it."

He frowns and rubs the back of his neck. For eons, we have worked side by side, and I know him almost as well as I know myself. He will do this for me. And for Willow.

"Very well. But the motion of this train is turning my stomach. I didn't explore San Francisco either of the last two times I visited. I'm going to remedy that oversight now. When you need me, say my name, and I'll find you."

He stands, closes his eyes, and bends the world to his will. His disappearance is no more than a puff of air to me, but several suit-cases split open from the pressure.

Rather than cause any further damage, I let my feet carry me back to the sleeping car. I will miss being able to appear and disap-pear at will, but a lifetime with Willow is worth it.

The electronic keypad next to the door blinks green. It should still be locked. Worry stabs my heart as I burst into the room. "Willow!"

My shout shakes the entire car. She's not here. Releasing the full might of my angelic power, I search for her.

Nothing. No trace of emotion. No spark of consciousness. How?

Kunchin bursts into the room. "Gabriel? What's wrong?"

"Willow has been taken!" I whirl around and shove him so hard, he flies back into the hall. "Where are Killian and Maddox? And where were *you*? I was gone for ten minutes, and they took her!"

The yeti lumbers to his feet. "I just got back from the dining car. Mad and Killian were in their room." He's at their door in three steps and pounds on it with all his might. 'Something's wrong."

I do not have the patience to tell him that something is much more than *wrong*. "Move."

Ramming the door with my shoulder, I splinter it in two. Killian and Maddox lie crumpled on the floor. The angel's arms stretch for his mate, but the warlock is just out of reach.

"Fuck!" I drop to my knees and check Maddox's pulse. "He lives. They both do."

I can sense them. Confusion. Fear. Anger from Killian. He is trying to fight his way free from...something.

"I'm calling Sinclair," Kunchin says.

"Maddox? Wake up." A gentle slap to each of his cheeks, and he groans. "If you do not open your eyes right now, you do not deserve to call yourself an angel!"

"You're a fucking asshole, you know that?" he slurs. "You...try to fight...a spell like that."

Rolling onto his side, he grabs his mate's hand. 'Killian? I'm right here, baby. Come back to me."

The warlock is slower to rouse—his human constitution needs more time to recover. Mad croons to him, soft declarations of love and devotion, until Killian lets loose with a string of curses the like of which I have never heard before.

I stalk over to the window and press my hands to the glass. Again, I search for Willow, but sense no trace of her left in this world. "Please," I whisper. "Fight, my love. Wherever you are, I will find you."

TWO HOURS. She has been gone for two hours and we are no closer to answers.

I pace the platform in Grand Junction, Colorado while Killian and Maddox arrange for the vampires' sleeping trunks to be transferred to something called a "U-Haul."

"Gabriel." Sinclair takes my arm, drawing me away from the handful of humans about to board the train. "Every one of the Bureau's witches is scrying for Willow."

"They will not find her." My anger has long faded, leaving behind an unending ocean of despair. I withdraw the notebook I found under the table in our room and show him the last line she wrote.

AURA's afraid I'll be able to...

"They have sent her to the void, Sinclair. They will not release her until they have the Blade."

The demon's deep blue eyes start to glow. "Two human police officers visited the farm in Nebraska this morning. When they did not return to their precinct by lunch, another patrol was dispatched. They found a husband and wife, a farm hand, and both officers slaughtered. Grayson sent me video footage from the scene. It was a bloodbath."

My legs do not want to hold me any longer. Sinclair grabs my arm before my knees hit the ground. "Look at me, Gabriel."

"Why? So you can use your *talents* and convince me this will all somehow 'work out'?" I shake off his hold. "It will not. And it is my fault they have her. Do you know where I was when Willow was taken? Fighting Azrael in the luggage car. The Angel of Death came to take me back to the celestial realm, and rather than tell him to simply 'fuck off,' I let him toss me around like a child's toy until I'd had enough and loosed my wings."

Sin's brows shoot up. "You showed Azrael the damage to your wings?"

A dry laugh scrapes over my throat. "No. In one of the Almighty's greatest jokes, my wings are almost completely healed."

He sucks in a sharp breath. "Can you fly?"

"Of course I can fly. But what does it matter? If those bastards release her from the void, I can get to her in an instant, wings or no wings."

"For an angel, you are a complete idiot sometimes," he mutters. "If you simply *appear* in front of Willow without knowing what you are up against, you will die. Perhaps by the very Blade you mean to destroy."

I turn away, unable to give voice to my greatest fear. Again and again, I promised Willow I would protect her, and every time, I felt the truth she refused to admit—even to herself.

If she is forced to use the Blade, the pure and beautiful soul I fell in love with will be gone. Her body may still draw breath, but Willow—*my* Willow—will die.

Zoe, who has been on the phone since she and Sin arrived, pockets the device and joins us. Maddox and Killian follow, though the warlock looks slightly...green.

"The vampires' trunks are safely stowed in the U-Haul. There's an abandoned shopping mall not far from the edge of town. Kunchin will wait for us there," Mad says and peels off his jacket.

I cannot see the point of any of this. "For all we know, those demented fucks could have Willow halfway around the world by now."

"It's possible," Zoe says. "But the Lieutenant just confirmed my suspicions. The grimoire is on a ley line that runs across the continental United States."

"And this matters...why?" This conversation is going nowhere. I am ready to take Lucifer's axe and cut this world in two. If only such a thing were possible.

"Because that same ley line runs through McCook Nebraska, several cities in Colorado, and continues all the way to Maine. If *I* were a power-hungry bitch hell-bent on destroying the world, *I'd* want that extra oomph of power." Zoe shrugs, and I gape at her.

"You think they knew. That they will force her to use the Blade somewhere along this ley line." A spark of hope ignites deep in my heart.

"I'd bet my formerly celestial ass on it."

I look from Sinclair to Maddox and Killian. Suddenly I understand why the warlock is so uneasy. "Tell me you can track them."

"Falling victim to a witch's spell leaves a bloody awful taste in my mouth. And a rather unique magical signature. The one who cast it was powerful. Ancient, even. But the old ones often don't know a damn thing about modern technology." He pulls a small device from his pocket. "If there's even a trace of the witch's magic left, this will find it."

"Well, what are we waiting for?" I remove my jacket and reach for the buttons on my shirt.

"For fuck's sake. Not yet," Sinclair mutters. "Too many eyes. Zoe, you'll stay close to Kunchin at all times?"

"I promise, demon-of-mine." She cups the back of Sinclair's neck and pulls him in for a swift kiss. "Go find the love of Gabriel's celestial life."

***

THE WIND WHIPS through my hair. Sinclair soars to my left, with Maddox—Killian held in his arms—on my right. We leave the Sierra Nevada mountains behind and follow the ley line toward San Francisco.

Maddox is half human, and though he has been in the earthen realm for two years, his wings are as powerful as ever. Sinclair's demon parentage left him with magnificent jet-black feathers, and a lethality to his flight I had not appreciated until now.

Killian keeps his gaze pinned to the little black box in his hand. Twice now, he has insisted we double-back, but the device stubbornly refuses to beep.

The four of us touch down in the Bureau's parking lot, where a magnificent gray and white eagle perches on a lamp post with a small bundle clutched in her talons.

"Grayson." I nod at Sinclair's lieutenant. "I am in your debt."

Her screech is harsh enough, I wince.

Killian bangs the small box against his hand. "It should have shown us *something*. Maddox, we need to visit the cathedral before we waste any more time. I have never been there, so I can't simply teleport."

"Flying will take time we do not have," I mutter and wrap my arm around the warlock's waist. I carry us to the antechamber in an instant.

"Fuck! he shouts when I release him. "You could not have warned me?"

"I did." I am baffled at his outrage. "What did you think I meant when I said, 'Flying will take time we do not have'?"

"I just *flew* across three states, Gabriel. The last time Maddox took to the air with me, I'd just been tortured half to death. Forgive me if I need a bloody minute!"

He huffs while I cast a glance around the darkened space. A few drops of Willow's blood stain the floor. I kneel to touch the only part of her that remains in this world.

"Gabriel? Gabriel!" Killian grabs my arm and jerks me to my feet. "It's working."

I shake off the fear I'll never see my love again, and meet his gaze. Then I hear it. The low, rhythmic beep coming from the device in his hand.

The black box is lit up like a Christmas tree.

He fiddles with the dials on the back of the thing until all the multi-colored lights turn green. "Take us to the others. As much as I hate saying this, we need to get back in the air."

TWENTY-EIGHT

Gabriel

Far below us, a lid of magical energy shimmers over the remains of an old storage facility. The roof is mostly gone. No windows. Only a single door that we can see.

On the other side of the building, a large reservoir stretches for miles. Approachable only by backroads, yet in the center of the ley line, this is certainly where AURA will bring Willow. If she is not inside already.

Two hours after leaving San Francisco, Killian's little black box alerted us to the faintest trail of magic. We followed it from the train tracks, down a steep hill, to a highway, then lost it again. He blathered on about some calculation involving miles-per-hour and the coefficient of drag, but I paid little attention to the specifics.

I can see my breath in the air. It is close to freezing in the Colorado mountains. Killian started a fire, then wove a spell around the area to hide the light and smoke—and trap as much heat as possible. I have not complained about its inefficacy. I suspect the warlock would react...badly.

The vampires care little about the cold. Nor does Kunchin

with his thick fur. But the rest of us are uncomfortable at best. Maddox said something about "human popsicles" not too long ago, and the term, while revolting, is accurate.

Zoe burrows deeper into Sinclair's leather jacket, eyeing the fire warily. I am not surprised. Only weeks ago, she and the incubus almost perished in the flames of Hell. I suppose I did too. My wings ache from the memory.

"My love, you are freezing," Sin says as he pulls Zoe into his arms.

Her lips take on a bluish tinge. "Better th-than burning."

"Let me bring you to the penthouse." I drop to one knee in front of the couple. "We cannot do anything until Grayson returns from reconnaissance. It would take only moments."

In truth, the idea of leaving Willow—though we have no proof she is actually here—terrifies me. But I know what love is now. I will not allow Sinclair and Zoe to lose what they have only recently found if it is within my power to save it.

"I'm staying here," Zoe says. "Non-negotiable."

The underbrush rustles to the west. I push to my feet and loose my wings. Sinclair cut holes in one of my t-shirts so I don't destroy them every time I—as Willow put it—"wing-out."

Fuck. She still thinks I am horribly broken. I suspect it was actually her words that healed me. She thought me worthy despite the devastation. She made love to me knowing I could not fly. She loved—*loves*—me for who I am. Not what I can do.

A tall, very naked blonde strides from a dense grouping of trees. Dirt stains her cheeks, and leaves stick to her elbows and knees. "Fuck, Grayson," Sin mutters. "Put some damn clothes on."

"My *clothes* are in that bundle there," the eagle shifter says and points to a pack next to the fire. "Did you expect me to leave them in the woods where bugs would crawl all over them?" She shudders. "Been there, done that. I found a centipede in my *ass crack* once. You try forgetting that sensation. I dare you." She unzips the small bag and pulls out a sweater.

"What did you find?" I ask, averting my eyes until she has covered herself.

Grayson runs her fingers through her rough-chopped blond hair and comes away with a handful of twigs. "There's a reason I prefer flying in the city." Still barefoot, she crouches down next to the fire and warms her hands. "I convinced a male to fly directly over the building. Or...try to."

"A male—do you mean an *actual* eagle?" Killian asks. "As in... not a shifter?"

With a huff, Grayson stares up at him. "Yes. These assholes are careful. Bordering on obsessive. And given what the male saw —before he smashed into a wall of magic and almost dislocated his beak—it's a damn good thing I took the precaution."

"Well?" I would shake the woman if I were not so fucking grateful for her help. "What did he see?"

"Cages. A lot of them. Several of the prisoners inside were screaming. After he spent ten minutes bitching me out for almost killing him, I made two passes myself—as close as I dared. The magic they're using is..." she shivers, "the strongest I've felt— outside of Killian's—in my lifetime. By my count, there are two men present—in addition to the prisoners. Eagles don't have the best sense of smell, so I can't tell you what any of them were. Humans, shifters, witches..." She shrugs. "I saw no sign of Willow, but that doesn't mean anything. She could have been in one of the cages."

My ass hits the log Sinclair dropped next to the fire to use as a bench. I have been searching for Willow's emotions since we set up our small base of operations here. She is still hidden from me. Either by the magical wards layered over and around the building, or because they have trapped her deep in the void. I do not know which is worse.

If the wards are as strong as Killian believes, I may not be able to pass through them to save her. But if she has been in the void since she was taken...will there be anything of her mind left when they finally bring her out?

"Enough of this," Kàra snaps. "Why are we doing nothing? If

Willow is in the void, she cannot be forced to wield the Blade. We should breach now."

"And what if she is not there?" Sinclair faces off with the vampire and her mate. "We need proof. If we're premature, they could disappear with Willow forever."

Killian lifts a pair of binoculars to his eyes. "Something's happening. Is that...? Fuck me."

I snatch the lenses from his hand and adjust the magnification. A large, black van rolls to a stop in the parking lot. From this vantage point, I can only see the driver's side. A dark-haired male emerges, looks around, and heads around the vehicle.

"That is the human. Isaac." I tighten my hold on the binoculars until the housing protests my grip. Fuck. If I am not careful, I will break them.

I let my power rush down the mountain, blanketing everything around me. The magic Grayson spoke of leaves a bitter taste in my mouth. I sense two souls in addition to Isaac. One is familiar. The Fae doctor. But I do not recognize the other.

Mist takes position next to me, muscles coiled and ready to spring. "Witch," she hisses through clenched teeth. "Fucking hell. Kàra. Get your ass over here."

The other vampires surround Mist so quickly, their movements stir the leaves at my feet.

Ewan peers down at the van, his dark blond brows furrowed. "I cannae tell what—"

Kàra grabs his arm and pulls a deep breath in through her nose. "The witch is blood bound."

"Blood bound? What the fuck does that mean?" I cannot tear my gaze away from the van. Hannah's brown hair shines in the vehicle's headlights as she strides toward the building. Another woman trails behind her, almost floating, with pale skin and jet-black locks long enough to brush her ass.

"The one you believed was Fae?" Kàra says, her voice taking on a haunted, rough edge. "She is much more than that. She is vampire, and the witch is in her thrall."

"Fuck me." Killian stalks away, muttering under his breath. "Is nothing in this world simple?"

The conversations around me fade into noise as Isaac comes back into view. Slung over his shoulder, her body limp and her soul still trapped in the void, is Willow.

Willow

I thought darkness was the absence of light. But even when my Dad used to take me stargazing during the new moon in the middle of nowhere, I could see...*something*.

Now, I'm trapped in a sea of nothingness. No sensation. No sound. No smell. No taste.

I can't draw breath. Can't feel my heartbeat.

Help me! Gabriel! Please, find me!

Minutes in the void feel like an eternity. I cry out—or I would if I still had a voice. A mouth. Lungs. But here, the endless scream is only in my mind.

Is this what it's like to die?

I'm slipping further and further away from my life. From any hope of rescue. From Gabriel. I'll never know the comfort of his arms around me again. Or his warmth. His strength. His voice.

I love him. I know that now—without any doubt—and I never got the chance to tell him.

Anguish tears through my consciousness. Rending one thought from the next, shredding them, and leaving my mind in tatters.

"I've been planning this for years."

"With your consciousness trapped...it's like you don't ever exist."

Hannah won't keep me here forever. She needs me to wield the Blade. Tonight, she said. They took me close to noon. How long can I survive here? Six hours? Eight? Ten?

Each moment feels like an eternity. Or...maybe each moment *is* an eternity.

If I could, I'd throw myself against the walls. Claw and scratch until my fingernails are bloody and my bones broken. Instead, it's my mind that fractures into pieces.

"You will obey me."

The sweet, lilting voice is so beautiful. It surrounds me, like flowering vines weaving through my hair, winding down my arms, my torso, my legs.

I can't help but agree. *"Yes. Of course. I'll do anything you want."*

"Good, sweet Willow. I knew you'd see reason."

Reason? I can't see anything. I don't *have* legs in the void. I don't have a body at all. Flowers don't exist here. The voice is a lie. The only thing here is pain.

"Gabriel. I want to see Gabriel."

Silence. Never-ending, oppressive silence.

THE VOICE CALLS to me constantly. It tells me to submit. To obey. To listen.

It's getting harder and harder to resist. When Hannah finally releases me from this endless nightmare, will I have any strength left to fight her?

Whispers push at the tatters of my mind. More of Hannah's tricks? It doesn't matter. The last shred of my sanity is fraying fast.

"Listen."

"Use her."

"We made the wrong choice."

"You hold the true power."

Each voice is stronger than the last. Familiar, yet not. I've been here so long, I can't tell what's real and what's an illusion. What's Hannah and what's...*me.*

They're all talking at once now. If my consciousness weren't being pummeled into dust, I'd clap my hands over my ears.

"*Stop!*" I scream with all the focus I can muster. "*The grimoire warned me, but I didn't listen. All I can do now is die!*"

The whispers get louder. Harsher. Now they're not talking to me, I don't think, but each other.

"*Make her understand...*"

"*How?*"

"*Show her!*"

Sensation returns in a tidal wave of pain. The voices are gone, replaced by the sounds of suffering all around me. Screams, whimpers, moans... All too real after the unending *nothingness* of the void.

Everything's too loud. Too big. Too bright.

Cold. I'm so cold. I can't open my eyes. Can't move. Can't speak.

I think...I'm kneeling. Sitting back on my heels. Someone grabs my shoulder and shakes me.

The chain wrapped around my throat burns, but I can't tell if it's fire or ice. Or both. My hands are numb. They're the only part of me that doesn't hurt.

Cool fingers trail over my cheek. "Open your eyes, Willow. Now."

No. I don't want to.

The chain vibrates, setting my nerve endings on fire. A thin whimper escapes my chapped lips.

"I will not ask you again. Calista? Send her to the very edge of the void, but keep her in *this* world."

My scream echoes through the frigid air. I topple over, my head slamming against rough concrete. Muscles seizing, I'm helpless to do more than cry until Calista releases the spell.

"Are you ready to cooperate?" Hannah asks. Dressed in a long, flowing white dress, she looms over me. "I do not have all night. The full moon will augment the power of the creatures I have lined up for slaughter."

I blink at her, begging silently for any shred of compassion. If I had the strength, I'd tell her... What would I tell her? I'd help. Of course, I'd help. She needs me. She'll take care of me. If I do what she wants, everything will be okay.

Calista flicks her fingers, and I'm lifted onto my knees once more. Blinking away my tears, I stare down at my hands. In the next moment, the red ropes unwind, disappearing into thin air.

I rub my wrists—or try to, as my fingers are only now starting to tingle.

Hannah's clipped footsteps retreat, and I blink hard. I can't focus through my tears and the lingering haze from the void. Something moves in my periphery. A shadow.

No. It's my whisper. She's here. Her hands press to her mouth. She shakes her head, then darts past Calista to throw her arms around me.

I can almost feel her. One of her tears hits my neck, just above the chain. It's warm.

I'm supposed to fight. But fight what? Licking my chapped lips, I taste blood. *Hannah's* blood. Blood bound. *I'm* blood bound.

"...lined up for slaughter."

Oh, God. She's going to make me kill them. There has to be a way out. Or...a weapon. But I don't have the strength to stand, let alone run. Even if I did, I don't know where we are.

"Bring the werewolf," Hannah snaps. "I want to feel his power running through my veins."

I crane my neck, trying to make sense of what I see. The walls are bare. Concrete. The building is massive. Football stadium big. High above, the moon is blinding in the night sky. How...? What happened to the roof?

The screams get louder. I can only twist my head an inch or two in any direction. Behind me, cages are lined up in a row. At least a dozen of them, full of men and women—some slumped to the floor, others shaking the bars like they think they can break free.

Several hurl obscenities at Hannah. Two men flank her, thrust long, black weapons through the bars, and electrocute the prisoners until they're howling in pain.

Isaac drags a young man out of the first cage by a thick, metal chain. Barefoot, emaciated, wearing nothing but a pair of jeans that look like they've been through a shredder, he can't get his legs under him.

A heavy, silver collar is locked around his neck, and as he fights and strains to get free, blood seeps around the edges. Once Isaac secures the short chain to a hasp on the floor in front of me, the man lunges and snaps his jaws. Another two inches, and he'd have me in his grasp.

I'll have to get close to him to use the Blade. If I hesitate—even a little—could he kill me first?

"Meet..." Hannah waves her hand vaguely. "Shit. I won't pretend I know his name. But he's one of the strongest werewolves I've ever seen. He'll be my first. *Your* first, Willow dear."

"Fuck you."

The ground rushes up to meet me, and a heartbeat later, my cheek and jaw start to throb. Blood trickles from the corner of my mouth. Did she...*hit* me?

"I have endless ways to cause you pain," Hannah says, kneeling at my side and flexing her fingers. "But I would much rather be kind. Don't you want me to be kind?"

I do. Of course, I do.

Calista flicks her wrist, and I'm lifted back to my knees. Her other hand twists in the air, forcing the werewolf to mirror my position. He yelps in pain. Fur ripples in patches over his skin. Hannah glares at him. "I forbid you from shifting. Your power is mine to control."

The werewolf's whimper is like a knife to my heart. The fur disappears in an instant, and his bare chest heaves with each shallow breath. His muscles cord and strain, but I don't think he can move.

Hannah steps behind me. I know the exact moment she picks up the Blade. Its fear scrapes along my spine, twisting until I can barely breathe from the weight of it. It *knows* what's about to happen.

"Claim your birthright, Willow, and I will take care of you." She holds the Blade over her head—well out of reach—and smiles down at me. "You want to please me, don't you?"

"Y-yes."

I *know* she's evil. I *know* I have to fight her. But I hurt. Everywhere. My heart most of all.

With her free hand, she traces the delicate links around my neck. "It's simple, really. Pierce the mongrel's heart with the Blade. You'll feel his life force—all his unique talents—flowing into the Blade. Once his heart stops beating, you'll use your magic to send that power flowing through this chain and into me. Can you do that?"

Can I?

My whisper floats behind Hannah, shaking her head and pleading with me.

"Willow? Answer me." Hannah uses the tip of the Blade to force my chin up until she can meet my gaze.

"N-no. I won't..." I start to sob, *knowing* that little bit of resistance was all I had left.

Her eyes harden, and her fangs lengthen to sharp points. "Calista!" she growls.

The witch's fingers jerk. My head snaps back. My lips part. Biting into her wrist, Hannah opens her vein. Crimson wells up, dripping onto her pristine white dress.

She shoves her wrist against my mouth. Cold, bitter blood flows over my tongue. Too much. I try to close my throat, but Calista pinches my nose shut.

Held by magic, Fae compulsion, and my own terror, I swallow.

TWENTY-NINE

Gabriel

"We have to go. Right fucking now! She will not survive this!"

Kunchin and Maddox hold me down, but they are no match for my strength. Not when the woman I love is about to lose her soul.

I throw off the angel and yeti, but before I can take to the air, Sinclair punches me in the gut. Retching, I stumble back, pull Lucifer's axe from my belt, and prepare to fight the first man on earth I thought could be..a friend.

"Put your goddamn wings away, angel," Sin growls. "That vampire-fae abomination needs her *alive*." He turns to Mist. "How long until Willow is unable to fight the pull of Hannah's blood?"

Mist shakes her head. "Not a fucking clue."

"What? You *are* a vampire, are you not?" I ask. Unbelievable. I am surrounded by idiots.

"Of course I am." Fangs bared, she stalks closer to the edge of the cliff. "If Hannah were a normal, run-of-the-mill vampire—and if this were the first time she forced Willow to take her blood she'd need to wait ten minutes to be absolutely certain Willow was in her thrall. But she's part Fae. No vampire in history has been able to turn a Fae. I don't think Hannah was made. She was *born* a vampire. We don't know if that makes her blood *more* potent or less."

Far below us, Hannah straightens and swipes her tongue over her wrist. Willow sways, head bowed, but somehow, remains upright.

"That's not our only problem." Killian turns away from the cliff. Rage pours off him in purple, green, and blue sparks. "If the witch is blood bound, she'll do anything to protect her mistress. She won't have a choice."

"So? You are the greatest warlock of all time. At least if the name you programmed into my phone is to be believed," Sinclair says.

"I *should* be." Killian tugs at his hair. "But no witch alive should be able to exert that level of control over another with only her fingers. She is hundreds of years old. And I would wager she's drawing on the vampire's power. If she turns her magic on you— on any of you—fighting her will be impossible."

With every minute that passes, I feel Willow slipping away. Once Hannah released her from the void, her pain and fear washed over me. But now...

"She cannot fight much longer." I sink to my knees, the agony of her loss cracking my heart into pieces. "We have gone over this plan a hundred times. I can get the vampires past the wards. Sinclair and Maddox too if need be. But if we wait, I will have no choice but to go alone."

Sin pulls his phone from his pocket and checks the screen. "Zoe and Grayson are in position. I do not like our odds, but...I suppose we have faced worse. Are you certain you do not want to call for Azrael?"

"He holds life and death in his hands. That is too great a power to risk. If I fall, he has vowed to see my soul—and Willow's —to the afterlife. I will not ask him for more."

Willow

A frigid peace settles over me. The world takes on a gentle glow. There's no pain. No fear. I could stay in this place forever, I think.

Hannah crouches in front of me. "Willow? Are you ready to begin?"

Begin? Oh, right. I'm supposed to help her. Magic sings in my blood, begging to be set free. I can hear it. Taste it. Almost touch it.

Don't listen to her!

What? No. I have to listen. I *want* to listen. I belong to Hannah now. She'll take care of me. She promised.

"Answer me, Willow. Are you ready to wield the Blade?" Hannah's cool fingers skim over my throat. A subtle vibration hums through the chain.

"Yes. I'm ready."

A shadow moves behind her. My whisper. Why is she here? I don't need her anymore. I have Hannah. I have the Blade.

But not Gabriel.

Gabriel? Gabriel's gone. But...where? I can't remember. Why isn't he here? I love him, and I never got a chance to tell him. My eyes start to burn. I need to run, but I can't move.

Hannah places the Blade in front of me, and I forget what I was getting so worked up about. "Don't touch it until I tell you," she says.

No. I won't. Of course not. I have to do what she says. Always.

The symbols carved into the metal come alive, swirling and twisting, faster and faster until I'm so dizzy, I'd fall over if I could move at all.

Why can't I move?

A man's weak whimper distracts me, and I lift my gaze. He's crying. His eyes hold so much pain.

I'm supposed to kill him.

My heart pounds against my ribs. This is wrong. So wrong. I can't do this. I won't. "Please," I say softly. "Let me go."

"How are you *still* resisting me?" Hannah shrieks. She wraps her fingers around my forearm and squeezes until the bone snaps in two.

I scream. My vision goes dark around the edges. The chain at my throat starts to vibrate again. Stronger this time. My shattered bone starts to knit back together. It's like ants crawling around under my skin.

I'm shaking all over, but still unable to move. Hannah shifts her hand to the back of my neck, and I can hear her *in my head.*

"Fight me again, you pathetic little witch, and I'll shatter your bones one by one. They'll heal—thanks to my blood—but the pain will be exquisite every single time."

My whisper's tears glisten in the moonlight. She floats behind the kneeling man—the werewolf, I remember now—with her hands over her mouth.

"I'm so sorry. I thought...I'd be stronger."

"Pick up the Blade, Willow," Hannah orders.

I try to resist, but it's no use. My fingers curl around the hilt. A wave of power rolls up my arm and settles somewhere deep inside me. My magic. Created by the very first coven, passed from generation to generation.

The symbols flow *into* my hand. Up my arm. They're a part of me now. As much as my name, my memories, and even my voice.

"Listen."

"Use her."

"We made the wrong choice."

"You hold the true power."

The voices from the void swirl around me.

"You hold the true power."

My whisper surges forward. Her lips move along with the voices.

"You hold the true power."

She's wrong. I can't fight Hannah's will. It's suffocating me. Drowning every ounce of free will I thought I had.

"Do you believe in fate?" I ask.

Gabriel arches a brow. "As in the Almighty's preordained plan for every soul throughout all of creation?"

"Yeah. That."

"Complete and utter bullshit."

"Strike, Willow!" Hannah shouts, her will wiping away my memories of Gabriel one by one. "Now!"

I raise the Blade high above my head. I can't take this man's life. But maybe I can take my own.

Gritting my teeth, I screw my eyes shut and focus on keeping Hannah out of my head. But she pushes back even harder. The hand on my neck tightens. The chain sends raw agony shooting through my entire body.

I can't fight any longer. I failed. Like all the Whisper Keepers who came before me. Has the grimoire already recorded my last words? Or will they come next?

I'm sorry. So sorry.

My arm swings down, the Blade arcing through the air.

A split second before the Blade pierces the werewolf's heart, a blast of power knocks me back ten feet. I land on top of Hannah.

Metal hits metal. Once. Twice. "Get the fuck out of here!" Gabriel shouts. The collar clatters to the floor. The man scrambles up and takes off at a run.

He came.

Hannah flips me onto my stomach, pinning me with her knee at the small of my back. "Calista!"

The witch flings her arms in a circle. Gabriel rises into the air, his limbs straining. The Devil's axe is still clutched in his hand. His muscles twitch, but Calista has him completely under her spell. His amber eyes tighten with pain. "Willow! Fight her, *deliciae*. You are the only one who can!"

"You hold the true power."

"Use her!"

A blast of magic explodes across the building. One of the walls starts to crumble. Isaac yells for the others to get their guns.

Shots ring out—so much louder than I thought they'd be. Hannah grabs the chain at my neck, and the void races closer.

"What will you do to stay out of the void, Willow dear?" Hannah asks.

"Anything!" As the word leaves my lips, I know it was the wrong thing to say. But she's so strong. And Gabriel...I can feel his fear. His pain.

Hannah laughs. It's not beautiful anymore. It's as ugly as she is. A shrill, cackling howl that makes my ears bleed. "I don't know what *he* is, Willow dear. But teleportation? Now *that's* a power unlike any I've ever seen."

Calista sends Gabriel flying into the wall of cages. My angel groans and starts to get up, but Isaac jabs him with a shock stick. His arms and legs flop helplessly, and his eyes roll back in his head.

With another wave of her hand, the witch slides my angel across the floor until he's lying in front of me.

Hannah digs her fingers around my left collarbone. The bone shatters. My vision goes white. I can't keep her out of my head.

I'm hers. I always will be.

With one final sob, I drive the Blade deep into Gabriel's chest.

Gabriel

I thought dying would hurt more. I feel only peace. Also...cold. Very cold.

Such an odd thing, knowing five inches of metal have run me through. Even odder to see the Blade sticking out of my chest, with Willow's hand still wrapped around the hilt.

"Gabriel. God, Gabriel. Why?" she sobs. Her tears fall, mixing with my blood. So much blood.

"I sensed your...despair, my love. I could not let you...lose your soul. My plan...was to destroy the Blade... Not...this." I struggle for each breath. My lungs rattle, and I taste blood.

The entire building rumbles. Another section of the wall collapses, this one closer. Killian's spells chip away at the wards protecting this place. The vampires should be close now. But not close enough. They were supposed to subdue the witch.

"What are you, *Gabriel?*" Hannah peers down at me. Her nostrils flare. "Your blood...it's intoxicating." With her hand tight around the back of Willow's neck, she leans closer. "Tell me, Willow. What is he?"

She's sobbing harder now, trying to twist out of Hannah's hold. Rage fills the vampire's brown eyes, turning them blood red.

"Answer me!" she screams.

Willow lets out a wail. "I can't! Gabriel, I...lov—"

A bone in Willow's shoulder snaps. She collapses on top of me, but whether because of the magic within her or the iron-clad control Hannah has over her, she can't let go of the Blade. My angelic power seeps into the weapon. Old wounds—long healed— open and bleed. The wings that carried me thousands of miles as we searched, blister once more. Soon, they will start to burn.

I have little strength left. But perhaps enough for one final miracle.

"*Mea amor. Mea lux. Mea deliciae.* Do not...be afraid. I will... always be...in your heart."

Another bone snaps in Willow's battered body. Her screams are getting weaker. As is her resistance. I feel everything. This vampire bitch will not continue to torture the woman I love. Not as long as I draw breath.

"Enough!" I roar. "You want...to know what I am? I...am the Archangel Gabriel. Bringer of...Justice. Revealer...of Truth. Inter- preter...of the Almighty's...Plan. And you...will let...Willow...go!"

"An angel? With your power, I will live forever!" She winds her fingers through the short chain around Willow's neck. "Take it, my pet. And give it to me. Now!"

Willow tries to resist, but a human body cannot hold angelic power for long. Her free will, her very soul starts to fade. The horror of what I have done washes over me. She trembles, her whimpers turning to hoarse sobs. "I...I love...you, Gabriel. I'm sorry..."

A blast of Killian's magic arcs across the cavernous space. The cage doors heave, metal screeching. The men and women trapped inside start to fight. But before any of them can escape, the silent witch takes off at a run, flicking her fingers at each prisoner until they are all screaming in agony.

I cover Willow's hand with mine and hold her gaze. "I chose this, my love. I go...to my death...at peace. Because *you* will survive. I will see you again...in the afterlife."

"Gabriel, no!" she wails.

Wrenching her hand from the hilt of the Blade, I loose my wings. I cannot make it far. Thirty, forty feet into the air. But I can see the reservoir beyond these walls. I know what I have to do. My heart slows. I struggle to draw the shallowest of breaths.

Hannah screams. "He has the Blade!"

The raven-haired witch has her hands full fighting off Mist and Kàra. She sends Mist to her knees, then lifts her hand to spell me.

I yank the Blade from my chest and fling it over the top of the wall. It flies end over end, passes through the wards, and splashes into the depths of the frigid water.

"I love you," I whisper, hoping somehow, Willow will hear me.

My heart thumps once. Twice. Then stops completely. Falling is so very much like flying. Almost...peaceful. I hit the ground, releasing one final breath. The Blade is gone.

Willow...someone needs to save...Willow.

THIRTY

Willow

Gabriel—my angel—his great, white wings stained with blood, but very much whole—locks his gaze onto mine.

He mouthes, *"I love you,"* before he crashes to the ground. I can *hear* his bones shatter. One last, final breath rattles in his lungs.

"Gabriel! No!"

His power coils within me. It's eating me alive. Pushing. Pulsing. Desperate to find its home. Hannah spins me around, one hand over my heart, the other tangled in the chain around my throat.

"Give it to me," she growls. "All of it. You cannot resist me, Willow. The Whisper Keeper is only a conduit. She cannot take the power for herself. *You* will never be an angel. I will."

The chain burns my skin. She's in my head. Whispering. *"Give it to me. You want to. You need to."*

The void races closer. Gabriel's power resists, keeping me on the knife's edge of nothingness and unending agony. I have to let it go.

Hannah's will consumes me. Willow fades away. Smaller and

smaller until I'm only a speck of dust in my own mind. All of Gabriel's angelic power rushes from my body in a blaze of pure, white light.

It knocks us apart. We're suspended in time, tethered by magic, until blood red wings burst through her white dress, ripping the delicate fabric.

For a breath, she closes her eyes, then her wings start to beat. "The power! I can feel everything!"

My magic releases the last of Gabriel's life force, and I collapse in a heap on the floor. He's gone. My angel is truly gone. Sobs wrack my body. The last few broken bones haven't fully healed, and each tremor brings more pain.

Gabriel tried to save me. He *did* save me. Not my life. Hannah will kill me. Or I'll find a way to meet my own end. But maybe... just maybe...he saved enough of my soul for me to see him in the afterlife.

Gabriel

I walk through an endless world of white. My robes are loose around my ankles. My wings flutter in a gentle breeze.

An overwhelming sense of peace settles in my soul. I...am home. Back in the celestial realm where I belong.

No. Pain flashes behind my eyes. I belong...

"Did you really think you could make a grand gesture like that and just...*die?*"

Whirling around, I come face to face with Azrael. His tailored black suit is still perfectly pressed, but in his hand...

"Is that a slice of pizza?" I ask.

His sheepish smile should anger me. But here, I cannot muster the emotion.

"Did you enjoy it?"

"Thoroughly. Have you tried bagels?" he asks and clasps my

arm. "Sea salt are my favorite. With blueberry cream cheese. Though Everything bagels have a certain appeal as well."

His breath reeks, and I wave my hand in front of my face. "I should have warned you, Az. If you consume more than trace amounts of garlic, you must brush your teeth soon after. Your breath is...vile."

He cups his hands in front of his mouth, exhales, and his eyes widen. "Fuck. Noted."

"Why are you here? With pizza, no less." We walk along the path to the Sea of Redemption. Azrael finishes his last bite of what I think was double pepperoni and swipes a napkin over his mouth.

The sea sparkles like diamonds, despite a complete lack of wind. There is no sun in the celestial realm. Only the never-ending light that touches everything here.

He stops on the edge of the shore, turns to me, and rests his hands on my shoulders. "You're dying, Gabriel. I'm here to carry your soul to eternal rest."

"Oh. Well, get on with it, then."

"Get...on with it?" Azrael shakes me, and when I do not react, arches a brow and punches me in the face.

"What the fuck was that for? Do you treat all your souls in this manner?" In the celestial realm, we cannot be injured. There is no pain. Only the shock of my brother's strike. He hits me again. Harder this time.

"Haven't you forgotten something down there?" He jabs his finger in the vague direction of the earthen realm. "Cr...*someone?*"

I have no idea what he's talking about, but before I can say a word, he looses his massive black wings, tosses me over his shoulder, and takes to the air.

Azrael is not only my brother. He is the closest thing to a friend I have in the celestial realm. So I let him see this through—whatever *this* is. He sets me down on top of a wall in the middle of the night. Frigid air swirls around us, and the sounds of war are everywhere.

Bullets whiz by a few feet away. A woman screams. The voice

is familiar. But before I can figure out why, another angel with sleek, black wings soars over the wall of the building, circles once, and dives into a lake.

A moment later, he bursts from the depths with a dagger in his hand. I know this weapon. My chest aches. I stare down to see a bright red stain spreading over my robes.

"Maddox! I have the Blade. Find Lucifer's axe!" he shouts.

"Oh, I've found it," another angel—Maddox, I assume—replies. "But you're not going to like where it ended up." I follow Maddox's gaze.

Three vampires battle against a woman with jet black hair and crimson lips. Her hands are in constant motion, sending massive chunks of the crumbling walls hurtling for the bloodsuckers. Lucifer's axe lies behind them.

"You look, but you don't see." Azrael points to the center of the building.

Blood red wings beat the air. The woman glows with power. The ache in my chest turns to searing pain. At her feet, another human screams. She clutches *my body,* sobbing, my name on her lips. My heart rends in two.

"Willow..."

In an instant, all my memories return. Holding her that first night in the cathedral. Marveling at her beauty. Breathing in her scent. Saving her from the vampire-fae abomination. Showing her my damaged wings. Feeling her fingers sift through the devastation with such tender care...

Making love to her.

Losing her.

Hannah grabs Willow by the throat and throws her against the wall. My love tries to get to her hands and knees, but collapses with a whimper.

"Your *friends* cannot save you, Whisper Keeper." Hannah advances on Willow, her wings outstretched, fangs glistening. "Nor will they ever find you again. Calista, get the Blade. Now!"

The witch turns, sending a burst of magic at Sinclair. His wings simply...stop...and he plummets to the ground. Bones break.

One of his wing bends at an unnatural angle, and he screams in pain. Calista flicks her wrist, sending the Blade flying across the building until it comes to rest in front of Willow.

"Pick. It. Up," Hannah commands.

Willow's strength—her will to resist—is almost gone. "Please, no. I killed the man I love. You can't take more from me!"

"I can take whatever I want. You are *mine*, Whisper Keeper. Mine to command. Mine to control." Hannah disappears, and an instant later, has Kàra held fast in her arms. "You will take this one's power next. She is the strongest of them. Ancient. A goddess among Valkyrie, I believe."

Willow screams as her fingers wrap around the hilt of the Blade. "Kàra...Fight her. Please!"

I turn to Azrael. "Why are you torturing me with this? I *died*, brother. Is that not enough?"

The Angel of Death holds up his hand. Time stops. There is no sound, no movement. I sweep my gaze around the building. Killian is frozen in mid-spell. The magic arcs from his hand in a magnificent burst of blue light. Maddox dives toward his brother. Calista sends a steel rod hurtling for Ewan, while Mist is pinned by a pile of rubble.

"You are hovering on the precipice of death, Gabriel. In seconds, I will have no choice but to release your soul to the afterlife."

"Then do it!" I grab him by his lapels, ready to beg if I must. "I cannot watch the woman I love lose anything more."

"Then don't," he says, a hint of a smile playing over his lips. "Get down there and save her."

"My heart no longer beats. My soul is *here*, tethered to the Angel of Death until he releases it to the afterlife. I cannot simply choose to live any more than you can choose to let me. Seraphiel would take your wings."

Azrael scoffs. "You are an archangel. One of the chosen. A celestial. You have the power to weave the very fabric of the universe. Surely your heart is not so difficult to mend. And Seraphiel is about to learn the true meaning of the phrase 'fuck around and find out.' Don't worry about me. I can take care of myself."

I press my hands to my chest. The wound is so deep. Can I really do this? Willow's cry echoes in my mind.

"I...I love you, Gabriel. I'm sorry!"

Azrael rests his hand on my shoulder. "I've given you all the time I can, brother. Are you ready to come with me or not?"

Shaking off his hold, I draw up to my full height. "Az? I love Willow with all that I am. I'm going to live. You can fuck right off."

My wings unfold, beating with a purpose I have never felt in all of my existence. I rise into the air, leaving Azrael standing alone. He nods once, and as my consciousness—my soul—dives for my body, all Hell breaks loose.

THIRTY-ONE

Willow

My world is crashing down all around me. Two of Hannah's goons are dead—shot, I think—but Isaac is still firing a very large gun through a gap in the ruined wall of the building.

Ewan screams. Kàra struggles, but she's as weak as a child against the angelic strength Hannah has running through her body.

"You hold the true power."

If I knew where that voice was coming from, I'd kick its ass.

"I don't! Not anymore!"

My whisper gets right in my face, but Hannah cackles. The chain brands my skin. A swirling vortex of pain and nothingness reaches for me, so close I can almost touch it.

A silent scream bursts from my whisper's lips. Her body writhes in pain, limbs flailing, and she starts to fade away.

"No! Stop! You're killing her!" I try to release the Blade, but my fingers aren't mine to control.

One step.

Two.

My arm swings over my head. The void tugs at my soul,

threatening to rip it from my body the moment I send Kàra's power into Hannah.

"Willow!" Gabriel's shout shakes the entire building. Chunks of stone sheer off the walls, each one larger than the last.

How? He...died. I saw him—felt him—die.

But he sits up, his shirt soaked with his blood, and a look of murderous rage in his molten amber eyes.

Hannah throws Kàra with all of her strength. The vampire screams. Her body slams into Maddox in mid-air, and the two of them go down together.

My angel roars as he staggers to his feet. His wings unfurl, perfect and strong and the most brilliant white, and his entire body glows with power.

He's so beautiful. Alive. Confident. And mine.

"This isn't possible." Hannah beats her own wings, rising into the air. Gabriel matches her position. Power crackles between them, sparking like lightning.

My whisper screams again, only this time, I can *hear* it.

Hannah and Gabriel grapple. My angel lands a punch to the woman's stomach. But she darts around him and tries to sink her teeth into his neck.

She's distracted. This is my chance to end it all.

I spin the Blade and drive it toward my heart. A hair's breadth from my chest, it stops. *I* stop. Hannah's voice booms in my head.

"Your life belongs to me, Whisper Keeper. Only I can take it."

"No!" I try again and again, but an invisible barrier stops me—impact singing up my arms—every time.

I can barely see through my tears. Hannah and Gabriel are still battling, disappearing and reappearing in mid-air. Hannah has all his power and more, but I can feel my angel's love strengthening him.

"We made the wrong choice."

"Use it."

"Use her!"

The voices from the void roar in my ears.

Use...her? I meet my whisper's gaze. *She's* the one who's been using *me*. She's in so much pain, but she still staggers to her feet.

Hannah knocks Gabriel halfway across the building then turns her gaze on me. "Your whisper really does look just like you. And how sweet that she wants to protect you. Use the Blade, Willow. Take her power. Now."

I lift the Blade over my head. My whisper pleads with me, the fear in her eyes shooting straight to my soul.

"Do it, Willow. Or Calista will shatter your ribs one by one," Hannah says sweetly. Gabriel roars as he dives for her. He catches her around the waist and spins her away.

But it's too late. Calista stalks toward me, drawing symbols in the air. My whisper's arms snap to her sides. Her legs glue themselves together. She can't move.

Centuries of knowledge, of pain, of regret slam into me. I understand now. Those voices in the void...they're all the Whisper Keepers who came before. They've been with me the whole time, but I was too afraid to listen.

They didn't need to die.

I don't need to die.

I refuse to move, and Calista snaps the first of my ribs. I don't even have the energy to scream.

Another, and my vision turns cloudy. This is my last chance.

"Trust me," I say softly. "I know what to do."

She sobs silently, terrified, so weak. But she nods.

"Please," I beg all the Whisper Keepers who have gone before me. *"Give me your strength."*

With my free hand, I grasp the chain wrapped around my neck. My magic flares to life inside me, vibrating through the links until the agony is too much for me to bear. At the same time, I reach for my whisper's consciousness. All those times I thought she stole my consciousness from my body? I was wrong. She didn't do a thing. *I* did.

The sudden sensation of nothingness as we're ripped from our physical existence leaves me disoriented. Dizzy. My thoughts fracture. Only a single shred of awareness remains.

A long, narrow tunnel pierces the darkness. I see through my whisper's eyes. She's straddling both worlds—the physical, where my body is, and the void.

But with my consciousness here, I collapse, and Calista has no reason to keep my whisper spelled. Not with vampires, angels, and a warlock to battle.

I let my consciousness float in the pitch black, searching. Suddenly, all the ones who came before surround me. They're afraid. Begging me not to fail. It's too much. So many voices, I can't make out the words.

"Everyone shut the fuck up!" At my outburst, they fall silent. *" One at a time. Tell me what I need to do."*

"Love and hate, light and darkness, life and death. Pairings as old as time itself. Love, light, and life created the Blade. Hate, darkness, and death came after. The circle begins where the circle ends."

The words are familiar. The grimoire. I read them at the beginning. It feels like a lifetime ago.

"The Blade was created by love," a single, scratchy voice says. *"Love can set the magic free."*

"I can't set the magic free. I'm blood bound. Hannah won't let me destroy the Blade any more than she'll let me destroy myself."

"You listen but you do not hear.. Love cannot be destroyed. Love exists, always. Accept it, cherish it, share it, and love will make you whole."

Share it?

Gabriel and Hannah continue to battle in the air. A blast of Killian's magic pins Calista to the wall. Kàra and Ewan reach Sin as Maddox snaps the demon's dislocated shoulder back into place.

Shots ring out. Isaac collapses, blood pouring from his gut. Mist finishes him off by snapping his neck.

I focus on my whisper—on our fragile connection. It was always mine to control.

Ideas start to filter through my weary mind.

"Wait. Can I use...all of you?"

The voices fade away for the infinite time that is each second in the void. Until they rise up, louder than ever.

"Refuse the call and your life ends here. Give in and your soul will sheer. Threads from the past can bind or break. The future is only what you make. When all is lost will come a choice. Love is yours to give a voice."

The words from the final page in the grimoire. The last line I didn't know until just now.

Hannah's strength comes from hate, darkness, and death. They're her weapons. Along with fear and pain.

I've been so scared of her—of what she'd make me do—I couldn't see what was right in front of me.

The Blade was created by love. Love is yours to give a voice.

I know what to do. But I can't do it from here. I reach for my whisper in the dark, pulling her close and praying she'll hear me.

"We have to break the chain, and we can end this. Together."

***

Gabriel

The punch sends me spinning thirty feet off the ground. My teeth rattle. I bite halfway through my own damn tongue, and blood fills my mouth.

My adversary scents the air. "You're tiring, angel. I'll taste you soon. Then bind you to me for all eternity. Or at least until I get bored and have my Whisper Keeper end you for good "

"Tiring? Hardly," I scoff. "I can do this all night."

I lunge for Hannah, but veer away at the last second. The move stuns her enough for me to grab the tip of her left wing and hurl her into the closest wall.

The impact should have left her body broken. Vampires can heal in seconds, but seconds are all I need to end her. If not for her stolen angelic strength, this fight would have been over long ago.

I slam into her from behind, banding my arms around her and pinning her wings to her back.

"Release me," she purrs.

I can feel her compulsion slithering through my mind. It would be so easy to let go. I *am* tired. Dying is exhausting. Coming back to life even more so.

No!

"Nice try, vampire. You *are* strong. But I have something you do not." I take us higher, scanning the ruins of the building until I find what I am looking for.

"And what is that?" Her voice is even smoother now. Sweeter. Her Fae talents are learning me. Searching for weaknesses she can exploit. She's wasting her energy.

"Love."

She laughs. "Love? The woman you *love* is mine. I'll steal every fond memory she has of you and lock them away until I'm done with her. But I'll give them all back the moment I make her take your life."

Thrashing with all her might, she manages to get a hold of my right arm. Her fingers crush skin, muscle, and bone. Still, I refuse to release her.

Sweat dots my forehead. Fire licks up my forearm, and the fingers of my right hand go numb.

Below us, Willow struggles to her feet. Power glows within her, the most beautiful golden light I have ever seen. And with her...my God.

Her whisper stands at her side. They're surrounded by eight other whispers, echoes of all the ones who came before. They hold hands, smiling, and focus all of their gazes on Hannah.

"I fought death for Willow—for love—and survived," I say in Hannah's ear. "It seems she has done the same."

———

Willow

Accepting my whisper was the easiest thing I've ever done. But pulling all the whispers who've come before out of the void *with* me? That was almost impossible.

More than once I thought I'd fail. But when my consciousness returned to my body, my whisper was smiling down at me. The Blade's fear—such a constant weight on my soul from that first afternoon in the cathedral—is gone.

I point the Blade at Hannah. She can't hurt me anymore. Not with so many whispers surrounding me. "You took something that wasn't yours," I call. "Time to give it back."

Magic heats the air. The Blade sings with it. The whispers do too.

Sinclair and Maddox flank Gabriel as he lowers Hannah to the ground. She shrieks obscenities at them, then turns her intense stare on me.

For a split second, I cringe, my mind cowering behind the weight of the blood bond. But I focus on the liquid gold of my angel's eyes, and all that power falls away. "I thought I'd lost you."

"You could never lose me, *deliciae*. I love you. There is no force in this world—or any other—strong enough to keep us apart." Gabriel lets Sin and Maddox take hold of Hannah, and the brothers force her to her knees. "You can end this?" he asks, cradling his left arm against his body.

"Yes. But..." I cup the back of his neck, pull him down, and whisper in his ear. "I can still feel her blood inside me, Gabriel. She's not in control," I add when a low growl rumbles in his chest. "I promise. But I don't know what's going to happen when I take your power from her. What if...what if it drives me mad?"

"Then I will use all my love for you to bring you back." He skims a knuckle along my jaw.

"All of it?" I shouldn't take the time to joke with him. Not when Hannah could break free at any moment. But...I'm not frightened of her now.

Gabriel brushes his lips to mine. The kiss is so tender—so full of all the things we didn't say to one another on the train—that tears spring to my eyes.

"Our love is an endless spring, Willow. It will never run dry. You are my whole heart. My soul. My everything."

He's right. Nothing Hannah—or anyone—could do to me will ever diminish my love for this man in front of me. I'm so light, I think I could fly. "I love you too, stud. Now go stand with all the whispers behind me."

I hold the Blade in one hand, the broken power chain in the other, and take a step closer to Hannah. "You thought you could control me."

She opens her mouth to speak, but Killian sends a blast of magic in her direction, and her jaw snaps shut once more.

"But nothing can *control* magic. Or love. The grimoire lied. To you. To me. To everyone. The Blade was created by love. For love. To preserve magic in this world until the end of time. Humans turned into something vile. And fear...fear killed the Whisper Keepers one after another. Not anymore."

My whisper threads her fingers through mine. We can do this. Together.

One by one, the other whispers lend us their strength. Their *love*. My whisper's hand is almost completely solid now. Spots of color darken on her cheeks.

One more step, and we hold the tip of the Blade over Hannah's heart. I don't need to make her bleed. Or suffer. That's not who I am.

"I thought I'd have to destroy the Blade—or myself—to escape you. But that's not the answer. I don't need to escape anything. I have everything I need right here."

I sweep my gaze from my whisper to the ones gathered behind us, to Gabriel. "I have my magic. I have this ancient artifact created by the first coven. I have friends. And I have Gabriel. An angel who loves me so much, not even death could keep us apart."

No one says a word. Even the prisoners still trapped in cages fall silent.

"The Blade isn't the weapon you think it is." I send all the love I have flowing through the Blade. My whisper does the same. "It's not evil. It's not even dangerous. It's Love. From now until the end of time. The Blade is love."

It takes nothing—only a single thought—to coax Hannah's stolen power back where it belongs. For a moment, nothing happens. Until she starts to scream.

Terror has a sound. I heard it the first time as the WCU sent me into the void, the second time when Gabriel died, and again now.

The bright, pure light swirls around her, picking up speed until the vortex lifts her high in the air. Her crimson wings turn to dust. In the next second...she's simply...gone.

Calista whimpers softly. Killian had bound her in ropes from her shoulders to the tips of her fingers before I emerged from the void. She turns, mouthing, *"Thank you,"* before her eyes roll back in her head and she crumples to the floor.

"Fuck me." Killian runs a hand through his messy locks and stares down at her. "Without the blood bond, she aged hundreds of years in...seconds." He checks her pulse. "She's gone."

"She wasn't evil." I press close to Gabriel—as close as I dare with the blood still soaking his t-shirt. "The way she looked at me just now...I think she's been praying for death for a very, *very* long time."

"I need to check on Zoe," Sin says. "Mad, help the vampires free the rest of Hannah's prisoners. Grayson and Kunchin will take their statements in a few minutes. Gabriel? I know you want to get Willow somewhere...*private,* but at least see that Lucifer's axe is secure. The last thing we need is Hell's greatest weapon falling into the wrong hands. There's been enough of that these past few days to last us a thousand lifetimes."

I don't want to let my angel go, but the axe is buried under an eight-foot pile of rubble. Kàra and Ewan take care of the cages, while Mist helps Gabriel toss huge chunks of concrete away like they weight nothing at all.

Killian limps over to me, his hands tucked in his pockets. "They do know I could have magicked that for them, right?"

"Gabriel died less than an hour ago," I say quietly. "Let him feel useful."

The warlock's rich laugh is comforting. Normal. And completely out of place. Every single one of us could have died ten times over tonight.

"You're sure the Blade will never be a threat again?" he asks.

I glance down at the ancient weapon in my hand. "The threat never came from the Blade, Killian. It came from the grimoire."

He frowns. "Want to run that by me again, luv?"

"The grimoire had me convinced the Blade was evil. That *I* was evil." A tremor of magic runs through me. My whisper appears at my side, concern in her expression. "I'm okay. We're okay."

She seems to accept my answer, because she fades into nothingness—along with all the other whispers. Unlike all the other times she's disappeared, I know I'll see her again soon. I'm even looking forward to it.

"When we get back to San Francisco, she and I are going to destroy the grimoire for good. This," I give the Blade a little spin, "from today until the end of time, is nothing more than a fancy, antique dagger. No more grimoire, no new Whisper Keepers, and no way for anyone to force this magic on the world again."

THIRTY-TWO

Gabriel

I feel slightly guilty entrusting Lucifer's axe to Sinclair. Also leaving him and the others to deal with nine, traumatized prisoners. But Willow has gone through hell the last fourteen hours, and when I pulled her into my arms a few minutes ago, she burst into tears.

"I...have t-to get out...of h-h-here. P-Please, Gabriel. Take m-me anywhere...but here."

I am not certain I have the strength. But for her, I will try. When my soul returned to my body, the pain was overwhelming. I cursed Azrael for not warning me. Though, perhaps he did, and I chose to ignore him. I have been known to do that. Often.

Zoe hurries over to us. She favors her right shoulder after laying down cover fire from a tree for over an hour. Without her, Hannah's goons could have shot me—along with Sinclair and Maddox—a hundred times over.

"Gabriel, are you strong enough to take her back to the penthouse?" Lowering her voice, Zoe adds, "I was only conscious for a few seconds after you and Sin pulled my soul out of Hell. But the *last* place I wanted to be was that old power station."

I smooth my hand over Willow's hair. "*Deliciae,* do you trust me?"

"How can you ask me that?" she says, sniffling. "I love you."

"Where is the Blade? You have been entrusted with its care. We should not leave it behind."

Willow shifts in my arms and points to a makeshift table Sin and Kunchin fashioned out of a slab from one of the walls and two of the now empty cages. The Blade looks so ordinary. Old. No more threatening than a letter opener.

"I'll get it for you," Zoe says, and shrugs out of her leather jacket. She wraps the Blade up tightly and passes it to Willow. "I'll text you the combination for Sin's vault. It's behind a false wall in our bedroom closet. The Blade will be safe there until you decide what to do with it."

I tuck Willow against my side. Her delicate hand presses to my heart, and she shudders. "I don't like feeling your blood," she says softly.

"Neither do I, my love. But we will take care of that soon enough."

Before I can carry us to Sinclair's penthouse, Zoe grabs my arm. "Gabriel? We won't make it back for *at least* twenty-four hours. You and Willow will have some privacy. But please...for the love of all that's holy in this world...no sex on the living room furniture."

THE LIGHTS of San Francisco cast glittering colors over Sinclair's black leather couches. Willow sags against me, utterly silent. This worries me more than her tears.

Once the Blade is secure, I lead her into the bath. But she stops me when I try to remove her shirt.

"You first. Please. I can't..." Tears brim in her eyes. "I keep seeing you die. Over and over again."

I lower my gaze to the gray t-shirt. The *formerly* gray t-shirt.

"Fuck." The material rips in my hands. But even balling it up and hiding it in the trash does not allay her distress.

My chest does not look much better. The wound has healed, but a jagged scar over my heart will remain for the rest of my existence. However long that will be.

Willow takes one of the soft, black washcloths, runs it under hot water, and starts dabbing at the blood staining my skin.

"Does it still hurt?" She only meets my gaze for a brief moment, and the pain in her eyes breaks my heart.

I wish I could lie. Her emotions are too fragile for the truth. But though I suspect I am no longer welcome in the celestial realm, I was, am, and always will be an angel.

"A dull ache, yes. I suspect I will feel it for the rest of my days." At her quiet sob, I cover her hand with mine. "Willow, look at me. Please."

She shakes her head and her tears spill over. "I...I killed you."

"No, love. *No*. It may have been your hand, but it was not you." I nudge her chin up, needing her to see the truth in my eyes. "I will *never* see that scar and remember the moment I...died. I will think only of my love for you and the moment I came back to life."

Willow's tenuous control shatters. Her entire body shakes as she sobs against my chest.

I sink down to the floor with her held in my arms, rubbing her back in slow circles, whispering words of love with my lips pressed to her hair until she has no more tears to cry.

Silence holds sway as I help her remove her bloodstained clothes, then shed the rest of mine and guide her into the shower. The water runs red, and as I brush Willow's hair away from her neck, my rage threatens to boil over.

Despite the healing power of the vampire's blood, deep purple bruises mar her collarbone, her arms, both shoulders, and several ribs. But that's not the worst of the devastation raged over her body. An angry red scar rings her throat. She shies away when I skim my finger just below the mark. "Don't...please."

"Killian said power chains were unbreakable. How did you manage—"

"Love." She shudders, despite the heat of the spray. "And the strength of all the whispers who came before. The grimoire condemned every one of the Whisper Keepers to death because that's all it ever showed them. They spent centuries trapped in the void. Afraid. Alone. But they figured it out. *We* figured it out. The only way to survive was to do it together."

Sweeping her against me, I claim her lips. Willow melts in my arms, but kisses me back with such passion, my cock springs to life, and a low growl rumbles in my throat.

"Gabriel," she pants when we come up for air. "I need... Make me feel *alive.*"

I press her back against the wall and turn off the spray. Avoiding her bruises proves difficult. My lips graze her collarbone. She whimpers, but it is not pain in her tone. It is need. So pure and raw, it almost overwhelms me.

Raining kisses over her skin, to the hollow of her throat just below the scar, down to her breasts, her waist, all the way to her mound, I savor every moan, every tremor, and the scent of her arousal.

"You are so fucking wet, my love. I would take you right here if I could wait another second to taste you."

Willow braces her arms against the shower walls as I swipe my tongue through her folds. She is rain. Spring. Love.

Sliding two fingers deep in her channel, I pump my hand in time with my tongue lapping at her clit. It takes only minutes for her to fly apart, screaming my name as her body quakes and her knees go weak.

I catch her before she falls. "Hold onto me, *deliciae.* For what comes next, this shower is much too small."

Her breath hitches, and a fresh wave of her arousal washes over me. "I need you inside me," she pleads, her voice husky from her release.

I wrap her in one of the black, fluffy towels and carry her into the bedroom. "You will have everything you need soon enough."

Her hooded eyes flutter as I lay her down, then suck one peaked nipple into my mouth. Willow's back arches. Her soft moans are life itself to me now.

"I am going to memorize every inch of you," I whisper against her skin. "What you like. What you need. What makes you scream."

She shudders as I kiss my way along her collarbone. "Gabriel. Please..."

Sinking her fingers into my damp hair, she angles my head and guides me to her mouth. Her tongue demands entrance. I let her take the control she needs—for now. I will claim her pleasure soon enough.

Pain prickles along my scalp as she tightens her grip. The sensation shoots straight to my cock, and I groan. How can this one woman wield so much power over me? I have laid my soul bare for her, and I would do it again a thousand times over.

Her hips swivel in the most delicious way. My hard length rasps against her clit. A drop of my seed escapes. Willow breaks off the kiss and licks her lips.

"Can I...?"

"My love, you never need to ask. I am yours until the end of time itself."

She scoots back against a mound of pillows, tiny lines of pain bracing her eyes. Fuck me. She is too fragile to have my cock in her mouth tonight. But she will not be deterred. "Help me. I need this—and what comes next—more than anything."

I get to my knees, straddling her so my cock is only inches from her glistening lips.

"You test my control, Willow. I want to be inside you in any way—in every way." Bracing one hand on the headboard, I give my length a stroke with the other.

Her eyes follow my movements. Another drop of my seed escapes. Willow scents me. She licks her lips. Her tongue sweeps over my crown.

Fuck. Willow teases me with the lightest of touches before she surges forward and wraps her hand around the base of my shaft.

I'm sucked deep in a single move. Willow hollows out her cheeks and takes me all the way to the back of her throat. She knows what she wants—and how to take it. That someone so pure, so innocent, so brilliant would want an angel like me for a partner is—"

"Not a partner, Gabriel. A mate."

I am halfway gone, but her words in my head are so shocking —and everything I could never have hoped for.

"Willow?"

Her lips curve into a gentle smile as she sucks my cock. She runs her tongue along the thick vein, hums, and with the lightest touch, skims her teeth over the sensitive skin.

"You are perfect, *deliciae*. Made for me, and I for you." I close my eyes, letting her set the pace for both of us. Her free hand wraps around my hip, fingers digging into the firm flesh of my ass.

"Harder," she demands without words.

My eyes fly open. "How...fuck. How are you doing this?"

"Don't know. But you're not listening."

"Well, I will remedy that with all due haste," I tease, thrusting my hips hard enough to make her gag, then pulling back with all my angelic speed. Again and again, I plunder her mouth. I'm desperate for her. Desperate to give her my seed. Desperate for her to see me break. To watch her lose control and break right along with me.

My balls tighten. "I am too close, Willow. I want...I *need* to finish inside you. In a way...I have never shared with another soul."

She pulls off my cock gently, pressing a kiss to my crown before she peers up at me.

"Do you trust me?" I ask for the second time this long night.

She nods. "With all that I am."

Fastening my hands around her hips, I angle them and slide home in one long, slow stroke. Her thighs tremble.

"Hold onto me, *deliciae*. Eyes on me. Always," I command.

Willow holds my gaze, obeying without question. She is mine, and I am hers. For the rest of our days.

Kneeling on the bed with her impaled on my cock, I release my wings. They unfold with a gentle rush of air, full and strong and powerful.

"Gabriel…" she breathes. "They're so beautiful."

"They are nothing compared to you, my heart. My light. My love."

I beat them gently, lifting us off the bed and high into the air. At the last moment, I twist us around to avoid the chandelier. "When we get our own place to live," I say with my lips pressed to her neck, "only lamps. No overhead lights at all."

I cup Willow's ass, thrusting my hips again and again. Her channel welcomes me home each time, little tremors and quakes for me to savor for the rest of our days.

"Can you take more, love?"

"Uh huh." Her breath escapes in shallow pants, and the most beautiful flush blooms on her chest.

With one hand pressed between her shoulders, I urge her to let go. To let herself do nothing but feel. She arches her back as I spin us in a slow circle, my hips moving faster, harder with each thrust.

My release races closer. Dipping my head, I suck one of her nipples into my mouth, and the sensation sends Willow over the edge with a scream.

Her channel clenches around me, tighter and tighter until I can no longer hold on. With a roar, I lose myself to my witch. My mate. My one true love for the rest of our days.

EPILOGUE

Two Weeks Later

Willow

I check my reflection in the mirror. The dark circles under my eyes are mostly gone, but the scar around my throat remains a permanent reminder of how close Gabriel and I came to losing everything.

Zoe brought me some magically-enhanced concealer yesterday, but I can't stand to touch the raised skin. Every time I try, I feel the void rushing toward me.

According to the Bureau's healer, Anastasia, the magic in the power chain is gone. It couldn't survive without Hannah and Calista. But I can still feel it long after Gabriel used Lucifer's axe to chop the thing into tiny pieces and Killian magicked them into dust.

Nights are the worst. Gabriel holds me when I wake up screaming, and the helplessness in his eyes is almost too much to bear.

My angel knocks on the bathroom door. "Willow? Are you ready, *deliciae?*"

Am I? This was *my* idea. But now that the day is finally here, all I want to do is burrow under the blankets and hide away from the whole world.

As appealing as that sounds, it won't help me protect the Blade—or myself.

He's pacing the hall when I finally work up the courage to join him. Shit. His shoulders are hiked up halfway to his ears. He's no more ready than I am.

"Hey, stud." I slide my arms around his neck. The delicious scent clinging to him—something angelic and powerful and *mine* —calms me, and I take my first steady breath since I woke up. "We're going to be okay. All the whispers will be there. Sin and Zoe too."

A muscle in his jaw clenches. Once. Twice. "Sinclair and Zoe caught a case this morning. They may be a few minutes late. Something about Sin *finally* getting to witness the aftermath of a vampire orgy."

All the blood drains from my face. I don't want to know what a vampire orgy looks like. Not after having Hannah root around *in my head* and force me to drive the Blade through Gabriel's heart.

A shudder wracks my entire body. I barely manage to stifle my sob.

"Fuck, Willow. I am sorry." Gabriel touches his forehead to mine. "I did not think—"

I silence him with a kiss. When my darkest memories threaten to drown me, Gabriel's touch, his warmth, and his *very* talented mouth pull me from the depths.

He saved me. And he keeps saving me over and over again.

Too soon, we have to come up for air. Licking my lips, I savor the taste of him. "I'm okay, Gabriel. Or...I'm getting there."

"We both are." He keeps me tucked against his side as he guides me down the hall to our living room.

"I will never get used to this view," I say. The floor-to-ceiling windows look out over the city, giving us a view *almost* as good as the penthouse one floor up. I almost fell off the couch when Sinclair offered us this place basically for free.

"Without Gabriel, Zoe and I would be trapped in Hell for eternity. I owe him much more than an apartment. You will be safe here. I own the entire building, and my wards will protect you until Killian can show you how to create wards of your own."

Gabriel plucks Lucifer's axe from the counter. "When we return, I will make you come pressed up against those windows, *deliciae*. Privacy glass is a wondrous invention."

This shudder is very different from the last one. "Promises, promises," I tease.

He pulls me against him so quickly, I gasp. "I am still an angel, Willow. You know I do not lie. When I make a promise, I keep it."

THE ANTECHAMBER HOLDS A BONE-DEEP CHILL. Someone—Sinclair, probably—set up floodlights to chase the shadows away, but they've done nothing to dispel the overwhelming sense of foreboding I feel being back in this room.

"Are you certain about this?" Gabriel asks. "We can go back home right now."

Am I? No. I'm still not sure about *anything*. Except the love we share.

I press my hands to the sealed vault door. "I have to do this. Putting it off isn't going to make it any easier. The grimoire killed dozens. It could have killed me, too. I won't let it hurt anyone else ever again."

The whispers of all the ones who came before surround me. *My* whisper offers me her hand. I can sense her unease, but it's nothing compared to her determination.

"You know how to get me out of there," I say, meeting Gabriel's worried gaze. "You'll feel me the whole time."

He wraps his arms around me, one hand cupping the back of my head. "Come back to me, *deliciae*."

"Always." I reach for my whisper, and as soon as our fingers brush, the world goes quiet and dark. A moment later, the first hints of blue flame start to glow.

We've been practicing for the past week, and I send all my power flowing into our connection.

She glances down at her hands and smiles. They're almost completely solid. The flames are brighter now, and the scent of incense is almost choking.

On the altar, the book waits for me—us.

"You've killed too many. Never again."

I can feel its fear. Its anger.

My whisper's hands snap to the grimoire's pages unbidden, and now I'm the one who's angry.

"No. You're not in charge anymore. We are."

All the other whispers lend us their strength. Love fills the room with golden light. The magical flames fight against it, but there is no power in this world greater than love.

"End this," I say silently, and my whisper smiles. She's ready. We're *all* ready.

She splays her fingers wide over the pages. My magic—our magic—flows through her, brighter and hotter with every passing second.

The grimoire fights back, but it knows it won't win. It can't.

The ancient pages start to burn. A haunting low cry fills the room until the entire book is on fire. We step back. Watching. Waiting. Until the last of the spelled ink has turned to dust, and the only light in the room is ours.

It's done. I'm the last Whisper Keeper. The last wielder of the Blade. And now, I'm free.

***

Gabriel

I sit on a folding chair in the middle of our darkened living room, shirtless, barefoot, wearing only a pair of loose pajama pants. Willow sleeps easily tonight—at least for now—but I have no such boon.

Seraphiel is trying to torture me. That is the only explanation.

He should have taken my wings two weeks ago. But I have heard nothing from him. Or Azrael, for that matter. The Angel of Death has been suspiciously absent since breaking all the rules and releasing my soul from death.

I cannot take this torture a moment longer.

"Azrael? Are you there?" I call softly.

The air in the room stills for a split second before he appears in front of me, knocking me—and the chair—halfway to the kitchen.

"I suppose I should have expected that," I mutter as I get to my feet.

"You have no furniture." He sweeps his gaze around the apartment, his brows furrowed. "Why do you have no furniture?"

"Because we have not decided what we want yet." The judgement in his eyes riles my anger. "It is a big decision. With consequences."

"Consequences?" He huffs. "Go to IKEA and get yourself a couch, Gabriel. It isn't that hard."

His words take a moment to register. When they do, I grab his arm. "How do *you* know about IKEA?"

With a chuckle, he shakes off my hold and turns to the windows. "You have a nice view."

"Fuck the view. Answer me."

Azrael shrugs. "I like it here. In the earthen realm."

"Seraphiel would certainly not allow you to spend all your days here—"

"Seraphiel is not in a position to *allow* anything at the moment." Azrael's lips curve into a wide smile. "The Almighty is quite displeased with him, and he has found himself *reassigned*."

"What the fuck does that mean? He's a Seraphim. What else would he do but lord over all the other angels?" I am ready to shake my brother. "Are you purposely trying to be as vague as possible? If so, that is a dick move."

His laugh echoes through the empty room. I send a burst of my power down the hall so he does not wake Willow.

"A dick move? Clearly, humanity is finally starting to rub off on you. I approve." He runs his hand through his hair, indecision playing over his chiseled features. "The story isn't mine to tell, Gabriel. Not fully. But Lucifer got that audience with the Almighty he was demanding, and...well...she was *not* amused when she heard the *real* story of what happened with Zoe."

Azrael's counsel as I was trapped between life and death comes back to me now.

"Seraphiel is about to learn the true meaning of the phrase, 'fuck around and find out.'"

"Where is Seraphiel now?" I ask. "And what is going to happen to my wings?"

Az claps me on the shoulder. "You are an angel, brother. In any realm. You will eventually become mortal. Your powers will diminish eventually. You'll age. You'll die. But your wings are a part of you and always will be. Seraphiel cannot take them away from you now, and none of the other angels would ever try."

Relief washes over me. I stagger back, unsure my legs will hold me much longer, and right the folding chair.

"I have to go," Azrael says suddenly. "There's something I... need to take care of. But I'll see you again, Gabriel. Soon."

"Wait! You never told me where Seraphiel was...reassigned."

The Angel of Death offers me a wicked smile. "I'll give you a hint. He's overseeing a place that's very hot, filled with screaming, and with gates newly locked from the *outside* for at least the next millennium."

"Hell? Seraphiel is the Underworld's new minder? What happened to Lucifer?" I rub the scar over my heart, needing the sharp ache to prove I am not dreaming this entire conversation.

Azrael chuckles. "He's somewhere in this realm, I believe. Having the time of his life. You should call him. I'm sure he'd love to tell you all about it."

With a burst of angelic power, Az disappears, leaving me in an empty room, stunned into silence.

"Gabriel?" Willow stands in the hall, her hand pressed to her heart. "Your wings...? Is Seraphiel demanding you go back to the celestial realm?" Her panic washes over me.

Fuck. I have tried to keep worries from her, but that was foolish. She is my heart. The other half of my soul. I can hide nothing from her.

"Come here," I growl.

She wraps her arms around my waist, and her nipples tighten under her t-shirt.

With a great *whoosh* of air, I loose my wings. Their celestial glow chases the shadows to the corners of the room. Sealing my lips to hers, I kiss my witch for so long, her knees go weak and my cock threatens to split my new pajama pants.

"I love you, *deliciae*. Until the end of my days. I hope that pleases you, because my wings and I are going nowhere."

THANK you for reading *Gabriel's Gambit*. I hope you enjoyed getting to know Gabriel and Willow. Azrael and Lucifer too. I can't wait to see where their books take me. Or them. Or all of us.

If you'd like a bonus epilogue from *Gabriel's Gambit*, you can find that here. You'll never guess what Gabriel ends up doing with his time in the earthen realm. Or maybe you will. But I'm sure there will be at least *one* surprise in there for you.

I hope you'll consider leaving a rating and/or review for *Gabriel's Gambit* on your purchase site of choice—or that you'll recommend the book to your friends, family, random readers on social media, or your local book club!

For updates on all of my books (including my plans for both Azrael and Lucifer), join my reader group on Facebook!

Thank you again for all your support. It means the world to me. Truly.

 Patricia

ACKNOWLEDGMENTS

This book wouldn't exist if one of my best friends, Jane, hadn't let me ramble on about the plot for hours and hours over voice message.

Jane, your restraint in not telling me to just get over myself and write the damn book is the stuff of legends. Thank you.

ABOUT THE AUTHOR

Patricia D. Eddy is a USA Today bestselling author who writes romance for the beautifully broken. Fueled by coffee, wine, and *Doctor Who* episodes on repeat, she brings damaged heroes and heroines together to find their happy ever afters in many different worlds. From military to paranormal to BDSM, her characters are unstoppable forces colliding with such heat, sparks always fly.

Patricia makes her home in Seattle with her husband and very spoiled cats, and when she's not writing, she loves working on home improvement projects, especially if they involve power tools.

Her award-winning *Away From Keyboard* series will always be her first love, because that's where she realized the characters in her head were telling their own stories—and she was just writing them down.

facebook.com/patriciadeddyauthor

x.com/patriciadeddy

instagram.com/patriciadeddy

bookbub.com/profile/patricia-d-eddy

tiktok.com/@patriciadeddyauthor

ALSO BY PATRICIA D. EDDY

Away From Keyboard

Dive into a steamy mix of geekery and military prowess with the men and women of Hidden Agenda and Second Sight.

Breaking His Code

In Her Sights

On His Six

Second Sight

By Lethal Force

Fighting For Valor

Finding Their Forevers (a holiday short story)

Call Sign: Redemption

Braving His Past

Protecting His Target

Defending His Hope

Trusting His Instincts

Saving Their Forever (an Away From Keyboard novella)

Guarding His Heart

Gone Rogue (an Away From Keyboard spinoff series)

Rogue Protector

Rogue Officer

Rogue Survivor

Rogue Defender

Rogue Operator

Rogue Mission

Dark PNR

These novellas will take you into the darker side of the paranormal with vampires, witches, angels, demons, and more.

Forever Kept

Immortal Hunter

Wicked Omens

Storm of Sin

Gabriel's Gambit

Elemental Shifter

Pick up the COMPLETE Elemental Shifter series for thrilling tales of werewolves and magic.

A Shift in the Water

A Shift in the Air

A Shift in the Earth

A Shift in Fire

By the Fates

Check out the COMPLETE By the Fates series if you love dark and steamy tales of witches, devils, and an epic battle between good and evil.

By the Fates, Freed

Destined: A By the Fates Story

By the Fates, Fought

By the Fates, Fulfilled

In Blood

If you love hot Italian vampires and and a human who can hold her own against beings far stronger, then the In Blood series is for you.

Secrets in Blood

Revelations in Blood

Holidays and Heroes

Beauty isn't only skin deep and not all scars heal. Come swoon over sexy vets and the men and women who love them.

Mistletoe and Mochas

Love and Libations

Targets and True Love

Restrained

Do you like to be tied up? Or read about characters who do? Enjoy a fresh COMPLETE BDSM series that will leave you begging for more.

In His Silks

Christmas Silks

All Tied Up For New Year's

In His Collar